SMOOTH

SMOOTH

MATT BURNS

CANDLEWICK PRESS

First edition 2020

Library of Congress Catalog Card Number pending
ISBN 978-1-5362-0438-4

20 21 22 23 24 25 LBM 10 9 8 7 6 5 4 3 2 1

Printed in Melrose Park, IL, U.S.A.

This book was typeset in Minion Pro.

Candlewick Press
99 Dover Street
Somerville, Massachusetts 02144

visit us at www.candlewick.com

For Adrianna

1.

End of Summer 2007

Sometimes I get this weird feeling that I might be attractive.

When you have acne, it's all about the lighting. I was in the bathroom at my dermatologist's office. It has these soft, fake-candle incandescent lights on the sides of the mirror, and one of them was broken. It was so dark, I'd soak the floor if I tried to pee. It was perfect. My jawline looked sort of defined and my cheeks weren't too bumpy. But maybe it wasn't just the light. Maybe my face was actually getting better.

"Kevin?" Mom said, knocking on the door. "Sweetie, are you doing okay in there? Dr. Sharp is ready for you."

I opened the door and squinted in the harsh light of the waiting room.

"Is your stomach upset?" Mom whispered. She thought I might have ulcers. In eighth grade I used to fake being sick all the time to stay home, so she did have a lot of evidence. Someday I should probably get around to telling her that none of those stomachaches were real.

I shook my head, told her I was fine, and stared at the floor while I followed a nurse through the hallways to the exam room. I sat on the padded table with my head down, and the nurse closed the door to leave me alone in front of a huge mirror and beneath about a dozen fluorescent lights. It felt like sitting in a police interrogation room.

I tried not to look in the mirror, but I caught one accidental glance when I lay down, enough to make me realize what an optical illusion the bathroom had been. My forehead and jaw were covered in purple-red splotchy scars. The skin around my mouth was inflamed and raw and bright red, like I had just finished eating a watermelon. My nose and forehead were shiny. There was always a layer of oil on my face, no matter how many times I washed it. Under those lights I felt like a buttered lobster. My face looked as bad in the mirror as it did in my head.

Dr. Sharp knocked on the door and stepped inside. "Kevin," she said, looking at my chart. "How are things?"

"Good," I said, leaving out the part about wishing someone would throw me into a pot of boiling water where I could scream until I died.

"How's your face doing?"

She always asked me that, and after two years it had never

become any less ridiculous a question. For one thing, she can see it better than I can. And my face doesn't exactly *do* anything, besides sting, leak goo, bleed, and highlight me in class photos. Her question always made me wonder if my face should be enrolling in art classes at the community college or something.

"It's, um, not any better, I guess. I mean, it's, like . . . bad." I pulled my eyes off the floor to look at her, wondering how she'd react. I'd never admitted defeat like that to her before.

"Okay," she said, setting the chart down and leaning in to stare at my face. "Have you been squeezing anything?"

"I mean, I guess. Not a ton. Sometimes."

"I know popping the whiteheads makes them go away for now, but in the long run touching your face and squeezing with your fingernails will cause scarring. I see there are some pustules around your nose and mouth."

What was I supposed to say to that? *Thank you for noticing—I grew them just for you*? I stared at the floor silently.

"May I extract them?" she said. I was a little offended she didn't get down on one knee to ask.

I shrugged. She had me lie back on the table and I saw her take two metal rods out of a drawer. "This may pinch a little," she said while poking the sticks into my zits and squeezing them dry. She did six of them and they all hurt. She wiped blood off my cheek with a napkin and I swear I saw the sides of her mouth curl up in pure delight. Of course she didn't want me popping my zits. If I did, there'd be none left for her.

She wrote a prescription on her notepad and handed me

a sheet. "I want you to stay on the Retin-A gel for a few more months to see if it starts working."

Tenth grade was starting in a few weeks. I didn't really have the luxury of waiting months for this gel to possibly, maybe, if it felt like it, start having any actual effect on my face other than continuing to dry it into a flaky croissant.

I stared at the prescription in my hand. *Ask her. Before it's too late.* I'd been prepping for days to ask her one question, and now was the time, but my mouth was dry and I kicked my heels into the side of the table over and over, annoying the hell out of both of us.

Ask. Her.

"I was, um, reading online, or, like, heard about, uh, you know, about this, uh . . . this thing . . ." *Get it out.* "Accutane?"

She sat down on the stool, looking concerned. "Accutane is really a last-resort kind of treatment," she said.

I bit my lip; heard my heart thump. After all this, was she just going to tell me no and send me home?

"You feel there hasn't been any improvement with the previous medicines?"

I shook my head and forced my heels to be still.

She said, "There are a lot of potential side effects," then opened a drawer and handed me the largest pamphlet I'd ever seen. It was like a full newspaper. "It's not something you can just test out for a month. You have to commit to at least a four-month regimen, taking two pills a day, and you can't miss any of them."

I nodded. My eyes flicked over the massive list of side

effects in the pamphlet: *depression, joint pain, yellowing of the eyes, breathing problems, irregular heartbeat, skin rash, thoughts of self-harm, swelling of the lips, severe headaches, dark urine.* The last one sounded like the title of a Japanese horror film.

"Do you want to try one more month on the Retin-A Micro gel? And then you can come back and see me in September and we'll see what you want to do?"

I swallowed. My instinct was to avoid this potential argument, give up, and do whatever she told me to do. Since my face had gotten bad enough to need prescriptions two years earlier, I'd always taken whatever Dr. Sharp felt like giving me, and nothing had worked. The constellations of zits on my face representing the Flaccid God of Guys Girls Don't Acknowledge had only shone brighter. My skin was awful and I hated the thought of suffering through tenth grade with a face like a red-and-purple tie-dyed scab. "I think I want the Accutane."

"You're sure?"

I nodded again. The side effects seemed worth the risk. All I wanted was to be able to look at myself in the mirror again. I didn't tell her that.

"There's a lot of regulation with this drug. You're going to need to sign up online for the iPLEDGE website. You won't be able to fill the prescription before you complete that. You'll need to go to that site every month and fill out a questionnaire in order to activate your next prescription. And you'll need to have your blood tested once a month to make sure there aren't any adverse internal reactions with your liver or digestive tract."

"Okay," I said.

"Your parents are okay with this?"

"Sure, they know," I lied. I'd never brought it up because Mom would turn it into a big deal and freak out, but if I just got the prescription on my own and slipped it into Mom's pile of stuff she took with her to run errands, she'd get the pills for me without even knowing what they were. I could get her to buy me a barrel of cocaine if I slipped the request into her stack.

"Okay. Your parents will need to sign off on this before the prescription can be activated."

Shit.

She tore off the new prescription and traded it for the Retin-A one in my hand. "I recommend the diagnostic lab on the first floor of this building for the blood tests. You'll need to have one done before you get this prescription filled, okay?"

I nodded.

She put her hand on my shoulder and looked into my eyes. "I hope it works for you." Then she opened the door and left. She'd never talked to me like that before. With the other prescriptions she'd just fling the paper at me and leave, cracking her knuckles in anticipation of the next kid's pimples she'd get to pop. I figure it's a big deal when your dermatologist touches your shoulder out of empathy and not just to scrape off a mole.

"You look happy," Mom said when I walked back into the waiting room.

I shrugged and said it went fine. I didn't bring up Accutane with her yet. I knew she'd have a million questions. I'd need to do more research and figure out responses to her fears about side effects before I even mentioned it to her.

But it would be worth it. Everything would get better when the pills cleared up my face.

"Did you have any more diarrhea in the office?" Mom said, two feet in front of the receptionist.

I stared ahead blankly, pretending I had no idea who that strange lady was. Whatever happened with Accutane, it could only be uphill from there.

2.

I got on our computer in the family room that afternoon, put in my headphones, and did more research. I'd forgotten where I'd even heard about it in the first place. Accutane is just a thing kids know about. It's like herpes or Aerosmith. No one ever sits you down and gives you a lesson about these things. They just exist in the ether and float into everyone's consciousness.

I read about a study done on acne that came to this gem of a conclusion: "People with acne are at substantially higher risk for depression in the first years after the condition appears. The reason for the association is unclear." Was there supposed to be a sitcom laugh track after that punch line? The reason for the association is as clear as the slime that leaks out of my pores when my face has run out of pus, blood, and yellow mystery wax: you walk around knowing you look like a god-damned monster, and if you're ever lucky enough to get distracted by a math worksheet and forget about your gross face for ten minutes, you're instantly reminded by people's horrified reactions to all the physical manifestations of your insecurities dotting your skin. How could anyone make it through this not depressed?

I found a bunch of blogs where people wrote about how they felt bummed out and didn't have much energy to do anything while they were on Accutane. There had been lawsuits against the company that made it, from patients who'd developed things like ulcers and Crohn's disease, and there were a few hundred official complaints from people who got depressed or had suicidal thoughts, and there were even some comments from the parents of kids who killed themselves while they were on it.

Their stories all started the same way — they'd tried every other prescription their dermatologist could think of and none of them had worked.

Under my sink in the bathroom I shared with my sister were dozens of clear-orange pill bottles and flattened tubes from prior failed attempts to clear up my face.

In ninth grade I'd been on adapalene gel, which made my face sting and shine like a glazed doughnut every night after I put it on. I'd lie in bed frozen stiff, keeping my eyes on the ceiling, paranoid that I'd roll on my side and get stuck to my pillowcase.

Before that there were minocycline pills that did nothing.

When I was taking them, I grew this marble-size lump on the corner of my left jaw that I couldn't stop fiddling with until it exploded in biology and I ran to the bathroom looking like a gunshot victim.

And then there was the Proactiv that Mom had subscribed me to back in middle school when the zits started sprouting up on missions to research if my cheeks were a good spot to colonize. I'd soak my face in that sting-y green juice twice a day, but I still had enough full bottles piled up from the monthly deliveries to wash a car.

I researched how Accutane works, and an article explained that Accutane is just a brand name and the actual medicine is called isotretinoin. Scientists still don't know 100 percent for sure how it works, but they know it shrinks oil glands and makes them produce less oil, and it slows down how fast skin cells regenerate inside pores, so the pores don't get clogged. A lot of research suggests it works by causing apoptosis — cell death — of the sebaceous gland cells that make faces oily. Of course it makes you think suicidal thoughts. It is killing the building blocks of *you*.

I'd read an article one time where this scientist said the cells in our bodies are naturally dying and being replaced by fresh cells constantly. He claimed the average life of a cell in the human body is seven years, which means we're technically an entirely different person when we're in tenth grade than when we were in third grade. And then we'll be another entirely new physical specimen when we're twenty-two.

There are some asterisks in the theory, and I think some

other scientists disagree with it, but the concept stuck in my head. It's not so much for the science. I like the poetry of it.

Every seven years I'll be an entirely new person. Every seven years I'll have a chance to start again.

Mom shouted from the kitchen that dinner was ready. Shit. I felt the prescription paper in my pocket and on the walk downstairs tried to cobble together some plan for convincing Mom and Dad to sign it.

When Mom says she "cooked" dinner, what she really means is she ripped open a frozen cardboard box from an international food corporation and microwaved the plastic tray inside. That night it was turkey with gravy, prepared with love in a Siberian sweatshop nine years ago.

Kate brought glasses of water to the table. If she were older, she might have been of interest to me, but as a twelve-year-old, she had no valuable information or advice. Everything that surprised or excited her happened to me three years ago and I no longer cared.

I wished I had an older sister. The kind of older sister who has sleepovers with friends who call me Kev and mess with my hair when they see me. A sister who could teach me enough about clothes so I can compliment girls without seeming like a creep. She'd let me read her magazines and I'd learn key terms like *scrunchie* and *camisole* and find out the secrets to coming off as understanding and nonthreatening. She would show me what movies girls watch when they're bored and alone, and what girls eat for snacks. She'd give me conversation topics that girls don't feel weird talking about in school. She'd leave bras hanging off the bathroom doorknob, so I'd be used to seeing them and when Emma's green bra strap was hanging out of her T-shirt sleeve in Spanish, I wouldn't have been temporarily paralyzed and unable to think about anything else for the rest of the day. Maybe after living with an older sister for fifteen years, I wouldn't think girls my age were a different species. My hypothetical older sister would be incredible. But I had Kate. Our main interaction was when I'd burp and she'd say I'd never have a wife.

Dad was at the kitchen table reading work emails on his BlackBerry. I stared at him for a while, watching the reflection of his in-box in his glasses. He scrolled through an endless list of charts and numbers, never looking up. He's a real estate agent, so he gets to pretend that he's working 24/7.

You know that feeling when a kid goes to your school for years but you've never talked to him and don't know anything about him but it would be weird to ask now because it would seem like you never cared? That's what it was like with Dad. I knew nothing and it was too late to show interest. I could have asked all the questions I wanted when I was eight, but I blew it.

"Put your thing down," Mom told Dad as she sat beside him and Kate sat next to me. Dad clicked off his screen and shook himself back to reality. Mom scooped hot reanimated meat onto our plates. "Do you remember junior year when Craig wanted to cook a whole turkey one night for no reason? And we drove around for hours going to different grocery stores and we finally found one in Gwinnett and by the time he cooked it, it was two in the morning and everyone was asleep?" She laughed.

Dad thought for a second. "I thought it was a chicken."

Mom turned to me and Kate. "You'd never know it from seeing him now, but our friend Craig used to be the wildest, most spontaneous guy we knew. One time he filled up his dorm room with little plastic balls, like the ones in a McDonald's PlayPlace."

Kate giggled. "That's crazy. Like, that's totally certifiably insane." She had recently discovered words longer than three syllables.

Dad said, "There weren't as many balls as he'd hoped for. Nothing really happened."

It's always like this with them. Mom tells a tall tale and Dad stands there next to her like some anthropomorphized Snopes.com and holds out a measuring tape and says, "Ma'am, I'm going to have to inform the audience here that this tall tale is in fact only a small story, hardly worth telling at all, that's been radically blown out of proportion for dramatic effect."

I've never been able to imagine them meeting in college. They were eighteen when they met, not that much older than me. I sat there watching them chew and thought about cells being replaced every seven years. My parents have been through, like, seven rounds of that. Were they completely different people back then? I've seen pictures of them in high school and they look like themselves, but I can never imagine the reality — them in 3-D, their voices, who their friends were, how much they spoke up in class, if my dad made jokes with other guys at his lunch table about jerking off, if they ever cried alone in the bathroom.

"How was Courtney's house?" Mom asked Kate.

"Wondrous," Kate said. "She showed me all her old report cards. Her parents say a B is good and they give her presents when she gets Bs."

"*B* stands for *bad*," I muttered. "You should get As. School isn't that hard." Her conversation was even more obnoxious than usual because I had something important to bring up.

"Are you saying Courtney's stupid? Mom, Kevin said Courtney's stupid."

"*Kevin*," Mom said, in italics. "Be nice."

"What? I'm giving her good advice to not be an idiot."

Mom put on her fake smile and said her favorite catch-phrase: "Positive mental attitude, sweetie." It was her vague, catchall advice any time I didn't have a phony Cheshire Cat smile plastered across my face. She'd been pelting me with it for most of my life, anytime I committed the sin of a neutral expression.

I sighed.

She added, "Where in your manners books does it say you can speak to your sister that way and roll your eyes?" She was talking about the dozens of books about manners she'd given me every birthday and Christmas for the last few years. I guess it was a parenting shortcut for her, to feed me printed instructions for being alive, like I was a punch-card computer from 1962. The books had titles like *Manners for Men, How to Be an Upstanding Gentleman,* and *Becoming the Respectable Teen*

You're Meant to Be. I'd never read any of them. They were piled up in a huge stack on a shelf in my room. Mom thought she was giving me helpful life advice, but it was more like giving me bricks, and soon I'd have enough to build my own house and move out.

I forced a smile. "Yeah. Right. Sorry." I took a breath and focused on the bullet points lined up in my head. I was going to talk about how Accutane works for most people, how it's just a supercharged form of vitamin A, and how I'd only be on it for a few months. I wasn't going to mention anything about depression and ulcers and all the stuff that would freak them out, but I had the counterarguments to those ready in case they brought them up. I was ready to debate them if they said no or tried to persuade me to try another medicine first.

Mom and Kate were talking about Courtney and I kept waiting for the right time to jump in, but there was never a gap. I finally just blurted out over them, "Dr. Sharp gave me a new prescription and I need you to sign it." I pulled the paper out of my pocket and flung it on the table.

"You didn't tell me about this earlier," Mom said, picking it up.

"How rude of him," Kate muttered, and folded her arms.

"I completely forgot about it until just now," I lied.

"It's a new medicine for your face?"

"I guess."

She stood up, got a pen from the kitchen, and signed it. "Okay. We can take this in to the pharmacy tomorrow."

Huh. Weird. No discussion, no screaming match. She

didn't seem to care, and Dad didn't seem to notice I'd said anything at all.

"Oh," I added. "I need to get a blood test before we can get the prescription. In the same building as Dr. Sharp. I have to go once a month."

"That's fine, sweetie. Whatever you need."

I nodded and ate while Mom and Kate talked about back-to-school clothes shopping or something. I looked at the prescription form on the table and wondered why it had been so easy. Mom and Dad didn't seem to know what I was getting into, or maybe they didn't care.

Now that Mom's signature was on there, it felt real. I'd been so set on getting the prescription signed that I hadn't really thought beyond that — the reality that taking this drug could mess with my head. I got nervous and stopped eating. I just sat there staring at the table, telling myself I should be happy I got the signature, trying to push out all the thoughts about side effects, all the stories I'd read online about it ruining people's lives.

It'd be worth it. It'd definitely be worth it.

Probably.

3.

Most afternoons that summer, Mom dropped me off at Luke or Will's house while she went to run errands, and we'd hang out all day. Every now and then we'd do something productive like make our own short horror movies, but mostly we watched movies, played video games, and talked about why my mom could possibly need to go to the grocery store, bank, post office, and dry cleaner every single day.

It was Tuesday, two weeks before school started. I was standing in Luke's garage holding a white PVC pipe as tall as me. Luke and Will dug through bins of cords and parts, looking for a grill igniter switch so we could finish building our hair-spray-powered potato cannon.

It was about a thousand degrees in the Georgia August heat, and the humidity made me feel like I was standing in a dog's mouth. I pulled the bottom of my T-shirt up to wipe the sweat off my forehead, and the cotton stung my bumpy skin. I thought about all the bacteria I'd just transferred from my shirt directly into my pores. I'd probably seeded an entire new field of zits. Shit.

Luke stood up from the pile, holding the small plastic grill igniter, which had two frayed wires dangling from its bottom. Luke's hair is long and messy but always looks right. He's a few inches taller than me and has chest muscles that are visible through his T-shirts and two small acne scars on his cheek that look deliberate — cool, even. Two different times — once when we were in sixth grade, another when we were in ninth — girls told me they thought he was hot. I told them both "Thanks" because I didn't know what else to say, and neither of them ever spoke to me again.

Will's straight-across-the-front hairline makes him seem like an intelligent alien from a TV show. His hair says, "I don't care what anyone thinks," and he really doesn't, whereas Luke's hair says, "I don't care what anyone thinks," but I know he really wants more random girls to tell his friends they think he's hot. My hair says, "I did not know what to tell the barber to do."

Our hair and my acne makes us look a little different, but you could make a Venn diagram of our interests, and it would pretty much entirely overlap: hanging out in each other's basements, horror movies, talking about testicles.

Will revved an electric drill and we walked into the dead

grass. I held the PVC pipe down while Will drilled a hole through it and Luke stuffed the igniter in. Then Luke sprayed enough hair spray into the pipe to make us all cough, and I screwed the plastic cap onto the back. Will crammed a potato down the front end and used a rake handle to jam it to the bottom of the pipe like he was a Revolutionary War soldier loading a musket.

"That it?" I said, standing with the end of the barrel in my hand, pointing it straight up.

"Yeah," Luke said, peering into the barrel. "We press the igniter, it makes a spark, the hair spray explodes and fires the potato."

I said, "How do we know the whole thing won't just blow up and slice us in half with plastic shards?"

"It probably will," Luke said, stepping back and shrugging.

"This seems like a really dumb way for us all to die," I said.

"Dude?" Luke said, looking down at Will, who was crouched near the ground with his finger on the igniter button. "You wanna do it?"

"Yeah, sure." He shrugged. His vote broke the tie and there was nothing I could do.

Will clicked the switch. I squeezed my eyes shut. Nothing happened. He clicked it again. And again. Nothing. I opened my eyes. He clicked it again and — *shit!* — the potato shot out with a *WHUMP* and the smell of burnt chemicals.

I let go of the pipe and ran under a tree, trying to find the potato in the sky. I couldn't see it anywhere. I imagined it smacking me in the forehead, making my whiteheads pop and bleed, fertilizing a giant purple bruise. I pictured it cannon-balling into my penis and scrotum, mangling the whole package before I'd even gotten to really use it, like wrecking a new car before you pull it out of the dealership.

The potato plopped onto the street at the edge of Luke's driveway. Luke and Will ran after it and I followed them. We leaned over the smashed lump.

"That could've been our dicks," I said.

Luke and Will both nodded.

"That's a good idea," Luke said while I watched Mom's minivan pull up behind him. Her window was down. "You boys want to cut our peckers off with the Bowie knife and shoot 'em into the sky next?"

"Hi, guys," Mom said. She'd definitely heard him.

"Hey, what's up, Kevin's mom?" Luke said, turning around and smiling at her. I have no idea how he can recover from saying things like that. He was never taught how to properly worry.

"You've got your appointment," Mom said to me.

"Oh, sure, yeah, I'll drive." I rushed over, took the keys from her when she got out of the driver's seat, and told the guys I'd see them later, trying to get out of there before either of them could ask what my appointment was for. I didn't feel like explaining Accutane and the mandatory blood test to them. They wouldn't be mean about it or anything, but they'd bring it up and make dumb jokes about the tests finding some disease in my blood you can only get from having sex with rodents or something. They'd ignored my acne for years, but once they thought it was acceptable to indirectly bust my balls about it, I wouldn't be able to deny to myself how obviously bad it was anymore. Plus, telling them would mean admitting not just that my skin was terrible, but that I hated how I looked badly enough to make this drastic step toward fixing it. It was too real an emotion to share with them. They wouldn't know how to handle it, and I wouldn't know how to handle however they reacted. It was just easier and more efficient to focus our conversations on our nut sacks instead.

I had my learner's permit, meaning I basically had my license as long as I could completely ignore Mom's existence. "Kevin, please. We have plenty of time," she'd say every time I eased into a stop at a red light. "You don't have to drive like a maniac."

"I'm driving ten under the speed limit."

"I feel like I'm on a roller coaster."

When I merged onto the highway, she squeezed her eyes shut, whispered a prayer, and crossed herself. Bold message from a woman who hadn't been to church in fifteen years. That was why I preferred driving with my dad when he was available. He hardly ever looked up from his work emails in the passenger seat.

When I pulled into the parking deck at the doctor's office, Mom gripped the handle above her door and made me drive all the way to the top level, where there were no other cars I could potentially scratch. She got out of the car and guided me into a wide-open space like she worked on an airport runway.

"Can I go in by myself?" I said after shutting off the engine.

I wanted to get it over with as fast as possible and to avoid Mom making it into a big deal.

"Oh," she said. "Okay. Do you know which office it is?"

I had no idea. I nodded and she handed me her insurance card that had my name printed in tiny letters as a DEPENDENT.

I found the diagnostic lab on the directory and went into their waiting room, which had four fish tanks, three awful abstract paintings on the wall, and two patients.

The receptionist was college-age with flawless skin that defied the fluorescent light above her. "Hi," she said. "Have an appointment?"

I nodded and stared at the ground. Under the overhead lights, my face must have looked shiny and sticky and red, like it was soaked in fruit punch. I handed her the insurance card and said to the floor, "I think the appointment's at four."

"Perfect. I see it right here, Kevin." It sounded like she smiled. "Is there a co-pay?"

"What?"

"With your insurance, do you have a co-pay?"

It was like she was speaking Portuguese. My parents had made me learn about sex from a book, and I guess they were even shyer about discussing insurance co-pays.

"Can I, uh, call my mom?"

"Sure."

I took a step away from the counter and called Mom. She told me there was no co-pay. She asked if everything was okay and if she needed to put down her sudoku and come inside.

"No, it's fine," I said. "I'm fine. I can do it by myself."

"No co-pay," I told the carpet in front of the receptionist.

"Great. Can you just fill out this information and get it back to me? You can have a seat wherever you like."

On one side of the waiting room was a scrawny guy sucking on his fingertips and muttering to himself, then smelling each of his fingers. On the other side was a girl who looked about my age. Her eyes were closed and she had earbuds in. I looked back to the guy, who seemed confused by the smell of his own fingers. I decided to sit near the girl, four seats down from her.

I filled out my name and address and checked the "no" box beside the hundreds of diseases I was pretty sure I'd never had and assumed weren't in my family's genes. I handed the form back to the receptionist, and when I turned back around, the girl's eyes were open.

She was looking right at me.

And as soon as my eyes made contact with hers, she looked at the wall beside me, and then the floor, and then shut her eyes again.

I sat back in my chair, leaned my head against the wall, and closed my eyes, performing indifference while I couldn't stop thinking about that girl. What was she in there for? She was around my age, but she definitely didn't go to my school. What school did she go to? Did she think I was weird for being there? Did she think I was a diseased freak? Was *she* a diseased freak? Wait, shit. Why did I jump to the worst-case explanation? She could have been there for some boring test, just like me.

I tilted my head five degrees toward her and focused hard on the music coming through her earbuds. One lyric was playing over and over: "Needle in the hay."

I lifted my right eyelid to look at her and wanted her to do the same. But not when I was leering at her. No, I wanted to look at her, and then after I'd looked away and appeared to be contemplating a deep thought while staring at a wall, I wanted her to open her eyes and look at me. Maybe she already had. Maybe while I'd had my eyes closed, she'd been secretly sneaking glances at—

Shit! She'd just opened her eyes directly into my creepy onslaught of direct eye contact. I hurled my pupils toward the floor and kept them there for a few seconds, mortified. When I dared to flick them back up, she was smiling a little at me.

Oh, shit.

I nodded back, excited and stunned stiff at the same time, a combination that likely produced the shiny-eyed-but-stoic facial expression of a remorseless serial killer. Was her look an invitation to move closer to her? Or just an acknowledgment that I existed? It was hard to tell, so the safest way to play it was to remain seated and limp and stare at the floor like I had a fetish for pale carpet.

"Alex?" the receptionist said. The girl stood up and I saw the outline of her bra through her T-shirt. I didn't want to seem like a creep, so I looked away, but my eyes locked dead-on with Mr. Fingers, so I had to flick them away again, bouncing them all over the room like I'd been electrocuted.

She disappeared into the hallway behind the counter and I settled into an imaginary conversation with her in my head. We hit it off. Imagined conversations almost always work out in my favor. I hoped she'd get back before —

"Kevin?" said the receptionist. "We're ready for you."

Damn it.

The receptionist led me back into a small room with a padded chair and a table; laid out on the table were a clear vial and a rubber tube with a needle at the end. My stomach got queasy. I'd been under the impression this was going to be a pinprick-in-the-fingertip situation. A nurse stepped in, sat on a stool, pushed up my sleeve, and tied a rubber strip around my arm. I shut my eyes.

"It'll be over before you know it. Just a little pinch."

I felt the needle go in, and then I made the mistake of opening my left eyelid. The tube turned dark red as my blood rose into the vial, which was the size of a prescription pill bottle. It filled up way faster than I thought it would, like the juice that kept me alive was rushing to evacuate my sinking ship of a body. The nurse pinched the vial off, pulled a second from her pocket, and attached it to the tube. It filled up even faster now that my blood had a running start and a clear path toward the exit. I felt like I was going to pass out and throw up at the same time. How many more vials did she have in her pockets? At the insane rate my blood was defecting from my body, it seemed liked I'd be drained to death in twenty more seconds.

"Almost," the nurse said, staring with twisted delight as

she topped off the second vial. She pinched it closed, slid the needle out of my arm, and pressed a cotton ball onto the tiny wound. She stuck on a Band-Aid, said, "We use the second vial to make soup," and laughed.

I didn't know how to respond, so I nodded as if I were agreeing that that was a good idea. The nurse said she'd see me in a month, and reminded me I had to go online to fill out some more forms. I stood up and was so dizzy I had to catch the doorframe to hold myself up. The nurse told me I should sit down, but I took some deep breaths, lowered my head so the overhead lights wouldn't shine directly on my zits, and walked back into the waiting room with this childish hope that the girl — Alex — would be there.

She wasn't, but her earbuds were on her chair. Without really thinking about it, I picked them up off the chair on my way out the door and put them in my pocket. If I ever saw her again, I could give them back to her, but I knew that would probably never happen. I just wanted some physical proof that I really had shared that moment with that girl, that it wasn't a daydream.

"See you next month," the receptionist said as I pushed open the door. I jumped guiltily and speed-walked toward the parking deck.

When I opened the car door, Mom asked if everything was okay. She said I looked out of breath. She was looking me over like I'd just shoplifted headphones.

"I'm fine," I said. "It was fine."

"You didn't have to pay anything?"

"No?"

"When you left, did the receptionist give you any paperwork?"

"I don't know. I just left."

Mom laughed. "They'll call me if there are any problems."

I turned the car's ignition on and backed out of the space. Mom said, "I was thinking we could go to a movie this afternoon if you want. My treat." She always liked to add the "my treat" part even though I didn't have any money, so it was kind of a necessary part of the deal.

"What movie?"

"Any movie," Mom said. She was not a discerning moviegoer. She wouldn't care if it was just two hours of a well-known celebrity poorly assembling a table. I think when she said she liked movies she actually meant she liked air-conditioning. "You can pick. You know, movies are a good thing for a guy to like. You'll make a great boyfriend someday."

Alex appeared in my head as I pulled onto the road. She was the first girl my age to look me in the eye. Store clerks and waitresses had looked at me, but they don't count. Her look meant something. Out of the infinite points in space around her, she'd chosen the precise coordinates where her eyes met mine. Not at the scars on my forehead or the dry red patches around my mouth. I didn't just like her because of how she looked; I liked her because she made me forget about my skin for a second.

"I don't think there's anything good out right now," I told Mom. I was thinking about Alex again, about how all I knew about her was her first name and that she liked a song that was probably called "Needle in the Hay." It wasn't much, but I'd have to try to find her online with those clues. I kept driving and pictured her back in the waiting room, trying to etch how she looked into my memory. She'd had jaggedly cut brown hair that stopped above her shoulders. She wore nonskinny jeans and a loose white T-shirt and sat with her head against the wall and her legs pulled up to her chest, flip-flops on the seat cushion. Her face was round, and it looked like she had a lot of makeup on her cheeks, but you could still tell her skin was bumpy underneath, and her forehead was shiny. She had acne scars on her jawline and temples. They didn't make her any less pretty. I wondered if she was there for Accutane, too. But her skin wasn't that bad, and the coincidence felt too far-fetched, even for one of my fantasies. Anyway, she looked like a girl you'd meet at a bookstore or a museum.

I have this fantasy of meeting my future girlfriend at a museum. It's probably telling that my fantasies about my future involve being a guy who goes to museums alone. But my dream girl does that, too, apparently, so maybe it'll all work out.

4.

Mom turned on the TV in the family room and I sat at the computer behind the couch, put in my earbuds, and went to the iPLEDGE website to fill out the questionnaire so Mom could get my prescription the next morning. There was some scientific language on the site confirming how disgusting I was:

Isotretinoin is indicated for the treatment of severe recalcitrant nodular acne. Nodules are inflammatory lesions with a diameter of 5 mm or greater. The nodules may become suppurative [ripe with pus] *or hemorrhagic* [ready to erupt blood all over my mirror]. *"Severe," by definition, means "many" as opposed to "few or several" nodules.*

I clicked to confirm that yes, indeed, I had a gross face.

Next was a page where I had to click about sixty "Yes" boxes to promise I would not have sex while on Accutane. Apparently if you do and the girl gets pregnant, she'll have a cone-headed baby. There were lots of diagrams showing this baby, like he was the mascot of Accutane. I agreed to that and all the other pledges to be a loser, too. It was like official, government-sanctioned cyberbullying. Some faceless agency was telling me, "There's no way you're drinking this year," and I shouted, "Yes, sir!" "There's no way you're doing drugs this year." "Yes, sir!" "And there's definitely no way a guy like you is getting laid this year." "Yes, sir!"

After I finished, I realized I'd been absentmindedly holding the tangled cord of Alex's headphones in my pocket. I took my earbuds out and put hers in. I searched for "Needle in the Hay," which led me to a clip from *The Royal Tenenbaums,* a movie that came out a few years ago, where a character cuts his wrists while the song plays. It was raw and painful and beautiful. It said a lot about who Alex was.

I started torrenting *The Royal Tenenbaums,* and while it downloaded I thought about how absurd it was to daydream about this girl I knew almost nothing about, but what the hell? Everyone needs an absurd goal to chase, right? Some idea of heaven you force yourself to believe in just to have a reason to keep moving forward. Guys at my school dream of making it to the NFL, and there's no chance they will, but that fantasy makes them try harder at practice. She was my NFL, my goal, my reason to keep hoping I could get better so maybe someday

I'd have another moment with a girl like her, and I could actually talk to her.

I wanted to carve the misshapen stalagmite of bumpy, mumbling stone I'd become into an upstanding, normal member of society who stands with his back straight and keeps his chin up and rarely drools or stutters incomprehensible half sentences often missing verbs. I'd refine myself over the year, whittling down and smoothing over the nervous, rough edges to find some better person underneath. The statue of David started out as a dumb-ass slab of rock, too, and if I wanted it badly enough, I'd be able to do it for her.

The white pharmacy bag was waiting on the kitchen island when I woke up. I snatched it and ran back upstairs to take the first pill. The night before, I'd imagined swallowing the pill and seeing a montage of the year, like time-lapse footage of a flower sprouting from nothing into something impressive and strong. It was an important moment, and in my head, I took the first pill in a sophisticatedly decorated, softly lit room.

Kate and I share a bathroom. It's windowless, with harsh overhead lights. It's a passageway linking our rooms together, but we've never been in there at the same time. We have two sinks and an agreement that neither of us would cross onto the other's side of the counter. On the wall on my half was a poster from an anime show I'd been interested in for two weeks in sixth grade that I'd been too lazy to remove in the four intervening years. Be careful with new interests on the day your mom asks you what you want for Christmas. You may be stuck with disturbing Japanese elves on your bathroom wall forever. On Kate's half was a poster of a horse with a smiling set of human teeth that upset me every day.

I decided to use the bathroom in my dad's office upstairs, which has no stupid decorations, a window with shades for soft natural light, dark-blue wallpaper, and dark-blue towels no one uses. Mature and serious. I looked myself over in the mirror and took a deep breath. I scooped handfuls of water into my hair to tame it with my fingers. There was a candle beside the sink, and I found a lighter in the drawer and lit it. I set up my iPod's portable speakers and played "Needle in the Hay."

The pack of pills was covered in small silhouettes of pregnant women with red Xs over them and a bold warning: DO NOT GET PREGNANT. I tore one of the expectant mothers off, threw her in the trash, and put the pill on my tongue. I shut my eyes, took a deep breath, and swallowed.

I heard my dad sniffing on the other side of the door. "Kevin! Why do I smell smoke?" He must have thought I was badly attempting to light my first cigarette.

"Sorry, I lit a candle," I said. "For the . . . bathroom smell."

"You playing music in there?"

"To cover up the, uh, noise," I said. He definitely thought I was masturbating. "I'll be done in a second."

"All right, take your time. Didn't mean to scare you."

I shut the music off and realized what a stupid scene I'd set up. I was taking a pill, not losing my virginity. I flushed the empty toilet and snuck back into my room, telling myself that once my skin cleared up, I'd be confident and in control and wouldn't find myself mock-shitting near my dad anymore.

That night I squinted at my stream when I peed, trying to tell if it was darker than usual. Sort of, but hard to blame that on the pill, since my water intake for the previous five hours consisted of one Mountain Dew. I looked my face over in the mirror. Maybe my cheeks were drier, but it was probably just wishful thinking. I took my second pill before I brushed my teeth, and when I was in bed, I shut my eyes, trying to feel the medicine in my bloodstream. If I focused hard enough, I could convince myself it was in there, running through my shoulders and arms like grains of sand. I felt a headache coming on, and I smiled. That was a side effect. I hoped it was real.

The night before school started, I went to my room, turned on my Xbox, put on my headset, and joined a lobby with Luke and Will to do a four-way prank call.

"George Foreman grill?" Luke said.

Will and I agreed, and Luke put his phone on speaker, set it next to his headset, and dialed the customer service number. I muted my microphone so no one would hear me laugh.

Once someone picked up, Luke said, "Hello, my name is Doug Ronald and my brothers are on the phone here, too. Chip Ronald and Kyle Ronald."

I had no idea where he was going with that, but the best calls were the ones we didn't plan out and just agreed with whatever Luke said. I unmuted and said, "Hey, Chip here."

"I'm Kyle," Will said.

"Right," Luke continued. "So this is more of a question than a complaint or anything. Honestly, our grill is working great. Doing exactly what it's supposed to be doing. It grilled up everything we put on it. So I guess we're looking for some advice. Essentially, my brothers and I accidentally grilled our dongs together on the Foreman. It roasted them up real good, seared them and everything. So, again, no complaints about the performance of the machine. It certainly did its job. But now our dongs are all fused together and the timing is terrible because tomorrow we each have separate business trips in Atlanta, San Francisco, and New York, and while I'd like to tell you each of us is hung well enough for that kind of cross-country stretch to pose no issue, I've got to be honest and own up to the fact that our gear just isn't long enough. So I guess my question is, what advice do you have for us?"

There was a pause before the customer service woman responded. "Sir, do you want a replacement grill?"

"No, it works great. Our peckers are fat free and seared with really nice grill marks. I guess I'm asking if you offer a product designed for unsticking penises that were fused together in your roasting-hot iron grill. Surely I'm not the first person with this request."

There was another long pause. "How old are y'all? Why is that funny to you? Grilling your . . . I don't even . . . That's nasty. You sound way too old for this. You boys don't have anything better to do than . . . Shouldn't you be talking to girls? You're not gonna lose your virginity calling me to tell me about your wieners."

Luke hung up. Will and I unmuted and burst out laughing.

"Good call to end summer on," Will said.

"Shit," Luke said. "Is school tomorrow?"

"Yeah," I said.

"Well . . . huh," Luke said. "Guess I have to fake all the summer homework tonight. Did any of us, like, do anything this summer?"

"We stood around talking in a lot of movie theater lobbies," I said.

"My dad knocked over that giant display of apples at the grocery store, and I think it'll be the funniest thing I ever see in my life," Will said. "That was back in May, and nothing topped it."

For a second I thought about bringing up Accutane and Alex. It seemed like maybe I should tell them, since they were the biggest developments to happen in my life in years. But it didn't feel right. They probably wouldn't care, or if they did, Luke would dominate the conversation and make me feel like I wasn't a part of my own story. Best to end the call on a high note.

"Nope. Didn't do shit," I said.

On the morning of the first day of school, I woke up an hour early so I could take my pill, take a shower, wash my face, rub green salicylic acid juice all over it with a cotton ball, and then coat my whole face with moisturizer. I'd decided to keep my external skin regimen going alongside the Accutane, so I'd flank my zits, imploding and exploding them at once. I used Q-tips around my nose and jawline to wipe off the extra shiny moisturizer goo, so I wouldn't look too buttery.

I was almost out the door when Mom held up her digital camera and said, "First-day-of-school picture?" In the one from last year, my skin didn't look too bad. At the time I thought I looked hideous, but compared to now, I was fine. I was just starting to get blackheads on my nose then, but that was when I started to hate having my picture taken. There are only, like, six photographs of me from freshman year, and in most of them I'm twisting away from the camera like I'm afraid it'll fire a bullet at me.

"Pretty please?" she said. "I can't have a gap in my collection." I smiled and she told me real smiles have teeth in them. I kind of opened my mouth a little. The flash went off. She showed me the photo on the screen and ruined my day. I had all these red splotches on my forehead and a bunch of red scabs on my temples where I'd been squeezing stuff last night. My cheeks were covered in pink sprinkles, and every inch of my face was shiny. The lighting in my bathroom had lied to me. I looked like a glazed Freddy Krueger.

Luke, Will, and I had agreed to meet at eight, and they showed up at 8:21, which wasn't surprising at all; order and structure never cross their minds.

Luke's desk in elementary school was chaos. The first time I saw it, it confused and stunned me and I've never forgotten it; it was my first clue that the world isn't the orderly, organized place children's television had promised. His desk was a whirlwind of crumpled papers, food debris, and broken pencils, like a thief was always breaking in and not finding what he was looking for.

Will's desks were always empty. I still have no idea how he passed classes without ever having books, or why he never had them in the first place.

My desks were always neat, deliberate, and so logical that I still picture one sometimes when I get stressed out.

I wish I could have some more interesting descriptions of Luke and Will. I mean, no offense to them, but none of us is really that interesting. Neither of them has diabetes or dead parents or a tragic terminal illness. And none of us has been chosen by a prophet to go on a quest to destroy an amulet and retrieve a magical scroll. We're just three white kids from the suburbs who like watching horror movies in basements. You can go to any tenth-grade hallway in any suburb and find our clones. We are highly replaceable.

The lighting in our morning spot by our lockers was brutal, like it was designed by the guy in charge of the before photos in the Proactiv commercials: fluorescent bulbs in the ceiling and the glare of the piercing morning sun through a wall of windows. It was a greenhouse built to grow low self-esteem. I shielded my face like a vampire while Luke and Will talked about *Halloween 4: The Return of Michael Myers*.

We looked at our schedules again and had all the same teachers except one. For math, I had Algebra 2, but they both got put into trigonometry because they got As on the ninth grade geometry final and I got a B-plus. I wondered if those two problems I messed up were going to someday mean Luke and Will would get jobs as nuclear engineers while I worked in a factory putting corn in cans.

For an unexplained reason Luke pretended he was a wrestler bouncing off ropes and knocked his shoulder into Emma, his ex-girlfriend. Emma had dark, thick eyebrows and long brown hair, and from the look of her cheeks, she probably didn't even know what a zit was. Like, she'd seen articles in girl magazines about how to clear up zits, and she didn't know what they were talking about, so she'd just turn the page. She was a member of the God Squad, a group of ambiguously religious girls who went to a lot of events that involved free T-shirts with crosses on them. For some reason, everyone knew about the abstinence pledges they'd made the summer before ninth grade, which was ludicrous because absolutely no one our age was having sex anyway. When I'd heard about it, I thought it would be equally valid to publicly announce I'd pledged to abstain from time-traveling.

"Yo," Luke said to Emma, laughing. "Sorry."

"It's all right," she said.

Luke thought it wasn't a big deal that he and Emma had gone out for, like, three months last year and now they had to see each other every day in school. It seemed like a huge deal to me. If I were him, I'd spend the entire school year in a bathroom stall trying to avoid her and the awkwardness. They never had a fight when they broke up. They weren't in any of the same classes, so they grew apart and decided to be friends. I still don't know how they could be so well adjusted.

"Hey, guys," Emma said to Will and me. There were a few times last year when she hung out with us on Friday nights at Luke's house. It was okay, at least until around ten o'clock when all of a sudden Luke told me and Will we should probably head out but Emma was going to stay. That was kind of weird. I never asked what they'd do after we left, and I didn't really want to know because we all sat on that same couch, and there was plenty of weird stuff two teenagers could do to exploit loopholes in an abstinence pledge.

"Did you go to the beach?" she said to me. "You look like you got some sun."

Goddamn it. I shrugged and looked at the floor and said, "Yeah . . ."

Will said, "Wait, when did you go to the beach?"

"No," I said. "I mean, I meant, 'Yeah, no, I didn't go to the beach.'"

"Oh," she said. "All right."

There was a silence just long enough to make me seem like one of the dumbest humans on the planet, and then the bell rang before I could change the subject, canonizing another episode of my confusing idiocy in everyone's heads.

5.

The first few periods were relatively normal — avoiding eye contact; racing to the backs of classrooms to secure seats; feeling my entire body tense, hoping teachers wouldn't make us stand up and introduce ourselves — until Luke, Will, and I had language arts with a new teacher, Mr. Meyer.

Mr. Meyer was this short, stubby, bald guy in khaki pants and a tie who looked like he should be plotting his suicide in a cubicle. So it was weird when he went on this long lecture — it was more of a performance, really, since he had weird tribal music playing off his computer while he spoke — about storytelling, like it was some mystical dark art. He said that most literature teachers we've had in the past have probably only talked about novels, short stories, essays, and poems. But those are just a small piece of what counts as storytelling. He said that just about every type of communication — songs, emails, phone calls, telling your friends about what you did last night, receipts, internet browsing histories — is storytelling, and no one form is any better or worse than the others.

"This year we'll explore, dissect, and analyze stories of all forms. It doesn't matter if it's a novel, a rap song, a recipe, or a shoe."

Veronica Wesson raised her hand. "How can a shoe be a story?"

"Who made the shoe?" said Mr. Meyer. "Why did they make the shoe? Why did they decide to put the laces there and color the sole the way they did? Did the final product succeed or fail? What's the narrative arc?"

"Oh-kay," Veronica said. "What if I just found the shoe in a trash can?"

"Who put it in the trash can?"

"Okay, fine. I get it."

I don't think she did. I think she just wanted Mr. Meyer to stop talking. I think only a couple of us got what Mr. Meyer was saying. It seemed cool to me.

"Stories can help us," he said. "They teach us how to communicate and give us examples of what to do and what not to do. I want you all to be able to identify why a story works for you, so that when you leave this classroom next May you'll be able to seek out ones that will enrich your life. Think about it this way." He drew a circle on the whiteboard and then made a small pie slice in it. "I think it's fair to say that about ninety-five percent of stuff — movies, books, songs — is pretty bad, right? This little five percent slice is what I think is really great. But someone else's five percent would be over here." He drew a wedge opposite his. "Meaning that all the things I love and cherish, this person thinks are complete garbage. It goes on and on, with billions of people on the planet, and everyone has a different slice of what they like." He set the marker down and turned to us. "So let's talk about the books you read in school last year. Who here loved *Nineteen Eighty-Four*?"

Five kids shot their hands up.

"Who hated it?"

A few kids' hands went up. Meyer pointed to Todd Lancaster. "Why'd you hate it?"

"All that stuff about new words, like 'doubleplusgood,' is, like, legitimately a better way to talk, but whoever wrote it was talking about it like it was a dumb idea, and that made no sense to me."

"Okay, sure," Meyer said. "Someone else, name any book you love."

Heather Derington said, "*The Lord of the Rings*," and Todd Lancaster groaned.

Meyer laughed a little. "See? One person's favorite is someone else's least. Todd, is it?"

"Yeah," he grunted.

"What is it about *Lord of the Rings* you don't like?"

"Hobbits are just gross little guys, you know? Nasty freaks and everything."

"But can you understand why someone else might enjoy it?"

"No."

"All right, let me put it this way. If you knew J.R.R. Tolkien when he was writing it, and you knew that in the future millions of people around the world would love his book and the movies based on it, even though you wouldn't, would you tell him to stop writing?"

"Definitely," Todd said, like a lawyer presenting the final piece of uncontestable evidence. "If I was back in time with J.R.R., or anyone, really, I'd tell them to stop whatever dumb stuff they were doing and head to the stock market to put it all on Apple."

Meyer narrowed his eyes and nodded slowly, smirking at Todd the same way I was. "Well, I can't argue with Todd's investment advice. But let's steer back to storytelling. So what's the point, right? Seems pretty depressing to think that the vast majority of the planet thinks your favorite things are stupid. We've got to realize we all have different tastes, and that's okay. It's great. It's liberating. It means that when you're creating a story, or doing anything creative or productive, it just doesn't make any sense to care what anyone else thinks. Being creative isn't like playing in a golf tournament. It's like playing golf by yourself, over and over, trying just to beat your own score. Figure out the story you want to tell and make it better until you love it."

He folded his arms over his stomach and straightened his

back. "I'm assigning you all a yearlong project with one goal: next May you'll tell us a story. That's it. You can work by yourself, or you can do it in a group, however many people in each group you want. Start thinking or talking about what kinds of stories you like and how you like them told."

Everyone shuffled their desks around to push them into little groups. I was already sitting next to Luke and Will, so we turned our desks to face one another. This assignment wasn't mentioned anywhere on Meyer's syllabus. He'd thrown us a curveball, but I felt excited in a way I never did at school. It was perfect for us.

"Movie?" I said. They both nodded. We'd been making movies together since middle school, but nothing longer than ten minutes. Goofy little horror movies with bad fake-blood special effects that never worked. They all sucked, to be honest, but I always thought if we actually put in effort, we could make something good. "Let's make this one, like, a real movie," I said. "If we have all year to work on it, we could make an actual ninety-minute slasher movie."

They both shrugged. Neither of them displayed the enthusiasm required to produce a feature film.

"Yeah, sure," Will said.

"What about football tryouts?" said Luke. "They're next week."

"So?" I said.

"We join the football team," Luke said. "That could be our story."

"And then we make a movie about it?" I said.

44

"No, like, not a movie," said Luke. "We actually join the team."

"We don't know how to play football," I said.

"We've played pickup games," said Luke. "I play with the neighbor kids all the time in the cul-de-sac. Me and Will crushed them last weekend."

"That's not, like, real football. Where guys who aren't nine years old tackle you."

"That would be hilarious. Getting tackled by football dudes who take it seriously. They'd be all intense and pissed off and we wouldn't care. We'd just laugh at everything."

Will shrugged. "I'm always looking for something to do."

I said, "*Playing football sarcastically* can't be a story."

"He just said anything can be a story," said Luke.

"Yeah, but not that." I turned to Will. "It's dumb, right?"

He shrugged again. "I'll try out. Got nothing else to do. But the movie idea is cool, too."

"Our story can't be *playing high-school football* and also a horror movie."

Mr. Meyer walked by and asked us how we were doing. "We're fine," I said. "We're making a movie."

"Excellent!" Meyer said. "You know, I volunteer as a jury member of the Goose Creek Film Festival. It's based in South Carolina, but they accept entries from anywhere. We screen features and shorts. We could enter yours."

"Whoa, seriously? That's awesome." I saw myself onstage accepting an award as Alex—the girl from the waiting room—smiles at me from the audience.

45

I shook myself back to reality and looked to Luke and Will. They seemed into the idea.

"Oh, and it's not a short," I said. "We're gonna do a full movie. Since we have all year."

"Even better," Meyer said. "What genre?"

"Horror. Definitely horror."

Meyer smiled. "Like Sam Raimi and his friends making *Evil Dead*. You guys could be next."

Holy shit. Yeah. We totally could.

"We're also joining the football team," Luke butted in.

Meyer looked confused. "Anything's a story. Can't wait to see how it all turns out." He moved on to the next group.

"Just come to tryouts, dude," said Luke. "Maybe you could be a kicker or something. What's the worst that could happen?"

"Seriously?" I said. "If, through some accident, we make the team, then what? *We played football.* That's our story? No one cares about football. It's not interesting."

"Okay," said Luke.

"Okay, you want to do the slasher movie?"

Luke laughed. "Jesus. Calm down. We have a year to do this project. Football's only in the fall. Why are you freaking out about it now?"

"Good point," Will said.

"Do either of you realize how much work it's gonna be to make something that isn't a total piece of shit? If we get our movie in that festival and people see it, we could actually get jobs and, like, *make* movies for real. This could be a big deal for us."

"Yeah, okay, cool," Will said, clearly not understanding the gravity of what I was saying at all.

"Just . . . Fine. You guys can go waste your time not making it onto the football team. I'll get started on the movie."

The bell rang and I walked out before they'd packed up their stuff. I was glad they weren't in my math class.

I took a desk in the back corner of the room. Mrs. Jenkins gave us a long worksheet to do while she sat at her computer doing a crossword puzzle. I did the first three problems to prove I could do them and then got out my notebook and worked on ideas for the movie.

I wrote down the horror ideas we'd all talked about at sleepovers and never followed through with. I mapped out a timeline over the entire year, blocking off sections for writing and editing the script, then figuring out the props and costumes and locations, making special effects that didn't suck, finding people to be in it, filming it in the spring, when my face would be clear and I'd actually want to be in front of the camera for the first time in years, and then editing and music. It was going to be a ton of work, but if we stopped bullshitting for five minutes and put some effort in, we definitely had enough time to do it.

My mind drifted to Luke and Will playing football. Imagining them making the idiots on the team laugh. Finding some weird niche they're naturals at, like being the guy who holds the ball up for the kicker. Gaining forty pounds of muscle. Chowing down on massive turkey legs all day long. Being carried off the field every Friday night on the shoulders of their adoring teammates, who deposit them at some diner, where they don't have to pay and all the waitresses wink at them and squeeze their shoulders when they bring out the food.

I didn't make much progress on the movie outline.

The final bell rang and after I got my stuff out of my locker, I went straight to the carpool line to find Mom waiting for me. She moved to the passenger seat and I got behind the wheel.

She asked me how the first day was. I told her it was fine. Pretty standard. Many syllabi.

She said something seemed off and I was being quiet, which only made me want to talk even less. I told her everything was normal and I was just tired. There was no point in telling her about Luke and Will's stupid plan to try out for football. Nothing was going to come from it, and there was no reason to stress her out and get her involved in our meaningless argument.

6.

We always sleep over at Luke's house the first Friday of every school year. When Will and I stepped inside his kitchen, Luke and his parents were sitting at the table with four pepperoni pizzas spread open in front of them. Every pepperoni was a little grease bowl waiting to fertilize a new pimple.

"Kevin, Will, how's it hanging?" Mr. Rossi said. Luke's parents treated me and Will like we were their kids. I nodded at him and reached for the slice that had the fewest pepperonis. I wanted to take a napkin and blot the grease off the top of it, but I knew everyone would think it was weird and ask me why I was doing it, so I ate an oily slice I didn't want.

"I'm so happy you guys are in almost all the same classes," Mrs. Rossi said. "Shame about math, huh, Kevin?"

I shrugged.

"Maybe the break will be good for you guys," said Mr. Rossi. "Who knows, Kevin? Maybe you can meet a girl in that class, since you won't have these two clowns embarrassing you."

I forced a laugh. "Yeah. Maybe."

"How are your parents?" said Mrs. Rossi.

"They're good." I shrugged, unsure what else to add.

"Has your dad sold any houses lately?"

"Uh, I don't know. He doesn't really talk about work. He just does it all the time."

Luke's mom laughed in a way that felt real, a way my parents had never laughed at anything I'd ever said. "What's your mom been up to?"

"Uh, she's good. I don't know. Driving around. Doing mom stuff."

She smiled and turned to Will and asked, "How's your mom?"

"Carol's killing it," said Will. "Her hydrangeas are off the charts this year."

That was a good specific detail. I wondered if he'd planned it. I'd forgotten to talk to Mrs. Rossi in my head before I came over, and now I was paying the price. Mrs. Rossi laughed. "Tell both your moms to come over here sometime for lunch so we can catch up."

Will and I nodded and Mr. Rossi said, "Hey, Kevin. Seen anything good lately? Besides *Slasher Massacre 8* and all the other trash you guys usually watch?"

50

"Oh, um, actually, yeah. *The Royal Tenenbaums?* It was good."

"Ah, then you should grab *Lost in Translation* and *Eternal Sunshine of the Spotless Mind.*"

"On that note," said Luke, standing up and closing one of the pizza boxes, "we will take this one to go."

We walked down into Luke's basement, where three huge couches formed a U in front of their giant TV and surround-sound system. Mr. Rossi's office was behind the couch. He worked from home, allegedly as some kind of "consultant," whatever that means. The coolest thing about him, though, was he used to own a movie rental store. It shut down a couple years ago, but Mr. Rossi kept pretty much all the DVDs and old VHS tapes and just moved the entire store into their basement.

I set my half-eaten pizza slice down on the coffee table, then went straight to the shelves and put *Lost in Translation* and *Eternal Sunshine* in my backpack to watch by myself later. Then I went to the horror section and said, "We should watch some new stuff tonight to help us think about our movie." We'd already seen most of the horror movies in Luke's basement — *Slaughter High, Class Reunion Massacre, Final Exam, Sleepaway Camp,* the *Halloweens, Elm Streets, Final Destinations,* and *Friday the 13ths* — but there were always more extremely disturbing covers and titles to check out. I took *Chooper* and *Slumber Party Massacre.*

Luke picked up a football off the floor and tossed it to Will. They passed it back and forth for a while, saying clichéd football terms like "Hut, hut, hike," and "Blue forty-two." They ran around the basement, throwing the ball back and forth, and when I came over, Luke threw the ball at me. I dropped all the movies on the table and caught it, then tossed it to Will.

"Let's watch this first," I said, holding up the *Slumber Party Massacre* tape. It was an eighties slasher about high-school girls. "It was written and directed by women and was actually, like, this feminist thing, almost like a parody of the whole genre. Maybe we could do something kind of similar in our movie."

Luke threw the football back to Will and leaned in toward the cover. "This is a feminist thing? Four babes with their boobs out staring up at some dude holding a big drill like it's his dick?"

"I mean . . . yeah . . . it is," I said. "Well, the woman who wrote it didn't, like, make the poster. There was this whole conflict between her and the producers, and—just watch it." I'd spent hours reading websites and forums analyzing the movie, and I understood its context but didn't feel like explaining it all to them.

I put the movie in and hit play, but Luke and Will kept passing the ball to each other and talking about how dumb and hilarious they'd look in football pads and uniforms at tryouts. Even ten minutes into the movie, they wouldn't shut up. I just sat there silently, staring at the screen like I was trying to shatter it with my mind. Eventually they started watching and making jokes about the movie, but I still didn't really say anything.

I'd planned to make a pitch to them about all my ideas and the deadlines we'd have to hit for the first draft of the script, but it seemed like a lost cause. They were in the mood to dangle their pizza crusts through their shorts zippers and slap them into each other. Luke and Will can both be legitimately funny, but sometimes they act like little kids and it's just not funny at all. There's a fine line between penis-related satirical prank calls designed to confuse and frustrate employees of major corporations and penis-related lame childish antics, and it was kind of depressing that they didn't seem to know the difference.

The movie ended and I went to the bathroom with my Ziploc bag full of skin care supplies to take my Accutane pill and wash my face and put on my salicylic acid. My cheeks were just as red and greasy as they'd ever been. Maybe even worse. Mounds of new lumpy whiteheads had sprouted all over my jaw and temples, and I smothered them in benzoyl peroxide cream that stung. My lips were a dusty, whitish purple, like dried-out old sticks of gum. I'd read that people usually get a bad breakout and their skin turns crazy dry as soon as they start taking Accutane, so hopefully my repulsive symptoms meant it was starting to work.

Luke found some dumb high-school comedy about prom and put it on to make fun of it. I'd called the big couch, so I lay there while Luke and Will sat on the floor. I didn't want my face to touch the leather because then Luke's old farts would get into my pores and make me break out, so I stayed on my back and kept my head upright and stiff like a mannequin. I imagined Alex sitting there next to me, telling me about the other music and movies she liked, things that were much more introspective and interesting than the dumb high-school movie Luke had put on.

There's a natural coating of grime that sticks to the human body during sleepovers, some signal in the morning that you need to have your mom pick you up immediately so you can begin the sanitization process. I told Luke and Will my mom was on the way and I needed a shower.

"Huh," said Will, sniffing his armpits. "I have no smell."

Mom pulled up into Luke's driveway with Kate in the front seat. "Mom and I are going to CVS together," she said. "*After* we drop you off.*"

"Okay."

"Do you want to know *why* you can't come?"

"I don't want to go to the store, so I don't really care."

"*Kevin*," said Mom. "Be positive."

"Well, the reason you can't go," said Kate, "is because it's for *woman things*."

I leaned my head back and closed my eyes until I was home.

It was Saturday, so Dad was in his office paying bills. His office is his fortress of solitude. He holes himself away in there for hours. I'm not sure what he does, exactly. I guess he keeps our family's finances in order while at the same time avoiding having to go browse the latest tampon styles with Mom and Kate. A win-win.

I got in the shower and shampooed and body-washed three times to get Luke's basement off me. Then I took my morning Accutane pill and washed my face with the white benzoyl peroxide scrub. It was the end of the bottle, so it took a lot of shaking and squeezing to get it out, and when I finally did, it exploded all over my hand and some of it shot behind me onto the wall. I wiped the goopy white stuff up with my blue towel. Then I put on the moisturizer with SPF and patted dry. Always pat dry. My dermatologist had hammered that into my head since my first appointment. Apparently wiping your face with a washcloth will destroy the last century of progress in the field of dermatology. Dr. Sharp would slap me across the mouth if she caught me wiping my face dry. If, on the same day, my dentist found out I only floss the night before my biannual cleanings, I swear to god the two of them would hop tandem on a motorcycle, drive over to my house in the middle of the night, and murder me in my sleep. So I patted dry.

Luke sent me a text saying he and Will were playing football with some kids in his neighborhood and I should come back to play. I told him I had stuff I needed to do at home.

I got out my agenda and looked through all the school assignments I'd gotten the first week and made a chart of when I'd get everything done. I divided the pages in a book about World War I by the number of days before the test and set a consistent schedule. There was a packet for chemistry due next week that looked pretty short, so I scheduled that early to get it over with. And then I listed our horror movie as an ongoing task that I should be thinking about every day.

I sat back to look over the finished assignment grid and was happy. I'd made my own megasyllabus for the rest of the semester. Everything in order, everything with a date and a place.

The only problem was I didn't feel like actually doing any of the assignments. Making the plan for the assignments was much more satisfying than reading thirty-one pages about the funeral of Edward VII. Instead, I got up from my desk, dug through my closet to pull out the worn pages of printed-out pornography I'd gathered and hid like they were religious texts, and jerked off.

Staring at a worksheet of quadratic equations or a history chapter on the Boxer Rebellion is so dull that my brain runs in the opposite direction. I wonder if teachers realize what they're doing when handing bland assignments to hormonal monsters, that the chemistry worksheet about catalysts is itself just a catalyst for a viewing of graphic pornography.

And then just as quickly as the obscene thoughts and images rush into my head — the instant the four minutes of magic are over — I forget about them. The urge to look at porn is no different from craving a Pop-Tart: it hits out of nowhere, and even though you know it's artificial and not good for you, you give in and then the craving's gone. All the urges and dirty thoughts disappear when I flush the tissue. Actually, while I'm walking over to the toilet, I've usually already moved on and am thinking about dinner, what's on TV, or that the Boxer Rebellion actually is kind of interesting.

I try to not feel too much like a disgusting beast just

because I occasionally allow myself to experience the greatest physical sensation available to humans in the most efficient way. Look, if Pop-Tarts had no calories and only made you feel morally repugnant for a few seconds after you finished, you'd eat one every day, too. Four when your parents are out of town.

I flushed the evidence, then meticulously put my sheets and pillow back in place like I was covering up my tracks after pulling off a museum heist. If my pillow had moved even half an inch from where it last was, I worried my parents would notice and start shrieking that I was a no-good, rotten self-stroker.

Dad knocked on my door, and I was still feeling so guilty and paranoid that it scared the shit out of me. He asked me if I had any trash he could pick up. I said yeah and he came in and asked how the schoolwork was going and I told him it was fine. He had a big trash bag with him, and he dumped my bathroom garbage bin into it. About a dozen tissues fell out. It looked like smoking-gun proof that I was addicted to beating off. I swear, though, they were from blowing my nose. When I masturbate, I flush the tissues like a gentleman.

Then he pointed to my towel, which was covered in white stains from the benzoyl peroxide cream I'd wiped up earlier. The wall still sported streaks of white goo, too. Yikes. It looked like I'd been doing butt-naked somersaults while cranking off in there for nine hours.

I stared into my notebook and told Dad the towel could use a wash. I flicked my eyes up and saw him carefully pick the towel up by one corner, facial expression neutral. He kept his eyes on the carpet when he wished me luck with the rest of my homework and left, shutting the door behind him.

Why do mothers and daughters get to bond over "woman stuff" while guys have to avoid eye contact over a stained towel? I mean, don't get me wrong: I'd rather slice my own head off with a rusty machete than have to deal with a period every month. And if blood ever came out of my penis for any reason, I don't think I'd scream with joy and write my pen pal a letter about it and rush off to the bathroom with six other boys to celebrate with red velvet cupcakes or whatever pastries the traditional customs might require.

Guys start to have weird bodily emissions around the same time girls get their periods, but we don't really get to romanticize some moment of "becoming a man." Dad and I never had a magic moment when I walked into his office, erection flipped up into my waistband, and proudly announced, "Father, it finally happened. I watched pornography and pleasured myself like an animal. I am a man now. Can you please drive me to CVS and recommend the best tissues for cleaning myself up while telling me that it's perfectly natural and everything is going to be okay?"

It's probably because girls don't get to choose when they get their periods, and then it happens naturally every month. Guys have to decide to peel down our running shorts, curl over like a hunchback under a bridge, whack off under cover of darkness, and then flush the evidence down the toilet. A girl's period is a flower blossoming in the springtime, but a guy's masturbation session is like a crime.

Perhaps they're not so similar after all.

Mom and Kate came back bearing boxes of feminine products I didn't want to look at, along with chicken fingers and mashed potatoes from the grocery store. I made a plate of food and took it back upstairs to eat at my desk, facing my TV. I pulled the *Eternal Sunshine of the Spotless Mind* DVD out of my backpack and put it on. The movie was emotional and romantic and sad, with this good music I'd never heard before and this crazy, smart, interesting structure. If we were going to have any hope of getting our movie into Mr. Meyer's film festival, our horror movie would need a unique structure like that. It couldn't just be another formulaic slasher movie.

Alex's earbuds sat on my bedside table, neatly wound up. I saw myself back in the waiting room, telling her about our movie. She'd be into it. She'd ask questions. She'd love it.

When I shook myself back to reality, I realized the DVD menu had been looping for fourteen minutes.

7.

Mom looked over the form with all the school-photo pack-
ages you could buy like she was studying for the SAT. She had
three brochures, two order forms, and a dozen sample photos
sprawled out on the kitchen island. She said she was buying
the super-premium package, which cost 140 dollars and came
with enough photos to give four copies to every single person I've ever spoken to in my entire life. It was like they were
expecting me to get kidnapped and wanted to be prepared to
staple my face on all the telephone poles in town.

"We don't need any copies," I said. "The picture will go in
the yearbook. You don't have to order anything. Right, Dad?"

Dad turned his head toward me but kept his eyes planted
on the newspaper. "Whatever your mother wants."

"I want to have lots of photos so that someday when I'm an old lady wondering about that high-schooler who lived upstairs in my house and spent all his time locked in his room, I'll be able to say, 'Oh, yes, it was Kevin.'" She smiled at me. I squinted at her.

"Come on," she said. "That was funny. Smile."

"You really don't need to waste the money," I said. "It's fine."

She put her hand on my back. "You'll never have to see them, sweetie. I'll keep them hidden, all for myself."

I shrugged and stepped away from her. There were about a million things I could think of that would be a better use of 140 bucks than a bunch of photos that will get dumped in the recycling bin someday when Dad's on a weekend trash run. But it wasn't worth the argument.

"What about these options?" she said. "They can do all sorts of stuff to your photo now. Whiten teeth, remove blemishes."

The blemish removal example showed this kid with a bowl cut from, like, twenty years ago with three big red bumps on his forehead and cheeks like stigmata. In the after-shot his skin looked like a freshly waxed car door.

Mom said, "Do you — would you want that?"

"I don't know," I mumbled. It looked strange and false. Isn't the media evil for Photoshopping celebrity pictures and making all of us have unrealistic ideas of how we should look? Wouldn't this just be part of that problem? On the other hand, by next spring when the yearbook came out, the Accutane would have cleared up my face and I'd look as smooth as the kid in the after-shot.

"I think you'll be happy you had it done," Mom said.

I kind of wanted it. But I was embarrassed to admit I did, so I pretended I was doing Mom a favor by huffing "Fine" and saying she could order it.

I stood in the yearbook picture line with Luke and Will, but they were mostly talking to Sam Hedrick and Patrick Baldwin, two guys they'd, I guess, become friends with at football try-outs. I couldn't believe Luke and Will had actually followed through on going to tryouts. They forget about 98 percent of the plans they make, but of course they remembered that one.

I'd known Sam and Patrick since fourth grade, but we'd never hung out with them outside of school or anything, so I felt like I'd never actually met them.

Sam has a buzz cut and is built like an ox. His dad has been training him to lift weights since he was an infant. He's my height but meaty, like a bowling ball made out of muscle.

Patrick has long, messy hair and is the bowling pin, tall and skinny.

They're always trying to attract attention together. The first time I ever saw someone get detention, it was those two, in Mrs. Yockle's sixth-grade language arts class, for charging at each other like a bull and a matador during quiet reading time. It wasn't funny at all. Patrick was the leader of the two. They were sort of like a comedy duo from the 1940s: flapping their limbs while the crowd goes nuts and you have no idea how anyone could find what they're doing or saying funny.

"Check out this nasty son of a bitch," said Sam, flicking the top of a whitehead in the crease of his nose. "I saved him up for right now so when I pop him, I'll be bleeding in the picture. It's gonna be sick."

All the other guys laughed, making noises like they were about to throw up. The zit they were so grossed out by looked exactly like any one of the twelve inflamed lumps on my forehead, nose, and jaw. "I'm gonna do it," he said, laughing. "Ready? Ready? Stand back."

Luke, Will, and Patrick backed out of the way and shielded their faces while Sam squeezed out the whitehead. It popped a minuscule amount of pus and the other guys all went nuts, hooting like apes. Sam laughed and cheered like he'd won a contest. It was an extremely weak pop, but I wasn't going to point that out. Considering how nasty they thought Sam's one pimple was, they must have thought of my face as some hellish nightmare that belonged in a photo of a Great Depression freak show.

"Excuse us," said Patrick to a few girls who looked at us. "Just taking care of some last-minute blemishes."

The girls laughed and smiled at him. The whole interaction was disgusting. Patrick is the kind of outgoing, arrogant, slimy jackass who once got away with addressing Mrs. Jones as "Barbara" in front of the entire class.

Luke said, "Did you guys see the retouching thing you can buy? If any guys paid for that, I hope they draw on a set of tits."

The other guys laughed. I folded up my order form and stuffed it as far down in my pocket as it could go. I stood two steps back from them and didn't say anything.

I finally got up to the front of the line. My heart pounded in my chest. I brushed my hair to the side and turned away from everyone and dabbed my face with the bottom of my T-shirt to get oil off it. The photographer called my name and I had to sit and smile. In a quarter of a second it was all over. The light was harsh and on top of it there was a flash.

I was glad Mom had paid for the retouching.

Mom called me downstairs that night when I was doing home-work in my room. She said she just got off the phone with Mrs. Rossi. Apparently Luke and Will both made the football team.

Goddamn it.

"I didn't even know you wanted to play football," she said.

"Right. I don't. They do."

"When were tryouts?"

"A few days ago or something. I don't know."

"Why didn't you say anything? You might still be able to get on the team as an alternate if you go to the practices. I can talk to the coach."

"Please, for god's sake, do not talk to the coach. I don't want to play football. And I don't think Luke and Will seriously want to play football, either. It was, like, a joke or something. I don't know."

"Oh. Well, Mrs. Rossi said they have practice just about every day after school now, and on some weekends, too. Are you sure you don't want to play with them? It might be fun."

"Sounds like a huge waste of time," I said. "I have stuff to do that's, like, actually gonna matter. A project they're supposed to be doing, too."

"What is it?"

"We're making a movie. Like, a real movie. I'm writing it and it could . . . There's this festival where . . . It's . . . just . . . a lot more important than whatever they're doing."

I went back into my room, shut the door, and tried to work on the script, but I mostly thought about Sam and Patrick's lame, obnoxious jokes infecting Luke's and Will's minds at football practice. They'd traded all their free time for the privilege of running up the bleachers until they puke and developing long-term head injuries via a hundred micro-concussions every day. They'd probably have brain damage by Halloween and wouldn't be able to contribute much to the movie's dialogue beyond incoherent mumbling and begging for ice packs on their groins.

I took my pill and spent twenty minutes on my face-washing routine while having this childish daydream about Alex somehow being there again at my blood test the next afternoon. The conversation we'd have played in my head and I locked in the perfect lines to say.

I went through my closet looking for an outfit to wear tomorrow like I was in a silent, lonely version of a teen movie makeover montage. I weeded through thirty dumb T-shirts to find the one button-down shirt I'd gotten for Christmas last year and had never worn. It was green and made me look older, or at least not so much like a child. I laid it out on my bed beside the least-wrinkled shorts I had. It was a decent out-fit. Maybe she'd like it.

Even assuming she was on Accutane, I was taking a leap of faith that she'd be there at the exact same time exactly four weeks after our first appointment. Accutane requires patients to stick to routines, and if ours aligned, it would mean some-thing. Synchronized schedules were a sign from the universe.

I closed my eyes and tried to picture her, but the harder I focused, the less of her I saw. I thought about her one part at a time, her legs or arms or shoulders, but I couldn't remember the shape or color of anything. All I knew was the impression she left on me. It was like staring into a bright light, then shut-ting your eyes and seeing the lingering glow stained against the dark. That was what I had of her, an imprint of how she made me feel that was more natural and real than measurements or a photograph.

Somewhere I read that you shouldn't worry about hypo-thetical bad things happening, because if they do happen, then you suffered two times. Maybe the opposite was true, too, though. That, as dumb and childish as it feels, you should let yourself hope because if you get lucky and the scene you play out in your head every night before you fell asleep comes true, then you get it twice.

8.

Holy *shit*.

She was there when I walked in, with her nose tucked inside the pages of a book, looking casual and confident in her messy ponytail. She held a half-eaten granola bar between the fingers of her left hand like a cigarette. I saw the scars on her cheeks, and she had a couple tiny zits on her forehead. She looked perfect. But she had to be on Accutane, right? The chances of her randomly being there at the same time as me again were zero. Unless the office paid her to sit there and attract guys like me into having our blood drawn.

The chair next to her was open. I reached into my pocket and blindly clicked buttons until I found play on my iPod, then rushed into the seat. My legs felt jittery. I pulled on the bottom of my shirt to tug the wrinkles out and make myself look less like laundry. "Needle in the Hay" blared through my earbuds at full volume. It stung my ears. I stared forward, my heart pounding, waiting for her to hear the song, ask me about my love of the song, then schedule the time and date when we'd make out to the song. My bleeding ear holes would be the sparks that set off the lifelong fireworks show of our romance.

Jesus Christ, it felt like the earbuds would explode inside my head.

I shut the music off, and in the sudden silence her eyes flicked up at me, then back into the book. Like she had no idea who I was.

Oh, no. Shit. Christ. *Abort mission. Abandon ship.* Forget all my hopes and dreams as I slap the eject button beside my chair and launch my head through the pockmarked tile ceiling. I couldn't give her back her earbuds now — she'd think I was a serial killer.

Get it together. I'd probably never see her again. If I didn't say something now, I wouldn't have another chance. I'd spent hours last night rehearsing this conversation in my head, fantasizing about this absurd coincidence that was now real.

"Hey," I wheezed.

A beat, and then she tilted her head toward me and shut the book. *Anna Karenina* by Leo Tolstoy. "Oh, hey," she mumbled through a mouthful of granola bar, spraying a few crumbs onto her lap. "Sorry," she said, swallowing.

I opened my lips, felt the dried crust all over them like pencil shavings, and no words came out.

Say the line, I told myself. *Say the goddamned line.* I'd spent six hours writing and rehearsing the script for this conversation, honing it into a slick, knot-free masterpiece guaranteed to make her laugh and realize how perfect we were for each other. But it would only work if I could nut up and say the goddamned first line. *Wait, what's the first word? Shit! If I get the first word, the rest will come. Get it together, you idiot. How stupid are you?*

Are you!

"Are you, uh" — I swallowed hard, then pushed ahead — "interested in grabbing a couple of burgers and hittin' the cemetery?"

"What?"

"Huh?"

"Did you say burgers?"

Sweet god. Holy hell. My face roasted and my armpits ejected sweat. My shirt's stiff collar scraped my wet neck. "Yeah . . . Do you . . . ? Uh . . . I, uh . . . *Royal Tenenbaums*? It's a line from that." I felt like I was being cooked in a rotisserie. I was such a moron. I'd spent forty-five minutes reading through *Royal Tenenbaums* quotes online to choose that one, and somehow didn't consider that when the other person has no idea you're quoting a movie, you're just asking her to eat fast food with you in a field of corpses.

She nodded. "Oh. Right. You really like that movie, huh?"

"Yeah. Yeah, I guess."

"Cool." She held out the last inch of granola bar. "Want any?"

"Oh, uh, I'm, uh—I'm good, thanks," I said. Wait. Fuck. Why hadn't I taken the granola bar? I *wanted* to take it. But there had been no granola bar in the scene I'd imagined. There were no snacks at all. It was a crumb-free fantasy with none of my lip smacks. She was supposed to recognize the *Tenenbaums* reference, and we were supposed to bond over our love of the same movies and music, so that when I gave her back her earbuds, she'd be primed to see me as the literate stud I'd scripted myself to be.

Instead I was a stammering kid strangling stolen earbuds in his pocket, wavering with indecision: Returning them would prove I was a thief and imply I was a stalker, but I'd backed myself into a corner and already looked stupid, so fuck it. "Oh, your, uh . . ." I trailed off while I wrestled the knotted mess of cords out of my shorts pocket. "You left these. Last time. I was, uh, keeping them safe."

"Oh, cool," she said. "I figured they just, like, vanished from existence. Thanks."

She set them in her lap, then flattened the granola bar wrapper and folded it in her hands and we didn't talk for a while. My face heated up. It felt like everyone in the waiting room was listening to me. Why was it so awkward? It shouldn't have been so awkward between us. Was it my dumb-ass button-down shirt? It felt huge on me. I looked like a third grader in an art class smock. This had all been a terrible mistake.

Finally she looked over and whispered, "You here for Accutane?"

I sat up straight. I had a comeback for that question: "How

can you tell?" I asked. "Was it the, uh . . ." *Shit.* I pawed around the cavern in my head, looking for the rest of that sentence and found nothing. I coughed. "Yeah."

"Same."

Holy hell. We took the same pills. It was the first time one of my romantic daydreams had actually been true. We had a connection. The same chemicals blasting through my bloodstream, potentially destroying my kidneys, were potentially destroying her kidneys as well.

She said, "How's it working out?"

"It's good," I lied automatically. Wait, what? Why had I glossed over the truth to her, like she was one of my parents? She wasn't part of the stressful, tangled-together mess of my friends, classmates, parents, and friends' parents. Anything I said or did to one of them rippled through everyone else. Alex was completely separate. I could be real with her. And some nurse would probably pop out any second to call one of us back and I might lose my chance to talk to her forever. "Actually it sucks. My face is still red all the time and it always kind of hurts. It stings and is dried out and feels pinched. I don't think the Accutane's doing anything yet."

She smiled. "Yeah, it tends to make your face worse for the first month. Then it gets better."

"Hard to tell if it got any worse, considering I looked . . . burnt before."

She laughed the tiniest laugh, mostly an exhale. I felt like I'd slam-dunked a basketball in front of fifty thousand screaming fans.

I said, "I'm still using all my salicylic acid and creams and stuff to try to make it work faster, but it's not really helping."

"Whoa, no. You're not supposed to be using any of that stuff while you take Accutane. Just take the pills and wash your face and moisturize. The pills dry your face out like crazy. Any peroxide or toner on top of that will, like, suck all the water out of your entire body. That's probably why your face stings."

"Oh. Huh."

"You can use basic stuff like Cetaphil to wash your face. Do you use that? The stuff that looks like camel spit?"

I laughed and nodded.

"Your dermatologist didn't tell you this stuff?" she said.

I shrugged. "I probably just wasn't paying attention. That's the tricky thing with advice. You have to be listening. I've probably let, like, dozens of inspiring quotes sail straight over my head because I was distracted wondering if, like, a hat exists that might look normal on me." She didn't really react to that. No laugh, no slam dunk. Not a big fan of the rambling. "So, um, you said it'll get better?"

"Mine's starting to. Thank god. Since this whole process is so annoying. My parents fight over who has to drive me to all these doctors' offices. And you know they test girls for pregnancy every month?"

"Your parents make you take pregnancy tests?"

"What? No." She rolled her eyes and smiled. She thought that was funny. I was just being a moron who misunderstood her. But I'd take the points. "The doctors do," she said. "To stay on Accutane."

"Wow," I said. "That, uh, that sounds like a lot of pee." *Jesus Christ, Kevin. Pee?*

"Well, no, it's just part of the blood test," she said, and for some reason didn't stand up and walk away and never speak to me again. "How are your hands?"

"What?"

She reached over the armrest and took my wrist. Her touch was warm and it shocked me, like I'd gotten a shot of adrenaline directly into my heart. She turned my hand over, inspecting it. "Mine got crazy dry and cracked at first. Yours look fine."

"Yeah, they're, uh, yeah, yeah, they're . . . pretty fine." I'd never thrown up from excitement before, but I sensed it brewing.

Before I vomited all over Alex's dry face, though, the receptionist called her name.

She put her book under her arm and her earbuds in her hoodie's front pocket. Before she stood up, she turned to me and said, "Your face does look better."

"Really?"

"You probably can't tell because it changes just a little every day. But compared to last month, yeah, it's better."

It took all my strength to suppress the audible gasp I wanted to unleash. She remembered me.

"See you next month?" she said, standing up.

"Ubbidah uh, uh — yeh, yeh, yeah," I Porky-Pigged at her.

Knowing she was about to disappear for another month, I felt the questions I needed to ask her slamming around inside my head: *Where do you live? What school do you go to? What's your last name? Give me all your contact information!* It sounded like what a stalker or murderer would ask. No, no — they were normal, necessary questions. *From a creep.* No, from a person interested in talking to another person. *Right. Quick! Ask the basic questions: Name and phone number.* Goddamn it, she was already walking away before I decided what to do.

She walked past the check-in desk and I watched her butt the entire time. It wasn't a conscious decision. I just instinctively stared at it, like I was a plant angling myself toward the sun.

When she disappeared to the back of the office, I replayed her telling me that my face looked good over and over in my head. I sensed her fingers on my wrist. I grabbed a magazine to hold over my face. I can't remember the last time I smiled like that.

A man sitting across from me with patchy hair and screwed-up teeth shot me a weird look. I realized my devious grin was buried in *The Women's Yoga and Pilates Journal.* I looked like a pervert and I didn't care. Alex had held my hand. She had said my face looked good.

That night I went through my bathroom cabinets and threw all my benzoyl peroxide creams and salicylic acid toners into a garbage bag. It felt important, ceremonial even. Alex had passed essential information on to me: *Stop coating yourself in acid.* We were bonded. Part of a distinct group with inside knowledge and secrets. The bag was enormous when I'd emptied the cabinets. A few years' worth of ineffective goo. When I lugged it downstairs, I felt like I was hauling a dead body out for disposal. It thudded into the bottom of the trash can in the garage and it was like I'd shed a younger, dumber version of myself. One big step in the evolution of Kevin. I'd just have to hurl five or six more metaphors for my own corpse into dumpsters over the next few months and I'd be set.

When I walked back inside, my parents looked over from the family room TV and asked what I'd thrown out. "Just some, uh, trash," I said, clarifying nothing. They nodded, each wondering how it was possible for me to have masturbated into so many tissues that the bag of them was heavy enough to make a hard thud. I stared at the floor and went back to my room, thinking about that classic riddle: Which is emotionally heavier for parents to hear being thrown away, ten pounds of acne goo they paid a lot of money for or ten pounds of evidence of their son's addiction to beating off?

When I closed the door to my room I stopped caring about that embarrassment and picked up where I'd left off thinking about Alex.

Over and over in my head, I replayed everything we'd said. Her touch, her soft smile when she laughed. My bland responses to her questions. My blank expressions. I started analyzing where I'd screwed up.

I'd flinched like I'd been electrocuted when she touched me. How weird was that? How noticeable was it?

I'd mumbled the few things I said to her. Completely

forgotten almost all the lines I'd prepared. The words I'd managed to force out had dribbled out of my mouth like applesauce down a baby's chin. I was such an idiot.

I'd barely told her anything about myself. I'd barely asked her any questions.

There were a million ways I could have handled it better. A million things I could have done but didn't.

But why did she touch me? Why did she talk to me at all? She could've just ignored me after I gave her back her earbuds, but she chose to talk to me. And she left me with a *See you next month?* Her voice definitely rose at the end; I was certain I heard a question mark. She asked me to confirm that she'd be able to see me again.

Was it possible . . . ? There was no way. But maybe? Did she . . . ? Did she *like* me?

No. Right? I just occupied her time for a few minutes in a boring waiting room where there was nothing else to do. I amused her. I was a novelty. I was a carnival game that lights up when you throw balls at it and holds your attention for three minutes.

No, it was more than that. She'd noticed me the month before and she'd remembered me. I remembered none of the other weirdos in the waiting room besides her. And she remembered me well enough to notice my face was getting better.

I let myself hope as I lay down in bed, shut my eyes, and saw us talking and holding hands under the waiting room armrests.

After a while I went downstairs, got on the computer while Mom, Dad, and Kate watched TV behind me, put headphones in, and read a summary of *Anna Karenina*. It was about this smart, interesting woman stuck in a marriage with this guy she hates, and she falls in love with this other guy. And, well, things don't really work out for her.

It sounded complicated and melancholy and beautiful. Mature. A step forward. It was exactly the kind of thing Alex would love. I made some notes to the movie outline and started thinking that our movie didn't have to be horror.

9.

In October, the high school's hallways get covered with banners for the homecoming game and dance. This year's had the same severe font as last year's, which Luke, Will, and I had made fun of for making the dance seem like a mandatory military draft we planned to dodge. I wanted to make fun of the dance with them again, but I barely saw them outside of school anymore because they were at football practice all the time. I saw them pretty much all day during school, but they mainly talked about football and it just wasn't the same.

At lunch they'd tell stories about what happened at practice the day before. They'd both experienced these events in real time, so I didn't get why they were even telling the stories in the first place. I mostly just sat back and observed them while I ate my peanut butter and jelly sandwiches. When the guys brought up that they were all going to the homecoming dance with some girls from Emma's group, I almost choked. "Wait, what?"

They claimed they were all just going as friends. Since when were they friends with those girls? Did they talk online? Did they call each other on the phone? When was the orientation held where everyone announced it was time to start having friendships with girls outside of class projects?

Whatever. I didn't care that I wasn't roped into their new, generic posse of kids I barely knew. Something about them playing football made me even more removed, more distant, more certain that I was different from all of them. They were just normal, boring high-schoolers; every day with them was a rerun of a TV show I'd already seen. I was writing a movie. I was fixing my face with medicine strong enough to mutate a baby. I had a girl outside of school none of them knew about.

On Saturday afternoon Mom forced me to go over to Luke's house, where their group was taking pictures before going to the homecoming dance, even though I wasn't going. I had better things to do than awkwardly stand around the gymnasium floor on a Saturday night watching Sam and Patrick try to entertain a bunch of girls by acting like animals in heat.

When I'd said I was going to stay home, Mom had said, "Kevin!" and I'd shrugged. Then she'd said, "Honey, what do you think? He only gets one sophomore homecoming dance."

Dad had bent down the corner of his newspaper and said,

"Whatever he wants to do is fine. Do whatever makes you happy, Kevin."

I'd drawn a blank. *Lying flat on my bedroom carpet thinking about Alex* would probably concern my parents, especially if I demonstrated the open-casket pose that was, honestly, just the most comfortable way to do that.

Mom said I could skip the dance if I went over to Luke's for pictures, and she told me I should shave so I looked nice. My probably-below-average testosterone levels mean I shave about once every two months, and doing it with acne is like running a lawn mower over a pile of water balloons. I didn't want to look at my face, so I shaved with my eyes focused on my bathroom sink and cut myself a dozen times and had to dab the cuts with toilet paper for fifteen minutes until they scabbed over. I covered my face in moisturizer and tried to think about how nice it would be when the afternoon was over and I could go back to my room by myself.

When I walked into Luke's house, I saw Luke, Will, Sam, and Patrick pretending to box each other and doing impressions of football coaches I didn't know, plus four of the God Squad girls standing on the deck taking pictures of themselves. I knew who they were — Lauren Gordon, Jen Evans, Veronica Wesson, and Haley Jackson — since I'd gone to school with them since second grade, but I didn't really know them at all. I probably wouldn't be able to identify any signature trait or article of clothing if one of them got kidnapped. They were bland background characters defined only by their snobbish blond-haired suburban Christianity. I'd spent thousands of hours in the same building as them, and everything remotely interesting about them could be written on a gum wrapper: Lauren cried when she'd get a grade lower than 90, Jen played either soccer or volleyball, Veronica was obsessed with adding more recycling bins to the school even though it was clearly only about puffing up her college application, and there was a rumor that Haley's dad was an extra in the rave scene of *The Matrix Reloaded,* but how was anyone supposed to verify that?

Seeing those girls outside of school felt wrong. I thought if I tried to touch them, my hand would pass right through.

Luke's dad slapped my back and shook me out of the trance I was in. "Where's your suit, Kev?"

"I'm gonna sit this one out," I said.

"Just here for the free snacks? I like it. Smart strategy. Help yourself, since Mrs. Rossi made enough food for the navy. Then get in there with the guys and we'll take some pictures."

I nodded at the guys and they waved back at me. Patrick gave me a salute, and I think he did it unironically. What a jackass.

Mrs. Rossi was taking pictures with the flash on; plus it was bright outside; plus they had all the lights on in the house for some reason.

Nobody saw me walk down into the basement, where I went into the bathroom and closed the door. I looked at my face in the mirror for the first time in a while. Once I'd realized my face wouldn't be immediately healed by Accutane, I'd started closing my eyes when I brushed my teeth and walking straight into the shower to avoid looking at myself in the mirror. But now there were cameras firing off from every angle upstairs, so I figured I might as well bite the bullet and see what I looked like.

It was bad. Even apart from all the shaving cuts. I don't know if it was just a flare-up or stress or if the Accutane was still making it worse, but in addition to my usual epidermal nightmare, I had a bunch of cauliflower-looking whiteheads sprouting up around my nose. I knew I shouldn't, but I squeezed them all out. It was so satisfying to drain every last bit of white goo out of them. Once I started I couldn't stop, in the zone like a pro athlete, focusing entirely on cleaning out every pore. They all bled, and I dabbed my face with toilet paper until the wounds congealed and I looked like I'd been stung by forty bees.

The guys and those girls were laughing upstairs. I didn't want to go back. I went over to Mr. Rossi's DVD library and looked through for stuff that Alex and I might like. I found a couple of the other movies I wanted to see — *The Virgin Suicides* and *Girl, Interrupted*. I was sure Alex liked them, or if she'd never seen them, I could recommend them to her after I watched and analyzed them.

"Kevin? Yo, Kevin?" called Luke.

"Yeah?"

"Get up here. You need to get in the pictures."

I brought the movies upstairs and stared at the floor, feeling and looking like a complete idiot. I was wearing a white

T-shirt and khaki shorts beside a row of girls in colorful dresses and guys in suits. I looked like a little brother no one wanted around.

"Perfect," said Mrs. Rossi, taking a picture every second. "Now the gang's all there."

I tried to smile, but I kept looking over at the guys and the flower thing pinned to their jackets that matched the color of their dates' dresses. In the same spot I had little dots of blood on my T-shirt that matched the color of my molten face.

It was like wandering through a dream, like there was a force field between them and me. Sam put his arm around my shoulder and smiled for the camera and gave a big thumbs-up. I made a confused face at him and thought, *Why is Sam putting his arm around me like we're friends?*

Jen Evans said, "Hey, Luke, did you hear Emma's going with Kyle Hornchuck?"

"Yeah, it's cool. I'm going to the dance with Haley, you know?"

He put his arm on Haley Jackson's shoulder. Everyone laughed. I watched them the way a scientist observes spores in a petri dish.

"Kyle's, like, such a dick," said Veronica Wesson, smacking gum.

"If he's mean to Emma, we'll beat the shit out of him!" shouted Patrick. He's the kind of cocky asshole who thinks he can cuss in front of adults.

They all cheered and laughed. Veronica said, "Dunk his head in a toilet for me." She stood on her tiptoes to grab the back of Sam's head and mimic drowning him in a toilet. Everyone went wild.

I moved over beside Will and tapped his arm. "Want to ditch this and watch movies at my house?" I whispered.

"No?" he said. "The dance is in twenty minutes. I already asked Lauren to go with me, bought the tickets, got this suit, and took all the pictures. I can't . . . I can't even tell if you're serious."

I shrugged. He walked out the front door to get into the cars with everyone else. Sam and Patrick had their licenses already and were driving. Once they'd all left, Mr. Rossi gave me a grocery bag to carry the movies in and I took it outside, dangled it over my handlebars, and pedaled my tiny bike out of their neighborhood and toward mine, the sack of DVDs knocking my knee.

While I rode, I thought about how Mr. Rossi had looked at me. It felt off, like he thought something was wrong with me. He didn't ask why I wasn't going to the dance. I kept wondering what Mr. Rossi thought about me, if he'd kept watch of me out the corner of his eye, worried I was some unhinged freak who might go nuts.

When I made it home, I tossed my bike into the wall of the garage, went up to my room, lay down, and thought about what Alex and I would do for homecoming if we went to the same school. We wouldn't go. We'd have a night in for ourselves. We'd be such an established couple there'd be no need to perform for anyone, to put on a stupid public show of our relationship for our classmates. We'd have nothing to prove and we wouldn't care about impressing anyone. We'd stay in my room wearing pajamas, building a fort, laughing at inside jokes we'd never tell anyone else.

Alex probably had plans to be at home in her room that night, too. Listening to introspective music and reading important novels, being quiet and thoughtful and alone, instead of at a school dance straining to hear some kid from chemistry scream over blaring pop music about which kid had been seen with a visible boner crease in his khakis and trying to avoid the sight of random kids from the cafeteria grinding their penises and butts together.

Her phone must have been right next to her. Mine was charging on my nightstand. All I needed was a ten-digit code to bring her voice into my room. It was like I was standing on the bank of a river and could just barely make out her shape across the water. I knew she was right there, and I knew she could see me, but not having her phone number — plus being fifteen and not having a license in a suburb where you have to drive everywhere — kept us apart. Next appointment, I'd ask her for her phone number. I'd get my act together. I had to.

I went to sleep wondering if she was thinking about me.

10.

My parents never have guests over, and Dad seemed stressed out the Saturday afternoon when he heard that his friend Tom from college and his wife, whose name I was 55 percent sure was Karen, would be staying at our house that night. I guess Tom was into monster trucks and there was some monster truck show downtown in the afternoon, and Tom figured it would be fun for them all to get together at our house afterward.

I dislike Tom and have for years. This is the guy who once called me out in front of our entire families at a restaurant because my jacket didn't have something called a "polar thermal matrix." He was talking about his new jacket's technology for a half hour, and apparently I was worthless because my jacket didn't have this bullshit thing some idiot made up and lied to him about on the Home Shopping Channel. He's a man who believes advertisements, and that's a man I want nothing to do with. Honestly, what had that guy ever done in his life to earn anyone's respect? I can't wait to be old enough that people assume I've accomplished things without any evidence.

When Mom got off the phone with Karen and explained what was happening, Dad said, "You know what would also be fun? Them staying in a hotel and we could stop by for an hour's worth of drinks and call it a night around eight."

Mom said, *"Paul,"* in the tone of voice she usually reserved for *"Kevin . . ."*

I was upstairs in my room when Tom and Karen rang the doorbell around seven. It's kind of embarrassing to admit this, but I army-crawled into the hallway where I could peer over the edge down into the foyer. Tom and Karen hugged Mom and seemed excited to be there. Dad stepped in a second later and, oddly, was all smiles and hugs, too. "Tom!" he said. "Cynthia!"

Cynthia? Where the hell had I gotten Karen?

He kept saying how great it was to see them. It was like he was running for mayor all of a sudden and became the friendliest guy around. They went into the family room and Tom sat down in Dad's spot on the couch, but Dad didn't say anything.

I could see the backs of all their heads from my perch upstairs. Only my eyes and forehead were poking out around the wall, so they'd never notice I was up there watching them. I felt safe and comfortable, like I had some superpower.

Dad seemed to have been suddenly struck by radiation, too. He was asking questions, smiling, laughing, looking Tom and Cynthia straight in the eye. He was like a talk show host. What happened to the dad who dreaded Tom and his wife coming over? Where was the shy, socially awkward guy who prefers email? He was fascinated by every uninteresting thing Tom said — how his job was going, what their kids were up to, how long it took to drive into town.

Kate walked in from the kitchen and they all said hi to her and talked about how they remembered her from when she was a baby. No one mentioned me at all, and it felt wonderful to be practically dead for a night.

I barrel-rolled across the carpet back into my room and watched *The Virgin Suicides* and wondered what Alex's bedroom was like and what she wore to sleep.

Hours passed and I could still hear them talking downstairs when I got up to take my pill. Dad hadn't stopped hosting the conversation, firing off questions. They eventually went to sleep, and I did, too, confused about where my real dad had gone and who that new guy was.

It was impressive. I wished I could just flip myself on the way Dad had. He was clear and direct, the opposite of my stuttering strangeness. If I could do that at school, I'd probably be the president of all the clubs and captain of all the sports teams, an all-around great guy who gets carried out of school on everyone's shoulders at the end of each day.

Or at least I could be slightly more normal. Just confident enough to talk to people without regretting every word the moment it trickled down my bumpy chin. I could be better around Alex. Ask her questions instead of nervously rambling movie quotes. Pass the ball back and forth instead of being a conversational ball hog. We'd be two normal teenagers bonding while exchanging information. I could find out where she went to school and who she hated. I could get her phone number. We could talk about face moisturizer and books and movies. There was so much for us to talk about if only I could get out of my head when I was with her. If I could lead a conversation like Dad just had, I would have known everything about Alex at our first appointment and by now she'd officially be my girlfriend.

I woke up to the sound of Tom and Cynthia leaving the house. As soon as the front door shut, Dad let out a huge sigh. "Aaaaaaaand that's over. Whew."

I knocked on Dad's office door that afternoon and asked if he had a second. He seemed stunned. I bet it's alarming to parents when you rarely talk to them and then, out of nowhere on a Sunday afternoon, formally ask them for some time to talk. I mean, yeah, from his point of view there was probably a 90 percent chance I was about to come out of the closet, so I got his surprise.

"Sure," he said. "What, uh, what's up?"

I sat on the filing cabinet beside his chair. "When Mom said Tom was coming over yesterday, I thought . . . I don't know. Like, you didn't want him to come over."

"I was just giving Mom a hard time. I don't always feel like entertaining."

"Yeah. But when they were here, you were the life of the party. You seemed really happy. How can you just, like . . . do that?"

"How do I host people?"

"Yeah." My throat felt tight and dry. I don't know if I was scared or embarrassed or what. At my age I probably should have been asking Dad how to have sex with my dream girl in the back of a convertible with an empty driver's seat and a brick on the gas pedal, howling through the desert 130 miles an hour. "How do you just force yourself to, like, be all social and outgoing?"

He leaned back in his chair. "Ask a lot of questions. When you meet someone new, or when you're stuck talking to someone you have nothing in common with, just keep asking them questions. You can always lead a conversation if you don't stop asking questions."

"What if there's nothing you want to ask them?"

"Oh, you probably won't care about their responses. That's not the point. You just need to keep them talking. People like people who seem interested in them. Repeat their answers to them to prove you were listening. Ask questions where the answer is just a number. There's always an answer when you ask, 'How long did it take to get here?' or 'How much does the new baby weigh?' or 'How far do you guys live from the stadium?' People get tripped up if you start asking them to tell you stories or about how they feel. Stick with questions about logistics. You won't surprise or offend anyone, and you'll keep them talking."

Huh. I nodded slowly, thinking it all over. He seemed calculated, robotic, and almost psychotic, but I figured he was right. Dad never asked me anything about how I was doing or to tell him a story about something that happened in school that day. All he ever wanted to know was how long a class period was or how old Luke's car was. And I always had an answer for him.

I said, "How did you figure this out?"

"I talk to strangers all day when I show them houses. I learned to ask a bunch of numbers questions up top and they think I'm fascinated by them. It always helps to have a plan, you know? Some people like to make it up as they go, and that's a mistake," Dad said. "You and I appreciate a plan."

"Right, thanks. That helps."

"Anytime," he said. And then, when I was walking out, he added, "How many more months do you have of school?"

"Um, well, it ends in May, and it's October, so I guess, like . . . seven?"

He nodded, and I left. I don't think he was aware that he just asked me a logistical question immediately after telling me that he often asks logistical questions when he doesn't care about the answer. Oh, well. Maybe he could use the information.

Dad's advice would work. I'd go to my next appointment with an arsenal of quantitative questions so specific they were guaranteed an answer. Dad had minimized the risk of stilted pauses and nervous stammering and maximized the chance of a clear response. I made a list of questions I'd ask Alex at our next appointment. I had a plan. I wouldn't have to worry about feeling weird or awkward or panicking if I forgot the script I wrote in a daydream. I'd fire off number-based questions and Alex would be on a roll answering them, chanting responses out like she was in a trance, and when I got to the most important one, *What's your phone number?*, she wouldn't hesitate.

11.

"I'm so sorry to have to tell you," Mom said Monday night, right after she got off the phone with Mrs. Rossi. "Luke and Will both got hurt at football practice. A sprained ankle and fractured collarbone. Luke tackled Will, or Will tackled Luke, or . . . Either way, the coach said it was one of the hardest hits he'd ever seen, like how the pros tackle. Truly. Like two eighteen-wheelers crashing headfirst. None of the damage is permanent, thank god, but they won't be able to play the rest of the season."

"Oh . . ." I said, trying to not smile.

I invited Luke and Will over that Friday to catch them up on all the work I'd done on the movie outline and schedule and get them excited and eager to dive back in. They'd be impressed that I'd actually kept up with the work while their stupid football plan exploded in their faces.

They both walked in looking completely fine and uninjured. They didn't even have casts, just soft fabric braces on Luke's ankle and Will's shoulder. We went to my basement and they sat on the couch in front of the fresh notebooks and sharpened pencils I'd set out for them. I stood with my printed-out sheets of notes and told them the movie is about this guitar player who's a genius, but no one knows how tortured his life is, and he dies, but this girl who loved him helps get everything he'd written out into the world. I mentioned how the structure would be nonlinear and incorporate some elements of memory and time-hopping from *Eternal Sunshine* and some parts of the doomed romance from *Anna Karenina*. And I'd read a lot about this French movie *Breathless,* so I said we'd use some of that, too.

"Wait, what are you talking about?" Luke said. "How is any of that a horror movie? We're making a slasher movie. Right?"

"It's . . . I mean . . . I don't . . . It's just a story. We don't need to put some genre or label on it."

"I'm kind of scared to ask this," Luke said, "but, like, the guitar player? The undiscovered genius some girl loves . . . ?" His face soured. "Is that, like, supposed to be *you*?"

"What? No. Come on. I don't play an instrument or anything. It's fiction."

"Because if this is, like, some weird fantasy of yours, it

might be the most embarrassing thing I've ever heard of."

"Well, it's not, so . . ."

Luke rolled his eyes. "All right. Well, what parts of *Breathless* do you want to steal?"

"Just, like, the way it's edited," I said.

"You've seen *Breathless*?" he said.

"I mean, I read a lot about it. I haven't watched it yet. I have it downloaded."

"I don't think you can just, like, take stuff from a movie you haven't seen," he said. "And what do any of us know about being a singer? Shouldn't this thing be about something we know about? So we don't seem like morons when someone who knows more about it watches it?"

Will, eating some of the Bagel Bites Mom had prepared, said, "He's got a point."

"It should be a slasher movie about a high-school football team," Luke said. "You've got, like, tons of weapons and tons of victims and suspects." He started jumping up and down on the sofa. "Dude, dude, dude, this would be sweet. Like, it could start with a receiver catching this huge pass and right as he gets to the end zone"— he ran across the floor, then stopped suddenly, stuck his tongue out, and fell down —"*fwoosh,* and someone throws, like, a knife into his neck."

Will nodded. "I like it." Then he looked at me. "Can we do that?"

"But you guys don't know that much about football. You only practiced for, like, a month. You never played in a game."

"What the hell do you know about music?" said Luke.

"You've been playing the same one song on my brother's guitar since sixth grade."

It didn't seem worth it to correct him that I had actually mastered *two* guitar tabs since sixth grade. And I didn't feel like explaining all the Elliott Smith music I'd been listening to since Alex introduced me to him. "I mean, I guess we might be able to use some of the football stuff. Maybe in one of the flashbacks the singer plays football. Or, I guess, maybe his band plays music in a halftime show. But, like, I don't know if it should be all gory. Like, I mean, horror is so . . ." I shrugged.

"Wait, what?" said Will. "Since when is it not a horror movie? I thought that was your whole idea."

"I don't know. I mean, horror movies are kind of all the same. It's always the same structure and you know everyone's gonna die. What's the point? They're just not interesting. Like, *The Royal Tenenbaums* or *The Virgin Suicides*? Or *Anna Karenina*? Those stories are more complicated and interesting."

"What?" said Luke.

"You haven't seen those movies?" I said.

"Let's just do a horror movie. What are you talking about?"

"How are we gonna do those special effects?" I said. "How are you gonna make a knife go into a football player's neck?"

"How we always do them: ketchup and that splatter thing we made from tubes at Home Depot. That thing looks ridiculous."

"It looks like shit."

"Remember when it sprayed all over the wall in my room? That was the best."

"If we do a serious movie without crappy effects," I said, "then we don't even have to worry about them looking horrible and taking people out of the story."

"You're the only one worrying," Luke said. "Let's just make a dumb movie where me and Will fight again and fall into a pool."

"That's the whole story?" I said. "That's a ninety-minute narrative to you?" I got hot and tense. We were already off track on my production schedule and I needed to steer us back. We couldn't give up already and make another five-minute waste of time that no one ever wants to watch and gets lost forever. "Why are you making this so hard? I feel like I'm in one of those documentaries about a cursed movie production that spiraled into disaster, like *Hearts of Darkness* or something."

Luke raised an eyebrow. "You think us sitting in your basement talking is as hard as filming *Apocalypse Now* in the jungle in the Philippines?"

Goddamn it. It was really annoying when Luke understood references I'd intended to sail over his head and make him feel clueless. "Look," I said, "you guys haven't even seen *Breathless*, so you don't know what you're talking about."

"You just told us you haven't seen it, either," Luke said. "You *just* said that. Your argument makes no sense."

"I downloaded *Breathless*."

"Yeah, that's the same thing," Luke said, laughing. "Like how I've been to China. Well, I mean, I've seen *Shanghai Knights*."

Will laughed. I shook my head and squeezed my eyes shut.

"Let's put it on right now. It'll be good. It's, like, a really important film."

I connected my hard drive to my Xbox and started *Breathless,* sitting on the far edge of the couch a few feet from the guys. The movie's in black and white, and it uses these crazy jump cuts, so time is rapidly shifting around. It's not like any regular American movie. It's really interesting. Better than most of the garbage movies they make now.

"Why are we watching this?" Luke said five minutes in. "Halloween is in, like, three days, so I don't know why we're watching a movie that's not about graphic murders. When did all this even happen? When did you start hating horror movies? Is some creepy eccentric billionaire paying you to make him a movie starring a bunch of young boys and you have to follow his orders very precisely or else he'll, like, lock you in a giant fucking birdcage?"

Will laughed.

"Yes," I said through gritted teeth. It wasn't worth trying to explain Alex to them. They'd make stupid comments and it would get complicated and annoying.

Luke said, "Seriously, what happened to pink-eye-blaster Kevin?"

"I don't know what you're talking about," I lied.

Will said, "That was, like, the thing you invented where you took an empty Mountain Dew bottle and ripped ass into it all through *Final Destination 2* and then you puffed your farts out of it at our faces."

"Did Godard blast his shit particles into his friends' eyeballs while he directed *Breathless*?" Luke said. I didn't respond. He added, "You know this whole mind-set of thinking modern movies are bad makes no sense, right? If you were around in Truffaut's time, you'd be shitting on his movies, calling them mainstream trash and obsessing over the 1920s, but if you were alive *then*, you'd say *all* films were a new fad of mainstream shit and you'd argue that blurry-ass 1820s photographs were better, and you could run with that annoying stance all the way back to being a caveman complaining about the first drawing and saying life was better before art existed at all."

I paused a moment, waiting for the perfect counterargument to find me. "Uh . . . no?"

"You're not gonna be this weird on the south Georgia trip, are you?" Luke said.

"I'm not being weird." I turned *Breathless* back on, but it was hard to pay attention because I could see, out of the corner of my eye, Luke and Will texting and not watching any of it.

I stopped the movie again. "Fine. Why don't we just try writing something?" They stared at me. "It'll be fun," I barked. "Okay? Let's just kick around ideas to get started. Anything. Whatever ideas you guys want." I was trying to be an inspiring leader, but I could hear my tone was more like a ruthless sweatshop owner. I considered shouting at them, *I'm being a cool boss here, you goddamned idiots,* but figured that probably wasn't the best thing for morale.

Before they kicked around any ideas, Luke's phone rang. He answered it, then said to me, "Yo, what's your house number?"

"Why?"

"Jen and Haley are gonna pick us up here so we can all go over to the game together."

"Uh," I said. "Since when?"

"What's your address?"

"Can you stop screwing around and pay attention?" It was like my plan to make something to impress Alex was a long line of dominoes I'd carefully arranged, and Luke was flicking pieces out at the start, sabotaging every other step down the line. "We're supposed to work on this all night to have a solid outline, so next week we can divide up the scenes and each start writing. Then we'll put all the scenes together and polish the whole script. We have to get that done in the next couple of weeks to stay on track."

Luke paused for a second. "Is it 2015 Lakewind?"

I just stared at him. Friends were better before cell phones.

"Kevin's buffering," he said into the phone. "Something's going on with his connection. Just go down Randal Parkway, make a right at the neighborhood sign that looks like a wiener, then it's the first street on the left."

I sighed and turned to Will. "Are you gonna help me work on the script?"

"Yeah, sure."

"Sweet. What ideas do you have?"

"Oh," he said. "I don't know. What you guys said earlier sounded good." He licked the Bagel Bite grease off his fingers. "Do you have any Sprite?"

I couldn't deal with them. Luke has the attention span of a cricket and Will is just kind of there. I'd have to continue doing the whole thing myself. They started playing pool and talking about the football game they were going to. It was hard to feel like I even knew them anymore. They didn't feel like friends. More like people who happened to be in my basement.

I switched the input away from the movie and sat there on the couch, staring at commercials on TV, waiting for them to leave. I was silent and pretty sure I looked extremely sullen, but neither one of them seemed to notice.

The doorbell rang and Luke looked at me. "Can we go let them in?"

I grunted and sulked upstairs. Luke and Will still didn't notice my exaggerated annoyance. How come Mom can notice I'm feeling off when I stare into the open fridge for one extra second, but my two best friends are oblivious when I completely stop talking to them?

Kate and her friend Courtney had already opened the front door. Jen and Haley stood in my doorway like holograms. "These girls are here for you boys," said Courtney, giggling.

"Have fun at the game," I said. "I hope our team gets the most concussions or whatever." Then I turned around to go back down to the basement.

"Dude, come on," Luke said. "Game's this way."

"Yeah, I know. Welp. I'll probably see you at school on Monday."

"Kevin, come on!" said Jen, which was weird because I'd never spoken to her in my life. What did she want with me? "You'll have fun."

"You don't want to go to the game?" whined Kate, tugging

on my shirt and making weird duck lips at me. "All high-schoolers go to the football games to kiss under the bleachers."

I nodded at her, wishing it were more common for healthy teenage boys' hearts to spontaneously combust; I wished to be a pile of ash.

"If he stays here by himself," said Courtney, "he'll probably *play* with himself." Then she motioned jerking off with her right hand, and with her left hand made this weird tickling gesture that I'd never seen before and which very much creeped me out.

"Jesus Christ," I said. "Who teaches you this stuff?"

Jen and Haley laughed. I'd definitely been planning to masturbate that night, but it would be hard to focus when just minutes before, my little sister's friend had demonstrated to some girls from school what I'd be doing, and she did it using a more advanced technique than I knew.

"Fine," I said. "Forget it. Whatever. I'll go."

12.

Freshman year we never went to any football games, so walking into the stadium, I had no idea what to do. It was starting to get cold outside, but we left my house so suddenly, I didn't think to get a sweatshirt. I was in a T-shirt and shorts, surrounded by people in hoodies and jeans. I felt like I'd walked onto the set of a Japanese game show. All the overhead lights were on. I didn't know what I should be looking at. I stayed at the back of our group. There were tons of open seats up at the top of the bleachers, but we walked past all that prime real estate and headed straight into the crowded student section, jamming our way through bodies until we got to the sophomore area. We were surrounded by people I had no interest in seeing outside of a classroom setting between the hours of 8:40

and 3:40, Monday through Friday, and I was sure they felt the same about me.

We settled on a spot and I stood on the very edge of the bleachers between the aisle and Will. Through some unspoken pact, everyone had decided to stand up the entire game. We'd all be happier sitting down, but I guess no one wanted to be the first person to do it. Everyone in the student section went insane every time something happened on the field. Some of them were painted and holding signs. How could anyone actually care? What difference would winning or losing this game make to anyone who was just watching it from the stands?

I tried to figure it out for a while, standing there observing everyone and wondering if my thoughts were profound or if I was just being an idiot and needed to stop thinking so much. It's tough for a fifteen-year-old guy to determine if he's the physical manifestation of Holden Caulfield or just a run-of-the-mill pompous jackass. Luke and Will clearly weren't thinking about anything. They were chanting and screaming for Sam and Patrick the whole time. I wondered if Haley and Jen were jealous.

Once our team finally scored a touchdown, all the guys freaked out and formed this mosh pit, jumping up and down and smashing into each other. Luke and Will dove into it and I watched. They looked like gorillas or cavemen or — or — I couldn't think straight enough over the noise of screaming teenagers and the school band's abrasive, jarring honks to decide what sort of uneducated beasts they exactly reminded me of. I couldn't focus, couldn't stop thinking about how bizarre the football game was. How strange the idea of sports was, like some pretend version of war. I wanted to stop thinking all those cyclical thoughts I knew a hundred million other guys exactly like me had already had. So ten minutes later, when our team scored again, I pushed myself into the mosh pit.

I don't know if *fun* is the right word for it. It was kind of satisfying, at least for the first few seconds, because I stopped overanalyzing high-school football culture, since my brain was fully occupied trying to keep me alive.

All of a sudden, James Dunne, whose personality is defined by his pet snake, looked at me like I had a spider on my face and said, "Holy shit, dude, I'm sorry! Are you okay?"

"Uh, yeah?" I didn't know what he was talking about.

All the other guys turned and stared at me. Their eyes lit up and someone said, "What the hell happened?"

I reached up and felt my forehead. It was covered in blood. "It's fine," I said. "Don't worry about it."

James Dunne said, "Dude, I'm sorry."

"It's fine."

I covered my forehead with my hands and squeezed my way out to the aisle, then ran up the stairs and into the bathroom to look at my face in the filthy mirror under the buzzing fluorescent lights. James Dunne had elbowed a ripe zit on my forehead and it had burst like a fire hydrant.

I wanted to wash it off, but the faucet spewed a yellow liquid that looked like pure E. coli. So I dabbed my forehead with dry paper towels until it was mostly clean. It was calm in the bathroom. Quiet and still. It reeked of stagnant piss and week-old turds, sure, but that was a fair price to pay for some solitude.

Two kids — probably in middle school — came in. As soon as they saw me, they started laughing, then smacked each other's arms to stop, which made them crack up harder. I felt my face turn red. Goddamn it. Maybe they weren't actually laughing at me — I had no way to know. It didn't matter, though, because even if they were laughing at some unrelated inside joke, the sound of them cackling reminded me how pathetic and out of place I was.

There were still fifteen minutes left in the game, but I didn't feel like going back to the student section and having to explain to everyone a million times that I was fine, it looked worse than it was, and it was really just one meaningless zit on the zit-covered forehead of Accutane Kevin. So when I left the bathroom, I went down to the parking lot, sat on the back bumper of Haley's mom's car, and folded my goose-bumped arms across my chest and squeezed them tight to keep from shivering.

This group of six freshmen was standing around talking and laughing and drinking those slushies from the gas station that kids put vodka in. I could have sworn those kids were complete losers. They spent the mornings sitting on the floor by their lockers drawing weird pictures of anime-style dragons, and it was verified school lore that three of the guys, on separate occasions, had been caught watching hentai in the computer lab. But apparently those freaks went to football games and were part of a group of friends that included girls.

Yet there I was, alone with my frigid nipples chafing against my T-shirt, trying to convince myself I was cooler than them.

I imagined what Alex was doing. Wearing a big, old T-shirt, leaning against her kitchen counter reading a French novel while Bright Eyes played and tea heated up in the microwave. Later she would call me and we'd talk about the pointlessness of homecoming, how weird it was to see my friends wearing suits before they went to the dance, why I'd never go to another football game again. She'd ask me questions and she'd think my responses were funny. I tried to remember those lines for when I'd see her next.

A river of my excited classmates flooded down to the parking lot. Before I could see her, I heard Haley say, "He probably called his parents. We should just go without him."

They stepped around the car and saw me. I stared at them, frozen, like they'd caught me trimming my pubes with the family scissors.

"Oh," said Haley. "What happened to you? Are you okay? We were worried."

"Uh, yeah, no," I said. "It's not a big deal. Like, nothing happened."

Luke said they were going to meet Sam and Patrick and some of the other players at Waffle House to celebrate the win. I told them I should probably just head home, since my house was on the way to Waffle House anyway.

Luke started trying to persuade me to go, but Jen said, "Whatever. Just let him do what he wants," and I crawled into the way-back seat.

They dropped me off at my house and I was relieved to no longer be a fifth wheel to their double date, or whatever that outing was. Luke and Will still hadn't explained their relationships with Jen or Haley or any of those other girls who'd suddenly been promoted from background extras to guest stars in the high-school TV show that happened around me.

I walked inside, told my parents I had fun and it was "good," and then sat down behind them on the family room computer and put my headphones on. I had to do the iPLEDGE thing to assure the government that I had not had sex in the past month. I thought for a while, trying to recall if perhaps I'd had a few sexual encounters and forgotten about them because they were so commonplace for a guy like me. Had I banged a few babes in the locker room before school? While waiting in Mom's minivan in the Kroger parking lot, had I gotten downright nasty with a couple of nymphomaniacs? I was pretty sure I hadn't, so I told the government it could relax.

I went upstairs to my room and closed the door. My brain replayed the scene of those two kids laughing at me — or near me — or whatever — in the football stadium bathroom and I got nervous for a second, like I was worried they'd pop out from behind my bookshelf and laugh again and I still wouldn't know if it was about me. Had I always been this paranoid and self-conscious? In middle school, did I cringe and tense up any time I heard laughter in the halls? Or was I the kid laughing at everyone else? When I'd fake being sick, was I just exploiting a loophole to stay in bed watching TV all day, or was there a reason I didn't want to go?

I pulled my sixth-grade yearbook off the shelf to try to remember. I looked at my picture. I didn't have acne, but I was chubby and had a bowl cut. I guess it was a trade-off. Maybe when my skin cleared up, I'd grow a potato-size cyst on my neck to keep my overall value even.

I found no clarity about my feelings in that picture. It might as well have been of some other kid. I remembered things I'd done but couldn't think back to feeling sad or stressed out or even happy or excited. My memories were all facts and information, all quantitative. It was like I knew the list of ingredients that made up my middle-school years, but I didn't remember how the recipe actually tasted. I couldn't decide if that was a good thing or a bad thing.

I shut the yearbook and fished around my desk drawer for my list of questions to ask Alex at our next appointment. I read through my questions over and over so I wouldn't forget them. I'd find out about her life and I'd tell her about my movie. Our snow-globe-waiting-room world would have no noise and no chaos, nothing but us.

13.

"Is everything okay?" is probably the least effective question a parent can ask. Despite its zero percent success rate, Mom persists.

"Yeah, I'm fine," I said. I had the minivan stopped at a red light on the way to the blood test place after school, trying to rehearse my questions for Alex in my head. Mom sat in the passenger seat and I could feel her staring at me as I accelerated.

"Mrs. Rossi mentioned earlier today that the guys and the girls they took to homecoming went out to Waffle House with all the other kids from school after the football game last weekend."

"Yes," I said, picturing myself asking Alex, *When do you —?*

"But she said you didn't go with them."

"Yeah," I said, trying to picture myself asking Alex, *How far from —?*

"It sounded like fun. You didn't want to go?" she said.

"No." *How long does it take you to —?*

"You know I don't want to be a mother who gets involved in her son's business, but . . ."

"But what?" *How many siblings —?*

"Did something happen between you and the guys?"

Goddamn it. "I just didn't feel like going. I'm sorry. I'll be grounded forever because I didn't want to eat Waffle House scrambled eggs and hash browns immediately before going to sleep."

"*Kevin.* She said Luke and Will have been going to all the football games this season. But you'd told me no one went."

"I just didn't want to go. It's not a big deal."

"Okay. That's fine." She was quiet for a minute. "Would you tell me if anything was wrong?"

"Sure," I lied. There was no point in spilling my emotional guts to her. She'd get on a conference call with every mom from school and let them all know that poor wittle Kevin was a sad wittle boy.

The stiff silence in the car made the last five minutes of the drive feel like ten hours. Finally I pulled into a parking space and told Mom I'd be back later. On the walk through the parking deck, I reviewed as many of my conversation notes in my head as I could remember. I didn't let myself think about the possibility that Alex wouldn't be there, about how much luck would have to pile up for us to once again be in the exact same place at the exact same time. I held my breath as I pushed open the door — and there she was, in her usual spot.

The bumps underneath her makeup hadn't gone away. Her hair was kind of wavy or something, and it wasn't in a ponytail; it was tucked behind her ears. The color was a little different from what I remembered — lighter, maybe — and it looked very good with her jeans and purple sweater. I don't know how to talk about a girl's appearance without sounding like some illiterate brute. Clothing is like another language I never learned how to speak. I wanted to tell her she looked good, or pretty or whatever, but I figured that would come off as creepy, so instead I played it suave by staring at the carpet and not saying anything.

She looked up from her book and our eyes caught each other's. She nodded at me. I sat in the chair beside her. It felt right. "Hey," she said. "Your skin looks good. Did you stop using salicylic acid?"

"Yeah." Holy shit, she'd remembered our conversation. Thirty days had passed and her memory of me had withstood it all. I froze for a second, zapped by her words into a smiling mannequin who couldn't string a coherent thought together.

Stop. Focus. Remember the questions. "So, how, uh, how long have you been here?"

"Ten minutes, maybe?"

"Cool. Any traffic on the way over?"

"Nope."

"What time did you get up this morning?"

"Uh . . . ?" She shifted her eyes around, confused. "Seven thirty?"

"Nice. So, uh . . . When, then, I guess, did you go to sleep?"

She sat up and leaned toward me. "Are you, like, wearing a wire?"

"What?"

"You're, like, grilling me with questions like you're trying to get me to admit to, I guess, not getting enough sleep?"

Shit. My questions made me sound insane. Dad's advice was not relevant to this situation at all. I was trying to bond with a girl, not make small talk to sell a condo. "Sorry. I'm just . . . I don't know. It's . . ." My face turned red and my whole body got hot.

She tilted her head at me. She looked me in the eye and I felt like I was being inspected. Something in her expression softened, like she let her guard down. "What happened to your head?" She reached over and brushed the hair off my forehead to reveal the scab where the pimple had exploded at the football game. I felt adrenaline surge through me as her finger made contact. I felt like Adam getting that touch from God, except, fortunately, my penis wasn't hanging out.

"I, uh, went to a football game I didn't want to go to. Made the mistake of trying to fit in and got elbowed in the face."

She pulled her hand away. "Sorry for, you know, touching your face. My hands are clean. Promise." She held up her hands to demonstrate how clean they were. Objectively I didn't give a shit about fingernails, but hers were purple and I adored them.

"It's okay," I said.

113

"I touched your hand last time, too. That was weird. Sorry."

Why was she apologizing for my favorite moments of my entire life?

She said, "What's going on in your life?"

"Huh? Oh, uh, not really, uh . . . not much."

"Really? Come on. How are you?"

I shrugged. "Fine. I guess." I hadn't prepared answers to any of her questions, so the standard autoresponses fired out.

"You sure there's nothing bothering you?"

Her eyebrow lifted and all my Dad-sanctioned robot questions evaporated from my memory and this corked-up emotional shit spray blew out instead: "You ever realize that everything and everyone is the worst?"

She laughed a little and slid her book into her bag. "Oh yeah?"

I nodded. "My best friends are . . . I don't know. They joined the football team, but then they got hurt and even though they aren't on the team anymore, they're still friends with all those guys — and girls, too — and I think they're, like, leaving me behind."

Oh, no. Why did I say that? Why did I let that self-doubt and weakness spurt out?

She leaned in closer to me. "Oh, wow," she said. "That sounds hard."

"Heh," I laughed nervously, feeling myself redden.

"Do you wish you joined the team with them?"

"Well . . . no. That's part of what sucks. I replay everything that happened to see what I'd change and there's nothing.

114

I'd do it all the same and always end up . . . like . . . alone and stressed."

I couldn't believe I'd said all that. It just spilled out of me and for some reason I wasn't embarrassed. Maybe it was the way she looked at me, with genuine interest.

She said, "Do they, like, not talk to you anymore at school?"

"No, they do. Everything's technically the same between the three of us at school, but it feels completely different. They brought these annoying new guys into our group."

She nodded. "That sucks."

I laughed a little. "It's all right. It's . . . I don't know. Did your school have homecoming and all that stuff?"

"Unfortunately."

"Yeah, it's such a waste of time," I said. "I don't even get the whole concept. It's supposed to be for people who graduated to come back to their high school? What kind of insane person would voluntarily come back to their high school after they finished?"

She smiled.

I said, "My friends and their jackass new friends went, but I skipped it."

"No girl to ask?" She raised an eyebrow. "Got a crush on anyone?"

"No," I lied, feeling my armpit birth a beetle-size drop of sweat. "My mom made me go to my friend's house when he and all his new friends and some girls were taking pictures for homecoming. I barely even know who those girls are, but suddenly Luke and Will are blowing me off to go watch dumb romantic comedies with them. It's annoying. I kept staring at the guys when we took the pictures. I'd never seen them in suits before. They looked like adults. I don't understand why school dances even exist. I'm convinced literally no one wants to go. It's entirely peer pressure."

"Could be. Did they have fun?"

"They talked about it like they did, but I always think that's, like, some teenage Stockholm syndrome, where you do all this stuff you don't actually want to do and then to survive, your brain convinces you that you had fun when you really just wanted to be curled in the fetal position under your covers."

She smiled and leaned her head back against the wall. "It sounds like things are really overwhelming."

"Yeah. Definitely overwhelming. That's the word for it."

"I get it. My mom moved out and . . . and I get being overwhelmed." She shook her head. "When you get stressed, do you ever worry about your heart stopping? For no reason? Sometimes I worry that if I think about it too much, about how I don't really get why my heart just keeps beating on its own, it'll be like shining a spotlight on it and it'll freeze up and forget its lines and just stop beating. Like I'll just be standing at Target and drop dead." She laughed and closed her eyes. "I sound crazy."

"No, it's . . . It's, uh . . ." I floundered, unable to think of anything except the fact that I was unable to think of anything. But then something clicked and I said, "Everyone knows the heart is like a sixth grader on the opening night of the school play." We both laughed and she had no idea I was feeling the same adrenaline and endorphin rush Tony Hawk felt when he landed the first nine hundred.

She looked over to the receptionist and rolled her eyes. "It's taking forever today."

I hadn't noticed.

"I wonder if someone back there's getting bad news," she said.

"Like, just finding out they have no blood at all in their veins?"

"Or they have a terminal illness."

"Right. Yeah. Yikes. I, uh . . ." I suddenly saw my opening in the conversation. I shifted closer to her. "What would you do if you found out?"

"That I was gonna die soon?"

"Yeah. Like, how would you end yourself? If it was ending anyway so you had to?"

Her eyes narrowed while she thought.

I pounced: "Sleeping pills for me. Or leave the car running in the garage. Fade out comfortably, you know? I don't think I'd have Cecilia's guts to jump, or Bonnie's arm strength to tie a noose."

She nodded, smiling. She got my *Virgin Suicides* references. Proof we were on the same wavelength, that we overlapped on the pie chart of things we liked. The thinnest little slice, this barely visible line where only the two of us lived.

"You wouldn't try to make the most of it? Definitely suicide for you?" she said.

"I mean, if you know you're gonna die anyway, is it suicide?

Or is it just taking control? Maybe I'm just impatient. Like, let's just get it over with."

She leaned closer to me and whispered, "Have you ever really thought about killing yourself?"

I leaned toward her and our heads were just a few inches apart. I whispered, "Just when life's at its bleakest, like when the internet goes out."

She laughed a little and I had to suppress the urge to sprint around the waiting room high-fiving nurses. She got me and my sense of humor. She said, "Wait, so, what's the project your friends are messing up?"

"Oh! Right! Well, we're . . . *I'm* making a movie. Our language arts teacher gave us this assignment that lasts the entire year and all we have to do is tell the class a story. Most people will just rush some lame comic strip or something two days before it's due, but we're gonna make a full movie to premiere at this film festival our teacher helps run."

Her eyes got wide. She was impressed.

"Or, at least, I'll make the movie. I'm the only one putting any effort in now, but — I'll figure it out."

"So . . . ?"

"What?"

"What's it about?"

"Oh! Right. Sorry. So, yeah . . . it's about this musician who's kind of like Elliott Smith, who goes on tour and . . . and he falls in love with this girl — or this woman — and he, uh . . ." Shit. I couldn't remember which of my thousands of bullet points I'd decided to use. "Well, he, uh . . ." My brain started writing new scenes on the spot. Things she'd like. "So he's in, like, Russia for a concert and he falls in love with this woman. They meet on a train and stay up talking all night."

"Is that a reference to . . . ? Isn't there some other movie . . . ?"

"Yeah, yeah, yeah. *Before Sunrise.*" I knew she'd get that and like it. Now I had to watch it. I had it downloaded, so I was halfway there. "And so he and this woman, they . . . they decide to run away from everything and flee to Italy." I was pretty sure that's what the people in *Anna Karenina* did.

"Wow. Cool."

"Yeah, yeah," I said through my smile. "And there's stuff kind of based on . . . all this." I waved my hand at the waiting room. "He gets sent to a hospital in Italy. He meets all these other interesting people, and — and there's this crazy structure with these flashbacks to memories and — and . . . I mean, I've got a ton more outlined."

"That's awesome," she said.

"Yeah." The movie I'd just described was nothing like the one I'd tried pitching to the guys, but Alex seemed really into it — maybe I was onto something. Chasing after her made me better. "Oh, and since music will be a big part of it, I wanted to talk to you about what other bands you li—"

"Alex?" the receptionist called from behind the counter. "For the fourth time, Alex Mae? M-A-E? Are you here, Alex?"

She sprang up from the chair. "I didn't hear her before. Did you?"

119

I shook my head. Why couldn't that receptionist have been eaten by a snake on her way to work that morning?

"Keep me updated on your movie. I want to read the script. And see you next month, right?"

I nodded and as she walked away, I imagined the two of us on the couch in our pajamas. We watch some French movie and she puts her sort-of-wavy, sort-of-light-brown hair up, effortlessly pulling together a knot she doesn't know is beautiful.

When I came out from my blood drawing, she had left and it felt like part of myself had gone missing.

That night the vision of my future life together with Alex — Alex *Mae* — crystallized in my brain. I stared at a chart in my chemistry textbook for an hour while I lived with her in my head. I didn't picture us at a bar or some dumb nightclub or any place people go hoping to be seen. We walk together down an aisle at Target in hoodies and jeans. We're unguarded, open, safe. The other halves of each other, barely having to talk. Understanding each other's glances and movements, bound by our secret language. Pointing at things and laughing, making other people wish they understood.

I closed my chemistry textbook, accepting that I'd get a zero on the homework. I went downstairs to the computer and started searching for her again. I'd already searched for Alex Mae, Alexandra Mae, Alexis Mae, Alexandria Mae. Nothing had turned up. Maybe she went by her middle name online. Or maybe she didn't bother with social media at all; maybe she'd decided not to participate in any of that mess.

Did I even need to find her online? Why would I want old digital photos of her, when I knew her in real life? What I needed to do was take a step forward at our next appointment. I'd told her the truth of how I felt about my friends, so I should tell her my real feelings about her: *I like you.*

14.

At the end of seventh period on Halloween, my teacher handed me the packet of hundreds of photos Mom had ordered back on picture day. I didn't want to see whatever weird airbrushing had happened, so I crammed the pictures into my backpack before I, or anyone else, could see.

At my locker, I shoved my books on top of the already-dirty, bent envelope. Will walked over to me right after I'd buried it. "So, are we, like, not going to your house for horror movies this year?" he asked.

"What? I mean, no, I hadn't really even thought about it." We always watched slasher movies in my basement on Halloween, but I hadn't planned anything. I didn't feel like watching more identical, crappy horror movies that were all rip-offs of each other, and I didn't want to have to deal with Luke inviting Sam and Patrick and probably the girls from homecoming.

"Okay, yeah," Will said. "Just making sure, since I guess we're all going to Jen's house."

"We are?"

"I think so. Patrick invited me. He didn't tell you?"

"I guess not."

"I mean . . . I'm sure you could just come. It wouldn't be weird. He probably just forgot to mention it."

"No, it's cool. I've got plans."

"Oh, okay, cool." Will walked away.

I spent the night alone in my room, working on my movie outline and watching my download of *Before Sunrise,* and I enjoyed every goddamned second.

After my parents and Kate were asleep, I went downstairs to the family room computer and deleted my bookmarks to the horror movie websites I used to read and saved new forums and blogs that covered the kinds of movies and music Alex and I liked.

The week after Halloween, we had an overnight field trip to south Georgia. I was rooming with Luke, Will, Sam, and Patrick. There were only supposed to be four people in each room, but Luke and Will insisted that I should be in theirs, so the school made an exception. I honestly would have been fine sleeping on the bus.

The night before we left, I was worried about the guys

seeing my pills or face washes and having to explain everything to them, so I spent an hour reading articles online about techniques drug mules use to smuggle contraband. One popular method was to use a body cavity as the transport container, but I thought that walked a philosophical fine line I didn't want to cross, where I might have to admit to myself and my dermatologist that I'd lost my virginity to a condom full of Accutane I inserted into my own anus. Instead I popped enough pills for the trip out of the cardboard pack, put them in a sandwich bag, stuffed them into a sock, then wrapped the sock in seven other socks. I tucked the socks and my face wash and moisturizers inside two T-shirts and buried the bundle in the bottom of my backpack under my other clothes.

I sat with the guys on the bus ride down and listened to them talk about fantasy football for hours, rattling off players I'd never heard of and stats that weren't interesting and would never matter.

Patrick noticed me at some point and tried to include me in the conversation. "Kevin, I heard you're writing, like, a romance novel for Meyer's lit project."

"What?"

"My mom heard it from Luke's mom or something. Is it like a funny romance book or something? I bet you could write a funny dumb romance book."

Everyone turned to stare at me. Like all twenty guys at the back of the bus. My face turned red and I could hear my heart pounding. "Uh . . . no," I mumbled. "Luke and Will are in the group, too, but . . . it's a different thing. We're making a movie.

Never mind. It's not a big deal or anything. Forget it."

There was a pause that felt like an hour. Goddamn it. I'd already made this vow to myself a thousand times, but seriously, I needed to stop telling Mom anything. How had she contorted a movie script into a romance novel? Suburban moms are modern-day versions of medieval minstrels, spinning minor events into bullshit legends. Makes you wonder if Homer was a middle-aged mother and Odysseus was just her son who went for a walk one time.

"Yo, Kevin," Luke said, "let's do a scene where someone gets hit by a bus. Or, like, no, the killer disguises himself as the driver of the bus for this football team! Shit, yeah, everyone's stuck on the bus with the killer."

The other guys screamed and piled on more bad ideas inspired by objects around them at the time they decided to think about the movie. The way a trout would come up with movie ideas. Christ, they were morons.

Eventually they lost interest and went back to their original conversation, which was basically just Luke, Sam, and Patrick saying, "Remember at football practice when the Measure Man or Job, Joob, Jerb, and Merb or Nip Juice J ate twenty-six mozzarella sticks or jumped off a roof and sprained his ankle or farted really loudly?" It was like Mad Libs for uninteresting people who don't think of new ideas.

At one point, Sam said to me, "Dude, why aren't you laughing? It was hilarious."

"Hearing about a secondhand fart just isn't as funny as hearing the actual fart," I said, like I was some ass scientist with a lab full of brown beakers. "I mean, I'm sure it would have been funny if I'd been right there next to the fart."

Sam nodded. He had no counterargument to my airtight thesis.

We spent the day listening to bearded old men explain how the forts and moats that lost the Civil War were designed by the state's most skilled racists. No one learned anything.

That night I unpacked my contraband in the bathroom under the cover of the noisy shower and was able to stick to my nighttime face-washing routine without anyone knowing. I stayed up pretty late in the hotel room with the other guys, listening to stories about the household objects they'd put their penises inside.

I didn't say much. I wasn't sure if I jerked off way too much or not enough, and it was too risky to say something weird in either direction. I felt like Goldilocks chasing that magic, perfectly normal, impossible-to-pinpoint median number of masturbation sessions per week. So I mostly sat on the bed against the wall listening.

I couldn't figure out if their stories were actually true or if they were just trying to top each other. They were so competitive about everything, even the strangeness of the pillows and coat pockets they'd had sex with. Either way, the stories were kind of funny. Maybe I was just too tired to think straight, but I started having a good time. It felt like a sleepover from eighth grade, like how it was supposed to be.

Around three a.m., we finally turned off the lights. Will

kept watching TV, but the rest of us tried to sleep. My face hurt from laughing as I drifted off.

Sam woke us up by shouting, "Shit!"

He ran to the bathroom and we asked him what happened, but he wouldn't say anything. Patrick looked over next to him in bed, where Sam had been sleeping, and screamed. "Holy shit! Sam had a wet dream."

I laughed harder at that quarter-size stain on the sheets than I'd ever laughed at any professional comedian, movie, or TV show. Patrick and Luke knocked on the bathroom door and asked Sam if he'd enjoyed himself. Sam said it was an incredible experience and we were all just jealous that we didn't have one. He said the dream involved a refrigerator and I don't know if he was kidding.

Throughout the day, while we learned nothing from old men about Native American burial mounds, Sam told all the other guys about his wet dream. He should have been mortified, but instead he got funnier every time he told the story. He'd spin this tale of his magical dream that kept getting grander and more ridiculous, like he was some traveling salesman pitching the world on his new discovery of nocturnal emissions.

I couldn't believe how confident he was about it. He took the most embarrassing thing ever and acted like he was proud of it and no one gave him any shit. The algorithm that decides what and who is cool in tenth grade continues to make zero sense.

* * *

The hotel bathroom was calm and quiet when I washed my face that night. I turned the shower on, locked the door, and spread my products out on the counter. The other guys had each only brought a toothbrush and a shriveled, crusted-over tube of toothpaste. Actually Will hadn't even brought those. He brushed with my toothpaste on his finger.

I lost track of time in the bathroom washing and moisturizing my face and taking my pill. There were lots of purple and pink scars around my mouth and nose, but there weren't any big whiteheads. Definitely an improvement. I focused on the spots between the scars: patches of legitimately decent-looking skin. I smiled a little.

Luke knocked on the door. "Yo, we're gonna meet up with Mac and Cheese and some of the other guys."

I'd never spoken to either Mac or Cheese. They were best friends named Marissa MacDonald and Brie Castillo, but ever since we all watched the *Passport to French Cuisine* videotape in sixth grade, they'd been known as the singular entity Mac and Cheese. They embraced the name and normalized it so even teachers addressed these two living human beings like they were a bowl of orange noodles. The only thing I really knew about them was that in seventh grade Marissa gave Luke a gift set of Axe body spray for Christmas. I was extremely jealous when he showed it to us on the bus. Not of the gift itself, since it sort of implied he smelled like garbage. But just the idea of receiving a gift from a girl. I would have been happy to get whooping cough from Samantha Shales, the girl who went to court in fifth grade for choking her brother.

I said, through the door, "What are you gonna do?"

"Sam said he thinks Lewis brought whiskey."

I barely even knew who Lewis was. And I didn't feel like sitting silently in the corner of a hotel room abstaining from drinking and mumbling excuses for why I can't have alcohol without giving away that I'm on heavy-duty acne medicine — all for the privilege of probably getting caught and then suspended.

"That's all right," I said. "I'll stay here." I started rubbing the moisturizer, in pea-size dabs on a cotton ball, across my forehead and onto my cheeks.

"Sure?"

"Yeah. You guys can go, though. I should stay back here in case a teacher comes by or something. I'll say we're all in here and not open the door."

I heard Luke walk back to the other guys and explain that I had a good point and would stay back to guard the room.

"He should come," Patrick said. "It's gonna be fun. Is he, like, scared or something?"

I stopped moisturizing and stood still.

"I don't know," said Luke.

"It's fine," said Will. "He just doesn't like hanging out with other people sometimes. We'll see him when we get back."

They overestimated how thick those motel walls were. I could practically hear the three gross, wiry hairs on Sam's chin crinkle when he spoke. "Is he embarrassed about his pimples?" he said. "He should just, like, wash his face with soap. That's all you have to do. It's not that hard."

Luke knocked on the bathroom door on their way out. "Thanks for holding down the room. We'll see you later."

"Yep," I said. "No problem."

Once the sounds of their footsteps faded, the room was completely silent. I finished applying my moisturizer, patted my face dry, and put on a clean T-shirt. I sat on the bed and tried to calm down by focusing on the sound of my own breathing. But Sam's words kept replaying in my head. *"He should just wash his face with soap. It's not that hard."*

What the hell did he think I was doing in the bathroom for the past twenty minutes? Should I show him the bag of pills I had to bring with me for those pimples? Should I point out the vein on my arm that gets drained every month and tell him it's slightly more complicated than washing my face with soap? It would be pointless. He had no idea what he was talking about. *Sorry we can't all be like you, Sam. Flawless, smooth skin, carefree attitude, proud of your nocturnal emissions, for whom stress is an alien emotion.* That's the kind of mind-set that gets you killed by a bus in an intersection.

What did Luke and Will see in Sam and Patrick? Why didn't they want to hang out in the room with me? We could have watched movies. Made prank calls. Laughed *at* Mac and Cheese instead of fake-laughing with them in some pointless attempt to make out with them.

Sam and Patrick were assholes. I'd made a great decision to stay back in the room.

15.

Sometime later, as I was flipping over the pillows searching for the TV remote, I heard a guy and a girl talking in the room next door. Their words were faint and muffled, so I got on my knees at the head of the bed and pressed my ear into the wall.

"Stop being boring," the guy said. "You're being lame as shit."

"Sorry. Why can't we stay here and spend time together, just us?" It was Emma, Luke's old girlfriend. The ass talking to her was Kyle Hornchuck, who had taken her to homecoming.

"Just come with me. All my friends are already there."

"Then go be with your friends. Tell them your girlfriend is back here sitting alone in her hotel room."

"What's wrong with you?"

He was getting angry. Without thinking it through, I pounded my fist against the wall. Kyle stopped talking for a second. It threw him off. *That's right, tough guy.* Look at me, standing up to a bully. I could handle tons of confrontation as long as there was a locked door and a load-bearing wall between me and the other person.

The distraction only lasted a second. He sounded even more pissed off than before when he said to Emma, "What's wrong with you? Just come. Okay? *Okay*?"

"'Okay,' what?" Emma said. "Just go. I don't care anymore. God."

I walked out into the hallway and pounded on their door. Then I lowered my voice so I sounded like an idiot and said, "Yo, Kyle, Mac and Cheese have their tits out."

I slipped back into my room as Kyle said, "We need to talk later," stepped into the hall, shouted, "Wait up!" and sprinted to the elevator.

I opened the door and poked my head into the hallway to make sure he was gone. Emma stuck her head out to do the same thing. She turned to look at me and I froze, eyes bulging, front teeth biting my frown like a beaver about to be decapitated by a Jet Ski. I figured I should have been proud, like I was some knight who'd saved her, but all I could think about was the phrase "Mac and Cheese have their tits out," which I had just said, out loud, and which did not seem particularly valiant.

"Hey," she said. "Did you . . . ?"

"Yeah. Um, that was me."

"Do they really have their . . . ?"

"Oh. No. Well, I have no idea. It's possible."

She paused for a second. "Are you doing anything?"

I shook my head.

"Want to hang out?"

I shrugged and she opened the door to let me into her room. It was a mess of girls' clothes and bags spilled everywhere, this fantasy realm that smelled like candy. I didn't know it was possible to make a hotel room smell good.

I'd hung out with Emma a few times when she was going out with Luke last year, but I'd never really talked to her much one-on-one. It's like the Sun-Maid raisin lady you've seen your whole life but never really gotten to know. Then all of a sudden you're alone with the raisin lady and start to realize she might have been a stone-cold babe the whole time. And she's wearing flannel pajama pants and a baggy T-shirt, and her brown hair is pulled back into this very casual ponytail, and you suddenly notice just how nice her lips are as she sits up against the headboard of the bed with her knees pulled into her chest, a casual pose you never see girls do at school. It feels private, like she's letting you in on a secret by being so comfortable with you.

I wondered if she'd been able to hear us talking about wet dreams that morning. Had she heard every disgusting, stupid thing I'd said the night before? I stood there looking like an anatomy class skeleton while my brain tried to process exactly how embarrassed I should feel.

"Want to sit down?" she said.

"Sure." I crawled across the bed, aware of my every movement. I felt like a gigantic baby. A real, genuine idiot on all fours. And the crawl felt like it took forty-five minutes. I finally sat next to her on top of the covers. I took a deep breath and accidentally swallowed a lungful of her shampoo and had to tell myself the feeling wasn't love.

She turned on the TV and flipped through movie channels. "Kyle's an asshole," she said. "I'd always kind of known it, but now . . . I don't know. Or maybe he's right. Maybe I'm lame. Maybe I am a prude. And I've been all bloated and gross since I started taking birth control, which is super annoying because the whole point of being on it was to make me feel *better,* not worse and — You okay?"

I'd frozen at the words *birth control,* eyes locked on what must have been the world's least-comfortable armchair. Birth control? What happened to her God Squad abstinence pledge?

She noticed my slack-jawed confusion and said, "Oh, the birth control is for period cramps. It's . . . Sorry. I'm still saying way too much."

"No, it's, um, it's fine. I was just . . . thinking about something else," I said, trying to shake the images of her and Kyle getting it on in that stiff chair. "Anyway, no offense, since you, like, liked Kyle or whatever, but he's been a dick since fourth grade. And he's got to be — again, no offense — a ridiculously huge dumb-ass to fall for what I did. That should not have worked."

She nodded.

I asked, "Where are your roommates?"

"They're all in Jen's room. I was supposed to hang out with Kyle, but . . . whatever. Where are your roommates?"

"They, uh, went out. Just went out. I don't know where."

"They went to see Marissa and Brie, didn't they?"

"That might have been on their agenda. I can't confirm or deny."

We both laughed a little.

She flipped through movies until she landed on a high-school romantic comedy. "Remember when me and you and Luke and Will used to watch movies in Luke's basement? We'd laugh at movies like this, saying how the kids in them are such morons."

"I still prefer movies over having to deal with, like, real-life high-school morons."

She smiled at me. I was pretty happy I'd said that. It just came out of me, unfiltered and real. For a minute I felt a wave of guilt, like I was cheating on Alex with Emma. No, it was fine. We weren't doing anything. If anything, it was a test run for when Alex and I would be together. It confirmed what I wanted in a relationship: staying in, watching movies, being untethered, safe, comfortably alone together.

We sat there watching the movie for a while. At some point I got up to go to the bathroom and saw about a hundred different bottles of face washes, toners, and moisturizers. Those four girls had enough product to stock an aisle at the drugstore. They spoke my language. I was home.

There was a little zip-up case that had EMMA embroidered on it. Inside I saw a bottle of the Neutrogena nighttime moisturizer I used. I gasped.

"Is that your Neutrogena moisturizer?" I said when I came back out.

"Oh—yeah. Sorry it's so messy in there. I meant to clean it up, but—"

"I use the same stuff."

"Cool?" she said, laughing a little.

I sat back beside her against the headboard. "It's good, I guess. Gets the, uh, job done."

"Yeah."

We watched the movie silently for a while. I couldn't tell what it was, exactly—perfume or shampoo or laundry detergent or some other liquid I'd never heard of—but she smelled as good as a human has ever smelled. I kept thinking about looking over at her, but it would be too risky. Our eyes touching could set off a spark I wouldn't be able to handle, causing some emotional reaction that would seep into the half of my head space reserved for Alex. *You're just friends. She went out with Luke. You're not allowed to like her.* I didn't pay attention to the movie at all. I just lay there like a corpse in a morgue freezer, thinking about how we had the exact same moisturizer on our faces.

Out of nowhere, she offered, "I think I'm gonna break up with Kyle."

"Really?" My eyes dilated with excitement.

"Yeah."

"Oh, wow. That's awesome. Cool. Really cool." Those words felt off-key. She was describing a relationship ending and I was describing a red electric guitar.

"I guess."

After a second, a Blink-182 song played over part of the

movie and Emma mentioned they were one of her favorite bands. I smiled and nodded, remembering when I used to be into them, and thought about sending her some links to other bands she could get into.

Before I could mention anything, though, her phone rang and she answered, "Hey, Mama." She got off the bed, motioned to me that she'd be a minute, and stepped into the bathroom. I focused my attention on the wall between us so I could eavesdrop better.

"Yeah, it's a lot of fun. Learning a ton. Did you know the Okefenokee Swamp got its name from the Indian word for trembling earth? . . . I know, right? . . . We're just all back at the hotel now, hanging out. . . . Yeah, they're all here. How's Mark doing? . . . Okay, well, give him a hug for me. I miss you all, too. Okay. Wait, you start or me?" She giggled. "Okay, okay. 'Now I lay me down to sleep. I pray the Lord my soul to keep. And if I die before I wake, I pray the Lord my soul to take. Amen.' . . . Love you, too, Mama."

The call felt honest, like I'd seen behind a curtain. I'd heard how she was with her parents. The little-kid names she still used for them. I saw a version of her that almost no one else gets to see. I'm not religious. Her prayer should have weirded me out. Talking about the Lord taking her soul in the night like he was a blade-wielding slasher crouched in a tree outside her window. But it didn't weird me out the way she'd said it.

"Sorry if I was loud," she said when she stepped back into the room. "Just a quick parental check-in."

"Do you do those a lot?"

137

"Every night I'm not home, yeah."

"Do they, like, make you?"

"I don't really mind. I know it's not, like, cool and rebellious and whatever to like your parents, but I do. I want them to know what's going on in my life." She shrugged and lay back down on top of the covers beside me and we watched the movie for another minute until she yawned and shut her eyes for a few seconds. I closed mine, too, thinking it might be nice if we both happened to fall asleep beside each other. But she said she was going to try to sleep, so I said I'd do the same thing and would see her later. That was probably for the best. My fantasy made no practical sense. Her roommates would come back, and after that Kyle Hornchuck would've found us, grabbed me by the ankles, and shot-putted me through the sliding glass door and into the dumpster in the parking lot.

I got in my bed and replayed the night. Emma had been so open with me, and I'd felt so comfortable lying there next to her. She had layers I never knew about, things I bet Luke never even discovered when they were dating. She actually liked her parents. I don't know why that was such a big deal to me. When everything about teenage culture is all "fuck adults, fuck teachers, fuck the establishment," maybe the most rebellious thing you can do is have a good relationship with your parents. And she was relaxed enough around me to let me in on that part of her life.

Was it possible that Emma liked me? She'd invited me into her room when she could have just nodded at me in the hall and shut her door. I'd shown her the kind of wonderfully serene evening, staring at a television, that she could have every night with a guy like me. And she'd told me about her birth control and being bloated and wanting to dump Kyle. Those aren't the sorts of things girls go around telling just anyone. My heart sped up as the clues piled up.

But *shit*. I couldn't ask Emma out, even if she did want me to. Mostly there was Alex. But even without Alex, there was still the fact that Emma was Luke's ex. If I asked her out, it would violate the unspoken agreement between us to not be weird and go out with girls the other one had gone out with.

I smiled at the ceiling in the dark. This was kind of a good problem to have. How had I gotten myself into a situation where I was suddenly so emotionally close to two different girls? I couldn't have talked to Emma so openly and directly without figuring out how to do that with Alex. It was working. Alex was making me a better version of myself.

Luke, Will, Sam, and Patrick stumbled back into the room around one thirty a.m., loud and amped up. They shut out the light and Luke got into bed with me, his feet next to my head, since I guess the prospect of us accidentally sixty-nineing in the middle of the night was preferable to making close-range eye contact. "Dude, it was insane," he said. "You should have been there."

I smiled, so happy I hadn't gone.

16.

The hotel breakfast buffet was just like the cafeteria, with kids sitting in the same groups, except everyone was adhering to a dress code of pajama pants, old T-shirts, and slippers that hadn't been communicated to me. I was the only person fully dressed in jeans and my brown coat. I sat down at a table with Luke and Will while Sam and Patrick got in line for food.

"You should have been there last night," Luke said. "It was the funniest thing I've ever seen. Sam and Patrick are insane, dude. They're the best."

"Yeah, they're all right," I said.

"No, dude, you don't even know them at all. You've never seen them in action. They're hilarious."

"It was funny," Will confirmed.

Sam's words from last night replayed in my head. Him saying that I should just wash my face with soap. That it really isn't that hard to have clear, flawless skin. That my own filthy, uninformed habits are causing all my zits. I could see him and Patrick in line, holding breakfast sausages up to their crotches and cracking up. Those guys are jackasses. Unfunny jackasses with a fourth-grade understanding of comedy. "What the hell did they do that's so funny?"

"Patrick got this bag of flour —" said Will.

Luke continued: "And we were all out in the back parking lot, right, behind the rooms, and Patrick and me got behind the dumpster and called for Lewis to come around the side, and as soon as he did, we threw huge handfuls of flour right in his face."

Will laughed. "He was so dusty. They call it antiquing someone."

I stared at them. I didn't laugh. Luke and Patrick both thought they were Ferris Bueller, and I felt like I was the only person who knew the truth, that they were just regular idiots. "All right," I said.

"It was hilarious," said Luke.

"They threw flour on Lewis. That's not that funny."

"You would have had to be there," said Will. "It was really funny, if you'd seen it in person."

I was getting sick of hearing them tell me that I would have had to be somewhere to see some stupid thing that wasn't funny. What a bunch of assholes. All that flour would clog up anyone's pores and seed a mountain range of pimples.

141

"We've gotta put that scene in the movie," Luke said. "Maybe the villain's, like, covered in flour all the time. Mr. Antique."

I sighed and rolled my eyes. "The movie isn't like that now. There's no . . . There's no villain or gory deaths or anything. It's about real people who meet on a train in Russia and —"

"Wait, what?" Will said.

Luke said, "Dude, you were yelling at us in your basement about how it was too hard to make fake blood so we shouldn't do a horror movie, but now you want to, what, like, build a Russian train?"

"It's . . . yeah, just . . . I'll figure it out."

"How the hell are you gonna *build a train*? And set an entire movie in Russia?"

"Well, part of it. But they flee to Italy and he goes to a hospital —"

"You're also planning to build an Italian hospital? Is that the name of your movie now? *Italian Hospital*? *Tony Has Cancer*? Where did any of this even come from? I don't understand."

"Well," I said, "maybe if you guys weren't wasting all your time with Sam and Patrick, you'd be writing with me."

Luke said, "You just don't get Sam and Patrick. Their humor. You don't get it."

"I get it," I said. "I just don't think it's that funny."

"No, it is," said Luke. "They're hilarious. They're the funniest guys I've ever met. You should have come with us last night."

My breathing got faster and I felt my face heating up. My

hands squeezed into fists and my shoulders tensed. Luke didn't know what I'd been up to last night without them. He had no idea about Emma and how there was a chance she was into me, but I was too good a friend to do anything about it. He just saw me as this pathetic shut-in loser covered in zits he wouldn't have if he *just washed his fucking face with soap.* "Why the hell are you so obsessed with Sam and Patrick? You sound like you're in love with them. When did you both turn gay for Sam and Patrick?"

They stared at me with wide-open eyes. I'd been loud. Really loud. I think I said it the exact moment the air conditioner had shut off and suddenly there was no background noise to drown me out. Everyone in the room stopped eating. They were all staring at me. Sam, Patrick, the football team, the band kids, Mac, Cheese, all the other girls, the anime kids. It felt like an hour passed. My face turned bright red. I could practically feel new zits sprouting from the stress.

"Dude," said Luke. "What are you so pissed off about? What did anyone do to you?"

I mumbled, "Nothing. Whatever," while Sam and Patrick walked over to our table.

"Who's gay for me?" said Patrick, dangling a sausage through the fly in his jeans onto Will's shoulder. Will turned and saw it, and they all burst out laughing. Without hesitating, Sam dropped onto his knees and bit into the sausage through Patrick's pants, and Patrick threw his arms in the air and unleashed an orgasmic "Oh, oh, oh, yeah!" Our entire class lost their minds. Applause. Screams. Thunderous roars

143

of approving laughter for Sam's fully committed performance of fellatio on his friend's breakfast sausage. Even the gay kids howled with laughter. Somehow Sam and Patrick were so beloved that no one but me was offended by their disturbing role play. Emma smiled at them and I felt like I could puke.

I got up and walked back to the room. I washed my face again, then put on more redness-reducing moisturizer while I wondered what my problem was. Life was so much easier before Sam and Patrick were in it. Were they the problem? Or was I the weird one?

Was I having mood swings? Was the Accutane screwing with me? If I wasn't on the medicine, would I have laughed with them and not gotten pissed? I used to be a dick-humor aficionado, but their stunt just made me mad. Was I more mature than they were, or was I mutating into a different person, spiraling off to the side instead of moving forward?

That afternoon we went to a nature preserve where no one retained any information about alligators. We went home after that. Nobody talked to me on the bus. I stared out the window and wished I could have discreetly fallen into the swamp and been devoured by an alligator and no one would notice I was missing until three days later when Mr. Davidson would realize I never turned in the worksheet on lagoon acidity.

We got Thursday and Friday off from school for Thanksgiving and I was glad to be away for a while from everyone who thought I was a buzzkill asshole. Mom invited my aunt Sharon, uncle Joseph, and my twin cousins, who are Kate's age. In the morning before they got there, it dawned on me that they'd be hanging out in the family room, and I'd look weird if I was doing my usual all-day internet browsing right there on the computer in front of them. So I dismantled the computer and put it back together on my desk in my room. I put my earbuds in, listened to Nick Drake, and read the new message boards I'd found where people discussed the kind of music and movies Alex and I liked.

Once everyone arrived, I had to go down and make an appearance. The cousins and Kate ran straight to the basement without acknowledging me. I was left stranded in the kitchen with the adults. I guess that's how you know you're not a kid anymore. Children don't see you. You're just a ghost who knows how to fix the TV when video games aren't working.

So I stood there in the kitchen, pretending to help by mixing things with spoons Mom had left in pots of food she'd already cooked and was keeping warm. Dad brought Uncle Joseph straight into the family room to grill him with questions about the square footage of the last hotel room he stayed in while they watched whatever football game was on. Aunt Sharon whispered to Mom that men only care about football. She laughed. What a groundbreaking observation.

Eventually Aunt Sharon noticed my existence and asked how I was doing. I told her I was fine and good, two solid answers that I thought would close the case on me and allow them to get back to discussing how the twins and Kate were coping with prealgebra. But it took all of two seconds before Mom said, "Kevin is writing an amazing movie script for his class. He's like our Steven Spielberg."

"You haven't even read it," I said. At least she wasn't claiming I was writing a romance novel anymore. Or had she ever said that? Had Patrick just been messing with me?

"If you wrote it, I know it's going to be good," she said.

"Steven Spielberg directs. He's rarely credited as a screenwriter."

"Oh, wow," said Aunt Sharon. "I remember your mom showed me some of the movies you made last year. They were . . . a good length. Very good."

I aggressively squinted at her, thinking that calling a five-minute movie "a very good length" was more of a straight-up insult than one of Aunt Sharon's usual backhanded compliments.

"Kevin is our film buff," Mom said. "He watches all kinds of foreign and exotic films."

"Really?" said Aunt Sharon. "Erotic films?"

"No," I lied.

"Things from France," Mom said. "Right, Kevin?"

"Uh, yeah," I mumbled. "I have watched one or two movies from France before."

"Incredible," said Aunt Sharon. "So you must be fluent in French? The language of love?"

"I, uh . . ." I didn't even know how to begin answering such an inane question. It would take days to explain subtitles to her.

"You do speak some French," Mom added. "You took classes all through middle school."

"I don't remember any of it," I said.

"Well, maybe you can add some to your play," said Aunt Sharon. "French things always lend some class. Sometimes I like to serve the kids French bread with their spaghetti. To add a bit of culture."

I nodded and wondered if it was too late to be adopted. There was a long silence until Aunt Sharon said, "Your face looks less red. Oh, last summer it was terrible. I remember thinking you'd been burned. Your mom told me you're on a pill now. What was it called again?"

I shut my eyes, and after a second I opened them just to glare at Mom.

Then Aunt Sharon added, "You know, the most handsome thing a guy can wear is a smile."

I don't mean this in an offensive way, but all I wanted to do in that moment was throw a chair at my aunt Sharon.

Mom tapped her on the elbow and said, "Let me show you the new curtains we got for the dining room." They stepped out of the kitchen. I stood there alone and looked to my left: Dad and Uncle Joseph sitting on the couch with a space for me beside them. I looked to my right: the staircase leading up to my room.

Two roads diverged in a yellow wood, and all that. I took the one most traveled.

I shut my door to block out the football noise from the TV downstairs, woke the computer up, and opened my document with all my screenplay notes. Dozens of pages of random bullets points — notes on characters, plot threads, genres, and scenes. There were a few worthwhile ideas, and I highlighted those, but there was a lot of garbage, too. I needed to weed out all of Luke's and Will's bad ideas and add more of the parts Alex would like so I could show her at our next appointment.

It was hard to dig through the clutter of ideas. Old slasher-horror notes and new parts about a serious relationship, all these completely different tones. It was a mess. My face got hot and my breathing sped up. Just looking at the seemingly endless document stressed me out. I only saw problems and dumb ideas, a list of mistakes backing me into a corner.

I closed out of the outline, figuring I'd deal with it when I wasn't so flustered by my grandparents' other offspring occupying the same building as me. I went online to check on Luke and Will, and saw pictures of them hanging out at Patrick's house the other night. Emma and the other God Squad girls were in some of the pictures. No one had invited me. I spent nearly all day with them at school and neither one of them had said a word about hanging out at Patrick's. Goddamn it. They all hated me. I'd looked like such a jackass on the trip when I blew up at them and asked if they were gay.

I clicked through more of Emma's pictures, wincing at her laughing in basement parties with the God Squad. Was I an idiot for thinking she might like me? She probably didn't even remember that I existed.

I fell into the black hole, scrolling through years of Emma's life, all these old pictures she'd scanned and uploaded, crawling all the way back to early middle school, wondering when those parties and school dances and hangouts had happened, and which part of space I'd been floating in alone during them. I dead-ended into her earliest picture, but my finger had momentum behind it and I kept going, clicking on some girl from her church playing a complicated-looking guitar chord. I hovered like a ghost through the last year of that girl's life at some other school. Everything was so disturbingly similar to my school, but it looked better, like everything was actually fun. I latched on to some guy at some other school with unbelievably white teeth, and I became a formless ghoul haunting his charmed life, frowning at old photos of his friends playing football and eating tacos and — *holy shit!*

It was her. She looked younger, but her eyes were the same and her face was the same shape. Her skin was clear and she was smiling, sitting on a sofa beside another girl in some basement.

It was definitely Alex, but the name Alex June appeared when I hovered over her. She'd hidden herself with a fake last name, made it a challenge to find her. The only thing she'd written in her profile was the year she'd graduate, which confirmed she was the same age as me. It felt like stumbling into a hidden treasure. I bit my lip to hide a smile. Holy shit.

My legs bounced in place and my arms twitched with all the adrenalized blood shooting through them like I'd tripped into an electric fence.

I hovered over the button to request her as a friend, but I clicked into her photos first. She'd posted fourteen pictures scanned in from her school's last yearbook. Some were those full-page collages the seniors get. She was always with this same group of kids and she was always smiling with this wide-open mouth, like she was having so much fun she was yelling about it. They played soccer in pouring rain. Picked apples at an orchard. Stuck their tongues out while wearing big floppy hats and giant T-shirts on a beach at spring break. Double-buckled with each other in the back of a minivan on some road trip. Held signs for their team at a football game.

Huh.

It didn't add up. Who were those older friends she had? Was she still friends with all those kids? She seemed so happy in the pictures and my stomach hurt.

I got annoyed at my annoyance. Why was I so dismayed to find out she had friends? Wasn't that a good thing? Didn't that mean she was probably a nice, likable person?

Alex was allowed to have friends. I had friends, technically. I should have been happy for her that she had a nice big group of tall, outgoing, friends with defined jawlines and sculpted hair who knew how to be spontaneous and have a wild and carefree time at the muddy soccer field.

I clicked through more pictures, hunting for something that would match the images in my head. All I needed was one shot of her alone in her room. Just one shred of evidence of her reading a book or listening to music would be all I needed to convince myself there was still hope of —

Shit. It was like I'd stepped on a land mine: There she was, tagged in a picture her friend posted from homecoming, just a few weeks before. Five couples lined up. Her smiling in a blue dress. Some tall asshole standing behind her with his arms around her waist like a lasso.

Goddamn it.

I clicked away as fast as I could.

I thought she told me she hadn't gone to homecoming. Or had that part of the conversation just been in my head? Shit. I couldn't remember.

I kept telling myself she was allowed to have a life. But she seemed different to me now. Alex in the waiting room and Alex in the pictures didn't match. Something changed. It was like when that young woman turns into a rotting old lady in *The Shining*. There was no picture of her in her room with Tolstoy, Dostoyevsky, Sylvia Plath, Sofia Coppola, and Elliott Smith. Instead it was her flashing peace signs on a roller coaster with Tommy, Danny, Sadie, Shannon, and Eddie.

I looked at my phone and knew Alex wasn't waiting on the other end. Even if I had her number, there'd be no point in calling. She was busy celebrating Thanksgiving with her pack of friends on the dock of some older kid's lake house, climbing into a human pyramid and smiling for a photo while her hands gripped a swimmer's massive back muscles. It didn't feel right to send that version of Alex a friend request.

Mom knocked on my door and it startled me like glass shattering. "Kevin?"

I instinctively closed out of my browser, even though I wasn't looking at anything questionable. "You can come in."

She stepped inside, eased the door closed behind her, took

a deep breath, then frowned. "Why's the computer in here? Did you move it?"

"Oh, uh . . . yeah. There was a virus and I decided to, uh, fix it up here."

She nodded for a second, then shook her head and refocused on whatever she came up there for. "Are you okay?"

"Yeah."

"We're all downstairs."

"Yeah, I have homework to do."

"You kind of embarrassed me earlier. When Sharon was asking about the script you're working on."

"Oh. Sorry."

"I just want you to know I'm proud of you. I think you're very impressive and smart, and sometimes I tell people, okay? It's what moms do."

"Yeah." I wanted to add that it was objectively ridiculous to think I was any more impressive or smart than thousands of other nearly identical kids at thousands of other nearly identical high schools.

In the singsong voice you'd use with a toddler, she said, "Positive mental attitude."

I got even more annoyed than I usually did when she brought up that stuff, since the dissonance from the two Alexes was still pounding shock waves through my skull.

"Okay," I said to my desk.

"Will you come down soon?"

"Um, yeah. Sure. I just have to finish some stuff."

She nodded and went downstairs.

I walked into the bathroom, turned on the light, and stared at myself. I was a scab.

Mom thought I was an asshole. My friends had moved on to cooler guys and didn't even bother to tell me. Alex was a stranger who only knew I was alive when I sat three inches away from her, once a month. She was too busy with her friends to think about me outside of the waiting room.

I had nothing to be thankful for. I wondered how the world would be impacted if I ceased to exist. If I just disappeared, would anyone seriously care? Would it change anyone's lives at all? There would be a lot of shrugging at my funeral.

Were those suicidal thoughts? Not really. They were more like postdeath thoughts, agnostic about the cause. Rational responses to being a friendless fifteen-year-old pepperoni.

17.

I wasn't looking forward to seeing Alex at my blood test at the end of November. She was a confident, well-adjusted, homecoming-attending girl, and I was an awkward dunce who wanted to resign from life and drive around on an electric scooter wearing a black sleeping bag and a motorcycle helmet, a larva who communicates exclusively via text message.

The instant I opened the door to the waiting room, I became aware of my brown jacket that was too big, the one Kate said makes me look like a drug dealer, and knew my dry, puffy, bushy hair made me look like someone's aunt. I did not look like Alex's friends.

I stared at the floor when I walked in and sat a couple seats away from her. She was reading a book. She nodded at me and

I nodded back. I stuffed my hands into my pockets, trying to hide my entire body inside them. I couldn't get those homecoming pictures out of my head, and I wasn't sure what to talk to her about. Maybe if I'd asked her the right questions at our first appointments, I would have known she was out of my league and could have saved a lot of time daydreaming about loitering in bookstores with her. But I blew it and stuck myself in a no-man's-land with a crush on a girl who used to make me feel safe but now reminded me of how lame and pointless I was.

I caught her looking at me out of the corner of my eye. I couldn't not look back at her. She got up and moved into the seat beside me.

She said, "It's you."

"Uh, yeah. Yes. It is me."

She bit her thumbnail. "How are you?"

I shrugged. "Fine."

"That bad, huh?"

"Eh. Fine."

"Fine usually means bad."

I smiled.

She said, "What happened? Talk to me."

That's all it took to shatter the ice around me. A direct question fired point-blank. I told her about Aunt Sharon asking me why my face is so red, and about sitting at the kids' table, where my sister and cousins ignored me so completely I'd nearly convinced myself I was dead. "So I took a plate of food up to my room and had Thanksgiving dinner with the audio commentary on the *Chasing Amy* DVD. So, you know, normal, cool stuff."

She leaned her head back against the wall. Looking at the ceiling tiles, she said, "Yeah, mine was kind of like that, too. We did Thanksgiving at my mom's new place and I know holidays make everyone crazy, but she's, like . . . like, just a lot to deal with. I was already feeling bad anyway about dumb friend drama, so I went to the bedroom that's supposed to be mine and just kind of waited for the day to end."

She closed her eyes and a new possibility blossomed in my head: She'd gone to homecoming reluctantly. She hated her friends and everything annoyed her, just like me. You wouldn't know it from pictures of us that the guys I hung out with bothered the hell out of me constantly. She could have been in the same situation. Everyone knows pictures people post online are bullshit, so maybe the version I knew was the real her, and the version of her online was the fake one. I had solid evidence she liked *Anna Karenina,* Elliott Smith, and *Before Sunrise.* Triangulated proof she was more interesting than most kids. Maybe she'd even moved on from her friends. All those kids in the photos were just old acquaintances from middle school she'd decided to cut loose but hadn't been able to shake yet, leeches waiting to be pulled off.

"Do you want to, like, I don't know, go somewhere after this?" I mumble-blurted. What? Where did that come from? How did I go from vowing to ignore her to asking her out? Although I don't know if what I said even technically counted as asking her out. I think I actually had just asked her *outside,* which seems different, like I just wanted to show her an unusual bird's nest.

She tilted her head. "You mean, like, to show me your movie script?"

"Oh, uh, yeah, right, right, for sure," I said as forty pounds of dense sweat oozed from every pore on my body like Play-Doh pushed through the spaghetti holes. "I was hoping you could help me, like, apply some of the structure from, uh . . . from *Anna Karenina*?"

"Oh," she said. "Yeah, okay. I could try."

"Cool, cool, um, so, uh, if . . ."

"There's this other book, too, that might be good," she said. "Shoot, I can't remember the name. It's really sad. My friend Chloe cried at homecoming because she'd just finished reading it. It turned into this whole scene where people thought something bad had happened to her, and we all were consoling her, but some song just reminded her of the book and it made her so sad, she started bawling. It was funny once we figured it out. Ryan and Mitchell were hoping some guy had said something mean to her so they could fight someone."

"Wait, who?"

"Who what?"

A sickening dread crawled from my stomach to my head and all I could wheeze out was "Ryan? Mitchell? Who . . . ?"

"Oh. Ryan's Chloe's boyfriend. And Mitchell's my boyfr —"

The world turned to static. Her lips kept moving, but all I heard were garbled, underwater sounds.

But one phrase penetrated: "We made out a little."

We made out a little.

She and Mitchell had made out a little.

My brain shut down the auditory system after that.

I nodded over and over, forcing a smile so fake it made me feel deranged. Her lips kept moving while I imploded. I fantasized about someone stuffing me into a cannon and shooting my limp body directly into a brick wall, hard enough to make my bones shatter like fluorescent lightbulbs.

Of course she had a boyfriend. Why had I tricked myself, out of some pathetic self-defense, into thinking the guy holding her waist in the homecoming picture was just an acquaintance? How dumb was I to think that?

I don't even know what I'd been thinking when I asked Alex to do something after our blood tests. What would I have said to Mom? She was out there in the parking lot waiting for me. Would I tell her that I was going to hang out with this girl she'd never heard of, and that girl's parents would drop me off back at home later? Would Mom insist on driving us somewhere? Would she take us to a bench, park directly in front of it, shine her high beams at us, and pretend to do a crossword puzzle while reading our lips through binoculars?

Well, luckily for me, the date, or hangout, or talk, or whatever it would have been, wasn't happening.

What would someone like Alex want with someone like me? She was a stress-free queen who made out in public. I had a better chance of being drafted into the NFL than I did of making out with a girl on the homecoming dance floor. She'd have to be a contestant on *Fear Factor* choosing between kissing my crusted lips and eating a yak's testicle, and even then it wouldn't be a sure thing.

I didn't want to get her phone number anymore. I had no use for the secret code to a stranger's bedroom. Besides, Mitchell would probably answer. And I didn't want to talk to that asshole.

A nurse stepped into the waiting room and called for Alex. She stood up and said something to me and I nodded.

She made this weird face at me and walked through the door with the nurse. I left her confused. That seemed to be my signature move. Some people leave others wanting more. I stare at walls, mumble into carpets, and leave 'em confused.

Sometime later — it might've been ten seconds or twenty minutes; it was all a haze — the same nurse called me to the back and I sat down, out of breath, and watched her tie the rubber strap around my bicep. I shut my eyes and saw Alex making out with that six-foot-three porn star of a boyfriend of hers. I felt sick. I opened my eyes — which was a big fucking mistake. At the sight of my black-red blood spraying into the vial, my emotional roller coaster sped into a corkscrew and my stomach blasted a hot, solid shot of vomit into my mouth.

I caught it with my teeth. My cheeks bulged out and the nurse looked at me, disgusted. I averted her gaze and tried to suck my cheeks back to normal, some ridiculous instinct to pretend nothing out of the ordinary had just happened. I watched the vial fill up like I was waiting for a bomb to detonate, and as soon as she sealed it off and stuck the Band-Aid to my arm, I lunged out of the chair and hurled the entire contents of my stomach into the sink, spitting chunks of stringy puke all over the metal while my red eyes leaked tears.

I wiped the sticky mucus off my dry lips with a hard brown paper towel and mumbled, "See you next month."

The nurse said, "Why don't you sit down for a minute?"

I waved her off. "I'm totally fine. It's just a stomachache. Don't worry — it's cool." I burped and stumbled into the hallway. All I wanted to do was collapse into the passenger seat, fall asleep, and let Mom drive me home.

But Alex was in the waiting room when I went back. *Shit.* She stood up and nodded toward the exit. "You ready?"

I stared back blankly into her eyes, tasting sour puke in my mouth.

"To go work on your script? Like we talked about?"

"Oh."

"Come on. I want to hear about it."

She looked directly at me and there was nothing I could do to resist.

I followed her outside onto a sidewalk that took us behind the building to this little courtyard with some bushes and picnic tables. She picked a table between a garbage can with that biohazard symbol on it and a doctor sitting at another table by himself, tearing into a roast beef sandwich like an animal.

We sat down across from each other and were both silent for a while. I wanted to talk to her, but it felt weird. I was certain Mitchell, shirtless and ripped, would pop out of the trash can and fire a lacrosse ball into my neck. *Just be normal. Have a conversation. Quantitative questions. How long have you been going out? How many times has he disappointed you? What about him annoys you, and where does he fail emotionally? Is his penis bent like a candy cane? How lopsided are those balls?*

Alex broke the silence. "So, your movie script? You wanted to talk about it?"

"Oh. Right. Yeah. I mean, it's really just a class project, and . . . whatever. It doesn't matter. It's a mess."

"Why?"

"My friends are just, like, making it more complicated than it needs to be. It's fine. I don't need to bore you by complaining. It's nothing. It's dumb."

"It sounds like things are still frustrating with your friends."

"Uh," I said. "I guess, yeah."

"Are they still hanging out with those new guys? The ones from the football team?"

"Oh, uh, yeah. Yeah, we all roomed together on this trip for school, and . . ." I trailed off. What could I tell her about the trip that didn't make me sound like a lame, unfun idiot?

"So your problem is that you now have too many friends."

"No, it's that these guys just aren't, like . . . They're just different from me and my friends, and now my friends are trying to be like them, or . . . I guess they're changing, too."

"Changing how?"

"Well," I said, "I had the movie all mapped out with all the stuff we talked about at our last appointment, but Luke and Will keep adding in all these plot points and characters that don't make sense, and Sam and Patrick are telling them that their bad ideas are cool, and there's too much stuff to cram in and I have no idea where to even start. I'm the only one actually working on it, so I'm not sure they should be contributing ideas to it at all. We're already way behind on everything and the schedule's all screwed up and —"

"Can I see what you've written?"

"Um . . . I've got some scenes planned, like this band is on tour, but . . . I don't have, like, the full thing written. It's all just a massive, unorganized tangle of notes right now."

"You haven't written anything yet?"

"I mean, the outline's really long."

"Maybe forget about the huge script for now. That's probably what's freaking you out. Just start with something small. Go one step at a time. When Mitchell and I were going out, we built these bookshelves in his room and it seemed impossible at first, but —"

"When you were going out?"

"We broke up after homecoming."

Good thing I'd already vomited, because if there had been anything in my stomach I would have blasted it all directly into her face, a pure shot of romantic excitement.

She said, "I told you that, like, fifteen minutes ago."

Goddamn it. I'd been too shell-shocked to hear. The Mitch Man was her ex-boyfriend. Micropenis Mitch, with his pea-size testicles and inexplicably gray pubic hair, was out of the picture. I couldn't imagine having an ex. It seemed impossibly mature, like smoking a cigar while deciding not to impulse-buy a DVD.

"Right. Yeah, yeah. I was, uh . . . Wait, sorry, what were you saying?"

She laughed a little. "Just that you should start small. Write something short I can read. I want to read a story by you."

I stared at the table, trying to hide my smile. "Yeah?"

"Uh, yeah. You've been telling me you're a writer. Bring me something you wrote next time. It doesn't have to be a movie."

"Okay," I said, feeling my heart race. "Okay, yeah, yeah, sure." I felt excited and eager. Motivated. I finally had something to do that excited me. A goal I actually cared about.

My phone vibrated and I opened the text from Mom: *r u ok.*

"Shit, my mom's waiting," I said. "What about you? Is your mom waiting?"

She reached into her hoodie pocket and pulled out car keys. "Licensed to drive, as of two weeks ago. Now my parents don't have to argue about driving me everywhere."

"Oh, wow, sweet," I said. My phone buzzed again. Mom: *r u hurt.* Then an immediate follow-up: *im coming in.*

Goddamn it. "I gotta go. Sorry. See you next time."

As I was speed-walking into the parking deck, it dawned on me that I'd barely asked Alex about her life and how she was feeling. Shit. There was so much more I wanted to know about her. There was still a chance she was annoyed with her friends and all she had was me. Still a chance that our backstories were different, but starting with the moment we made eye contact at that first appointment, our lives converged. We were two wavy lines on a graphing calculator that intersected and became one, stretching into infinity. The past didn't matter because we had each other now.

I walked up the concrete stairs and considered how she had a license and I had a phone, and I should have texted Mom that Alex would drive me home. We could have kept hanging out all afternoon. Jesus Christ. We could have lived out *Before Sunrise* together, but instead I was having my mother drive me back to my room so I could browse the internet. Goddamn it, I was an idiot.

If I brought her the right story at our next appointment, I could give some made-up excuse to Mom so Alex and I could stay out all night driving through our town together. At two a.m. we'd connect the dots between Walmart, QuikTrip, and Waffle House. Errands would feel like adventures when we'd do them at night. We'd bring a laptop in her car and watch a movie in there, our own space, our alternate universe when everyone else was asleep and the world was just us. The only thing I needed to do in December was write a story she'd love. I could ignore everything else. It felt great to have a clear goal.

I got to Mom just as she was getting out of the car, and I took the keys from her and drove her minivan back home, feeling so good that I didn't even get stressed out when she screamed at me for rolling straight through that bullshit stop sign in our neighborhood.

18.

Luke hosted a LAN party at his house in December with a
bunch of guys from the football team and I didn't go. At school
the Monday after, Sam and Patrick talked about a horren-
dously unfunny prank call Todd Lancaster had made to the
number on the Proactiv commercial. The premise was just that
his face was really gross and he looked like he had the bubonic
plague. Todd Lancaster is probably the dumbest person I've
ever known. He's the kind of idiot who refers to any shape of
pasta as spaghetti. The more they talked and laughed about
the call, repeating lines about nasty zits and pus, the more I
realized they were making fun of me. They'd wanted to say that
stuff every day all year, and they finally found a way to do it

without saying it directly to me, a hidden underground passageway to calling me disgusting.

I had no regrets about lying to Luke that I'd had to stay home that night to help my dad pressure-wash our driveway.

Stress from finals made me want to squeeze out every whitehead. At school I had to condition myself to not touch my face. In all my classes I kept a pen in my right hand and I sat on my left hand. If training myself to not rub my oily fingers on my chin meant looking like I literally had my thumb plugged in my ass during math class, then so what? I really didn't want to give myself any more breakouts to inspire some not-funny joke Todd Lancaster would amuse himself thinking about.

On the back of the test packet for Meyer's final was an extra-credit question: *How is your group progressing with the Tell Us a Story project for next May?*

Ah, shit.

Ever since Alex had asked me to write her a story, I'd been actively trying to not think about the movie. Luke and Will hadn't even mentioned it in the past few weeks. I tried to picture the messy notes document from my computer and remember any of the bullet points about the musician.

I leaned over to read what Will was writing and saw his outline for a horror movie about Japanese gangsters.

Then I sat up to look over Luke's shoulder and read his notes about an inbred farmer stalking a high-school football team.

The bell rang. I felt a pit in my stomach. Why were Luke and Will ignoring all my ideas and the effort I'd put in? Both of their ideas involved dozens of characters and car chases and explosions. How the hell would we film any of that?

When I handed in my test, I mumbled to Mr. Meyer that I wanted to talk to him if he had a second.

I nodded at Luke and Will when they left, and after everyone else filed out, Mr. Meyer spun a chair around to sit in it backward. I wondered if that was a move they teach you in teacher school to appear casual to the youth. "What's up?" he said.

"It's, uh, the story project," I muttered. "I thought we were doing one thing, but now me and Luke and Will all have different ideas. They don't work together at all."

"It's not due for another six months. Don't stress about it."

Don't stress about it. Great idea in theory. Absolutely no practical application.

I stared at the floor for a while. Some genetic thing prevents guys from asking directly for life advice, so we have to get it in roundabout ways by pretending conversations are about some project. When guys are in Home Depot asking other sunburned men how to build a shed, they're really desperately searching for any idea of what happiness is and how to get it.

I finally got the words out: "I need help. I know what I want to do, but I don't know what to do about . . . them."

He leaned back and stroked his chin. I couldn't figure out if he was a wise, inspiring teacher who would someday be the basis of a feature film or if he was just a regular dope impersonating a wise, inspiring teacher.

"Your friends? This project is getting between you?"

I nodded and shrugged, playing it off like it was no big deal. I was just a normal, cool, laid-back teenage dude asking his teacher how to maintain his friendships.

"This project's not worth losing friends over. Can you write the story you want to tell as prose and do it yourself?"

The idea of deleting all of Luke's and Will's ideas from my outline felt incredible. And just writing it as prose? Holy shit, I wouldn't have to deal with cameras and costumes and actors and props and me yelling at the guys to stop dicking around because the sun was setting and we were losing all our light. It could just be me sitting alone at the computer. Not having this project stuck between us anymore would be a huge relief.

I'd have to break the news that I was abandoning them, and they might be pissed because I was the only one who'd actually been doing any work. But a lot of the reasons I'd been annoyed with them were because of this project. It would be good for us. The most fun we'd had together all year was that night in the hotel room on the south Georgia trip, when none of us had brought up the project.

"Yeah," I said. "I've actually been thinking about writing, like, stories instead of a movie lately, so I think I'll work alone and start from scratch with just my ideas and see what happens."

Meyer smiled. "You know, I also volunteer as a reader with the *Sopchoppy Review,* a literary magazine down in Florida. We're always looking for submissions of short stories and poetry."

My face lit up. "Oh, wow. That's cool. That's awesome.

Yeah." Meyer had so many connections outside of our dumb school, outside of our dumb town, outside of our dumb state. He could help me publish a story. It wouldn't be just a pointless class project like everyone else was doing. It would be a real thing.

"Oh, so, can I add an extra-credit answer now that I know what I'm doing?"

"Do you think you earned extra credit?"

"Uh . . ."

"Did you make progress today on your project?"

"Yeah."

"Then you did great."

"But, like, how many points will it add to my grade?"

"If you feel good, then you did great. Remember, no one ever gets any answers, but we all find our own solutions."

I nodded and walked into the hallway, not sure what he was talking about. Mr. Meyer was a weird hippie and I suspected he made his own candles, but I liked him.

I found Luke and Will by their lockers. "Hey, Mr. Meyer just told me I have to work by myself for the rest of this story project," I lied. Was I a coward for blaming it on Meyer? Probably. But I'd never suspected I wasn't a coward at any point in my life, so it was fine.

Will said, "Wait, what?"

"Just, like," I said, "because of our extra-credit answers. We have different ideas of what to do. We're not in trouble or anything, but he told me I should just write my own thing and you guys can do, like, a movie or whatever about the football team slasher yakuza whatever. You guys can write it and cast all the people and set up the lighting and test the special effects and choreograph all those car chase scenes however you want to do them. It's totally up to you now."

Luke shrugged. "All right. We'll figure something out."

Will said, "Yeah, it's fine."

I nodded and said, "Cool." I was annoyed they didn't make any attempt to stop me, that they didn't realize they were screwed without me and crawl on the floor to beg me to stay with them. That would have been nice. They didn't care at all. "Well. Okay."

"Yeah," said Luke.

"All right," added Will.

"I guess I'll go to math," I said.

"Cool," said Luke.

Will brought our intellectual discussion to a rousing conclusion with an "Okay."

For the rest of that week in school, while we finished taking our other finals, I saw Luke and Will every day, but something felt off. Before first period, I'd stand in our circle with them, Sam, and Patrick. But without the project to link us together, I felt like I had no reason to be there and mostly stayed silent. They'd talk about movies I didn't care about and other kids in our grade I barely knew. Sam and Patrick repeated stories about the driver's ed class they all took together over Thanksgiving break. Will would laugh at their jokes. I just sort of stood there.

We were like Venn diagrams that had rolled apart.

My plan to excise the project from our relationship like it was a tumor hadn't fixed anything. Instead of Meyer's project being the thing getting between us, had it been the only thing that was keeping us together? Without being officially bound together into a group, were we just not friends anymore? I wondered if the subconscious reason I'd decided to do such a ridiculously complicated, time-consuming project was that it would force us to hang out together all year. That it would force us to have fun making a movie like we used to. It didn't work at all. I was like some out-of-touch divorced father in a movie who makes his biological kids go with him to see a movie they all hate when the kids just want to hang out with their cool new stepdad who takes them to football games.

I tried to remember why we'd become friends in the first place. I started being friends with Luke in fourth grade when Mrs. Owens had us all mark our houses on a map of our town and Luke's was closest to mine. My parents picked our house because there is a magnolia tree in the side yard. If a gust of wind hadn't pushed that seed into that spot fifty years ago, who knows who I'd be friends with now? We were friends because of proximity and decisions our parents made, the platonic male equivalent of an arranged marriage. Will showed up in middle school with the same generic interests as us, and the two of them were still putting up with me mostly due to inertia. We were all too lazy to make it stop. The project wasn't what had been killing us — *I* was. I was just a disease Luke and Will had been stricken with from middle school through ninth grade, and Sam and Patrick were the cure helping them flush me out of their systems forever.

A few years ago some kid wrapped his car around a tree, so his parents pressured people to pass this state law that requires every kid to sit through three days of driver's education classes before getting a license. When Luke and Will had said they were doing driver's ed with Sam and Patrick over Thanksgiving break, I'd told them I was doing it later without clarifying when or why. I couldn't stand to be the fifth wheel in their group 24/7. I needed a break.

Everyone at school always talked about driver's ed like it was the biggest pain in the ass in the world. To me it seemed like an opportunity to get away from everyone. Press reset and try to have normal conversations with new people who didn't know me.

I'd go in there for those three days pretending to be confident and outgoing and personable, able to freely ask everybody questions because I'd never see anyone in there again in my entire life. No risk. If I discovered that acting like a normal, socially engaged person made me feel like a phony dipshit, then I could go back to being uncomfortable and maladjusted. I'd be trying on the persona of a well-formed human being like it was a coat. Maybe driver's ed wouldn't be so bad if you treated it like experimental theater.

So far, all I had was Dad's terrible advice about asking number-based questions. If I was going to succeed at approximating a functional human being, I needed better instructions.

I eyed the stack of manners books Mom had given me every Christmas since fifth grade. I'd vowed that I'd never read them because they were objectively stupid, but it turned out that by avoiding them, I'd become the clueless, desperate idiot those books were written for.

I made sure my door was locked, then opened one of the books to a section called "The Gentleman Says the Right Thing." That seemed appropriate. It said I should be able to strike up a conversation with any pleasant person I encounter by asking a positive, noncontroversial question that does not bring attention upon myself.

That seemed like some decent advice. Similar to Dad's advice, but instead of grilling people for cold, hard facts, I'd just ask generic, boring questions. The next page in the book was a scan of an article from a British magazine originally printed in 1779 called "The Art of Pleafing in Converfation." It was from that era when printers hadn't yet realized the letter *f* wasn't an *s*. This part stood out:

> There is not a man of common sense who would not choose to be agreeable in company; and yet, strange as it may seem, very few are; not arising from the want of wit, sense, or learning, but for want of the proper judgment of applying them. Too much eagerness to shine often makes a person intolerably dull; misapplied wit becomes impertinence, and even learning, introduced improperly, sinks into pedantry. Conversation may metaphorically be styled

a well-seasoned stew, in which no one ingredient should predominate, but be made palatable to all the guests present. Much attention should be paid to the complexion and disposition of your companions.

Had whoever wrote that watched me mumble at Alex through a two-hundred-and-fifty-year-long brass telescope? Had morons like me really been blindly bumbling their way through one-sided conversations for centuries? Back then, people openly fired diarrhea onto public streets and slept on mattresses made of their dead relatives' teeth. They'd dust their chests with crumbs at night and invite swarms of rats to be their blankets, and anyone with acne was hurled onto a funeral pyre to roast with the witches. So much technological progress had been made between then and now, but casual conversations remained our species' albatross.

My stomach growled. Mom, Dad, and Kate were downstairs laughing at some shitty TV special of the "World's Funniest Commercials." They'd called me down to come watch it with them a few times and I told them I was busy. Mom had said the other day we don't have any Christmas traditions and she wanted to start one, but I'd rather have no traditions than a horrible one of literally watching advertisements. Besides, I thought I had my own tradition of hanging out in my room most of Christmas break, making my parents think I'm masturbating. They can never truly know. I'm a human physics paradox. Simultaneously jerking off and not at the same time. Schrödinger's masturbator.

I went downstairs to make a PB&J and I tried to think of a positive, noncontroversial question to ask my family that wouldn't bring attention upon myself.

After thirty seconds of me standing there drawing a blank like a slack-jawed idiot who forgot his lines on the opening night of the school play, Mom told me to close the fridge door.

I made my sandwich and went back upstairs, annoyed that this plan to become a normal, polite person would require some real effort.

19.

At seven thirty the first morning of driver's ed, I stepped out
of Mom's car in the parking lot and didn't look back when
she walked around from the passenger seat into the driver's
seat and drove off. I could see my breath in the cold as I stood
outside the driver's ed door, which was nestled between a dry
cleaner and an off-brand cell phone store in the middle of
a beige concrete strip mall, with three other kids who'd also
shown up before the teacher.

The two guys and one girl looked like they were around my
age and I didn't recognize them, thankfully. They must have all
gone to other schools. "What's up?" I forced through my teeth,
looking one of the guys in the eye and nodding. He kept his

hands tucked into his hoodie pockets and nodded but didn't say anything.

More kids showed up, and a few adults, and I said, "What's up?" to all of them and got the same lack of reaction. The words felt stilted and unnatural, like I was trying to push open a door that needed to be pulled. Being the life of the party was much more difficult than it looked in soda commercials. I hadn't injected enough Mountain Dew into my heart to be that guy.

One of the older people, who I guess were there to get speeding tickets taken off their record, looked at emails on his phone. He seemed to be in his midtwenties. I walked beside him and said, "You cold?" which was one hell of a pleasant and noncontroversial question.

He shrugged and briefly made eye contact. Bingo. I was bonded to him like a newborn duckling and the first thing it ever saw. I tried to think of a follow-up question about anything other than the weather, but I drew a blank. I figured it was okay to take it slow. I had three days to forge a lifelong friendship with my new mentor.

Finally the teacher showed up — a heavyset woman named Paula Freeman who waddled up to the door with a folder of papers clenched in her teeth. She said, "Come on in. Excuse my tardiness. I got caught up this morning writing my stand-up jokes." She turned on the fluorescent lights and we all took our seats at two long tables. "You can see me perform at the Chuckle Cabin every Tuesday and Sunday night at two fifteen a.m."

Paula handed out packets of worksheets and some battered

textbooks and then had us write our names on little cards and put them in front of us. My new friend was named Carson. He had a few purple scars on his jawline, but they were covered by a layer of the kind of stubble I was looking forward to having someday. He scrolled through more emails on his phone.

I leaned over and said, "Work sucks. I know." I wasn't sure why I'd said that. I'd never had a job. And then a second after I'd said it, I realized it was a very well-known Blink-182 lyric, and I suddenly became embarrassed. Luckily he didn't seem to have heard me, because he didn't react at all.

Paula sped through a memorized paragraph about the importance of our worksheets and the VHS tapes we'd be watching, then told us to open our books to chapter four. In health class, too, we were always randomly skipping around chapters. The teachers tell you the class is so valuable and will save you from a car wreck or a disgusting growth all over your genitals, and then in the next breath tell you that chapters one, six, seven, nine, thirteen, and fifteen are wastes of time and you don't need to worry about those. I'm convinced that I'll one day die in an entirely preventable way that was covered in great detail in chapter seven of the ninth-grade health textbook.

We had an hour to read the six-page chapter and answer a ten-question quiz at the back about proper conditions for driving. It took five minutes, and then I sat there and tried to think of something to talk to Carson about. The one thing I knew, based on sneaking glances at his phone, was that he worked some kind of office job. I tried to think of something I knew about the business world. I leaned over and whispered, "What's your take on that article about Pepsi in *Time* magazine?"

"What?"

"You see the article about Pepsi in *Time*?"

He stared at me for a second. "I don't read *Time* magazine."

"Oh."

"When was it?"

"Uh . . . I guess a few months ago."

He squinted at me. "Did something happen to Pepsi?"

I tried to think. I honestly couldn't remember anything about the actual article. It was only, like, half of one page. It had something to do with business. That was all I remembered. Shit. Apparently not all adults subscribe to the same magazines as my dad.

I gave him a shrug that I intended to convey *I don't know, dude — the world's a crazy place and me and you are just cruising through it together,* but I think it looked more like *I'm a strange idiot with poor reading comprehension skills.*

I flipped through the textbook, scanning for dumb photographs of people from the early '90s. One page featured a teenager with a bowl cut and sunglasses giving a big thumbs-up. Someone had already drawn a half dozen penises surrounding his head and hands. They were wiry and long, unusual and well done. Whoever drew them had an artistic voice.

I laughed at them, and Paula Freeman said, "Kevin? Something's funny about proper conditions to drive?"

"No," I said, staring down at the table. I could feel the entire class's eyes on me like heat lamps.

"Kevin, tell me, is it safe to drive while feeling angry or upset?"

She was speaking to me like I was three years old. I bit my lip and shook my head to answer her question.

"No? That's right. And what should you do if you get behind the wheel feeling angry?"

I didn't care enough to give a real answer, so I shut my eyes and mumbled, "I don't know."

"You don't know? Well, *I* know your face is turning redder than a lobster in a marinara hot tub."

A few kids laughed at her horrible joke while she frantically searched for a notebook on her desk and wrote down her punch line. My face felt pressurized. My entire head felt like one massive, ripe whitehead about to burst.

"Lobster," Paula Freeman repeated, "in a marinara hot tub!"

My embarrassment was becoming the big closing joke of her stand-up set.

"Y'all need to pay attention to the tips in this book and not just chuckle at the ancient ding-dong doodles like Kevin over there. Driving angry or upset is distracted driving and it's dangerous. You should pull over and wait thirty minutes to calm down. Got that, Kevin?"

I nodded, but I still didn't look up from the table. I'd been an idiot for thinking I could just suddenly change my personality because I was in a room full of strangers. It wasn't the Breakfast Club; no one wanted to open up and learn from each other. We all just wanted to sit there like potatoes in a microwave, waiting to get a piece of paper saying we could drive, and then put the memories of ever having been in that classroom in a temporary folder of our brains where they would quickly be overwritten by something more memorable, like an unusually long banana we saw at the grocery store.

For the rest of the day and the two that came after it, I didn't speak to anyone. I brought headphones and avoided eye contact. During our lunch breaks, when most people went as a group to the deli at the corner of the strip mall, I went around behind the building, sat on the ground against the wall, turned on music, and shut my eyes.

At the end of the last day, Paula Freeman handed us all little certificates of completion. We never got inside a car, but somehow that class proved we were good drivers. It was like a weird miniature graduation ceremony. We were supposed to walk up to the front of the class, take our certificate from her, and then go back to our seats to watch the rest of the class get theirs.

I was one of the first to pick my certificate up, and as soon as I did, I walked straight out the door. I heard Paula Freeman say something behind me, and then everyone laughed. I didn't even care what it was anymore. Probably another obvious comparison of my face to a tomato or a fire truck. Her entire act was a list of things that are red. What fresh, satirical observations she was making. What a unique point of view. I stood at the entrance of the strip mall waiting for Mom to pick me up, wondering if she'd even be able to see me, since my red face must have camouflaged into the stop sign behind me.

20.

On Christmas morning, my parents gave us all a new computer for the family room and told me I could keep our old one in my room. I'd kind of forced them into letting me keep it because I'd been holding it hostage since Thanksgiving and I was the only one who knew how to take it apart and put it back together. Kate had screamed about me taking it at the time, but Mom let her use her laptop and she got over it, and now the desktop was officially mine. Perfect. I could continue to do my internet browsing alone without hearing some awful sitcom laugh track behind me.

As soon as I set up the new computer, Dad looked up a traffic report and then frantically collected all the wrapping paper scraps and hauled the bag out to the garage trash can to erase any evidence of Christmas. Then he rushed into his car and told us to put our shoes on faster if we wanted any chance of beating the traffic on the way to Grandma's house.

Hardly anyone else was on the road.

Few things make a fifteen-year-old feel more insignificant than Christmas with extended family. Here are the gifts I received: *The Beginner's Guide to Card Tricks,* a child's acoustic guitar, an expensive Harley-Davidson motorcycle figurine, a framed photograph of a lion, a set of poker chips, and a jar full of baking supplies that could someday become brownies. There was no pattern, through line, or consistency to that spread; it was a collection of random items that had probably never been put together before and never would be put together again. It was like a dozen delivery trucks had crashed together on the highway and my uncles and aunts had pulled over and said, "Oh, shit, did anyone get anything for Kevin?" and then pointed to a smoking pile and decided, "That'll do."

On the drive over, Dad had reviewed the plan for the afternoon: a half hour of mingling with relatives followed by an hour of basketball on TV, an hour for eating, and then a half hour to open gifts and "wrap things up" and be the first people to leave. It aligned almost perfectly with my own schedule, except during his mingling and basketball windows I'd penciled in "hiding in low-traffic areas." The idea crossed my mind of blocking out a section to masturbate — not out of any real sexual desire, more as a way to kill time — but I ultimately decided against it. It felt like a mature and wise decision.

Instead of giving frankincense or myrrh, I'd eliminate the possibility of my family members walking in on me beating off in an upstairs bathroom. It was the greatest gift they'd never know they'd received.

Dad dove right into the fray, shaking hands with all of his brothers and sisters-in-law, asking them these insanely specific questions about their jobs. I have no idea how he keeps track of all those personal details about people. Either he has some serial-killer-style archive of notebooks in his office or he was born with a dental hygienist's infinite memory for small talk.

I tried to avoid everyone, but my uncles and aunts piled on the standard questions that I never had any good answers for:

"Kevin, how are you?"

"Good."

"Kevin, how's school?"

"Fine."

"Kevin, are you studying anything interesting?"

"Just the normal classes everyone has to take."

"Kevin, have you read any more books about World War Two fighter planes?"

"Not since I was seven, no."

"Kevin, have you started thinking about colleges yet?"

"Uh . . . no?"

"Kevin, do you have a girlfriend? Any special lady in your life? A crush?"

"I'm gonna help my mom in the kitchen."

I went upstairs to the playroom with toys and stuff for the grandkids. There was a computer in there, too, and I turned it on and sat in the tiny kid's chair in front of it. I tried to go online, but my grandma had installed such insanely strict anti-porn, antiviolence, antianything content blockers that a siren would go off if you searched for *Moby-Dick*. Her internet was unfit for anything but images of baby ducklings and Crock-Pot recipes.

Microsoft Word was on there, though, so I opened it and typed SHORT STORY at the top. I had a bunch of bad ideas from the movie outline that could have become the story for Alex — things about musicians, people falling in love, modern twists on old stories — but I didn't write any of those.

What I typed, almost without thinking, was "I went to a driver's ed class that didn't even let you drive a car. They probably knew I'd try to steer it off a bridge."

I thought it was kind of a funny way to start. From there, I described the first day of driver's ed exactly how it had happened. I mentioned that guy Carson I had tried to be friends with, and all the other teenagers in the class. I spent a few paragraphs explaining how Paula Freeman looked and sounded and I attempted to get inside how her brain worked as she wrote her horrible comedy act. I lost track of time up there. I was putting in more and more detailed descriptions and even some jokes. I felt charged up, being able to just focus on telling the story and not having to worry about how we'd film it or what Luke or Will would want to change. It was entirely my story and I could put whatever I wanted into it.

It was basically nonfiction, until I got to the part when Paula Freeman had called me out in front of the whole class for

185

getting a question wrong and pointed out how red my face was. What had really happened was I sat there, folded my arms, and stewed in silent frustration. But instead I wrote:

I stand up and slam my textbook shut. They watch me, unsure what I'm about to do. I walk to the front of the class and snatch a set of keys from Paula Freeman's desk, then stomp out the door and into the parking lot. I unlock the driver's ed car with two steering wheels, and as I close the door behind me, I see Paula Freeman in the rearview mirror sprinting through the parking lot, screaming and shouting and flailing her arms. "You ain't licensed to drive that car!"

Fat chance a maniac like me respects the authority of a piece of plastic issued by the DMV. I start the car and rev its decrepit engine. It coughs like I'm trying to keep a dead man alive against his will, but once it's going, it's pure lightning and I peel out of the parking lot and whip onto the highway faster than a once-caged eagle clawing his way to freedom.

Paula Freeman huffs her way back into the classroom. "He's gone," she says. "I lost another one. He ain't never coming back."

"I bet he's robbing a bank," one girl says. "He had that look about him. The look of a bandit."

A guy says, "No, he's on his way to Mexico, where he will change his identity and become an entrepreneur. It's always risky to start your own business, but something about that guy makes me confident he'll succeed."

Paula Freeman says, "No. I've seen this before. That boy is gonna drive for a hundred years without ever slowing down. Long after we're dead and buried, he'll be watching the world burn through the gaps between bug corpses on his windshield."

"But, Paula," a girl says, "won't he run out of gas sometime between now and one hundred years from now?"

Paula laughs. "Y'all have a lot to learn about driving if you think that stone-cold lunatic could possibly run out of gas. Open your books to page —"

The class shrieks as I kick in the door and walk back to my seat, holding a bag from the grocery store. I pull out a bottle of redness-reducing moisturizer, unscrew the cap, and smear it over my face.

I keep rubbing until my face is caked in white slime. I withdraw a long stick lighter from my pocket and click a flame out of it, lighting my face on fire. I roast stoically, with my eyes closed. The smell of burnt hamburgers circulates.

"No!" Paula Freeman shouts. "No!"

The class members scream and hurl chairs through windows; they beg forgiveness from false gods; they hide under the tables, and I crouch down to their level. They each open their eyes, and once they are all staring at my flaming face, I say, "Boo."

Every student's head explodes.

As I cross through the fiery gates into hell, Paula Freeman weeps into her hands, wailing, "Not again, dear Lord, not again."

The end.

I didn't know what any of that story was supposed to mean. I wasn't sure if it was symbolism. It was just a weird and sort of gross image that I thought was kind of funny and naturally came out when I was writing. I didn't question it.

"Kevin! Dinner!" Mom yelled from downstairs. "Kevin? Are you upstairs?"

I'd been up there for over an hour without realizing any time had passed at all. I emailed the story to myself and went downstairs. I had to sit at the adult table and endure small talk about work and diseases afflicting great-aunts I'd never heard of, which ordinarily would have made me want to take the ham's place inside the oven. But I felt good. I'd been creative and productive. I'd made something that hadn't existed an hour before. I wanted to write more stories. Every time an uncle said something offensive or an aunt asked me if I was still interested in that thing I was into when I was seven, I didn't get mad. I just thought about the story it would inspire and all the things I'd be able to do once I put myself inside it.

The night before our next blood test, I edited my story over and over while imagining what Alex was doing at the same time. She could have been sitting in her room alone just like me, or she could have been out at an elf-themed party with fifty of her hottest friends. Daydreaming about Alex had become a test of my emotions. If I felt any hope, I'd see her with her headphones on in bed, reading Sylvia Plath poems and novels that won awards I'd never heard of. But if I started slipping into pessimism, that vision morphed into the opening credits of a reality show, where Alex was one of ten hyperconfident, popular babes introducing themselves with one-liners about wanting to hook up with everyone.

Those mood swings were probably just from the Accutane, right? I knew Alex. She'd introduced me to singers and bands I'd never heard before, thoughtful songs about real emotions. I was no longer an oafish boy wearing AC/DC and Led Zeppelin T-shirts his mom bought him at Kohl's, forcing himself to listen to lame-ass cock rock because that's what guys are supposed to like. I was past all that. Luke and Will hadn't left me behind; I'd left them, and she had led the way.

21.

The afternoon of our December blood test, I still felt a little hopeless about having a normal conversation with Alex, but I felt good about my story. I was decent at expressing my thoughts when I spent hours alone obsessively editing them.

She was in the waiting room when I got there, wearing a giant jacket that made her look like a turtle poking her head out of a big, poofy shell. I sat beside her.

"Did you change something in your face-washing routine?" she whispered. I shook my head. "Oh," she said. "Well, your skin looks really good."

I forced the childish smile away and shoved my hands in my jeans pockets. "Did, um, you . . . ? How was Christmas?"

"Eh."

"Eh?"

"My brother was home from college, so that was good, but he and my dad are just, like, I don't know . . . They're hard to figure out. We did a lot of packing at my dad's house. Then Mike and I went to our mom's, so I guess we had two Christmases. Both were better than last year's, since our parents weren't yelling at each other. First Christmas since they're, like, officially divorced. Well, maybe better's not the word. Quieter and weirder. At both I just thought about the parent who wasn't there. I don't know. Sorry. I'm rambling."

I stared at my shoes, trying to process all that. She was opening up to me. You'd only do that with someone you trusted, someone who mattered to you. I needed to prove to her that her trust in me was warranted. I needed to ask her something polite and noncontroversial about her parents' divorce. Shit. What a complicated subject I knew absolutely nothing about. All the advice from Dad and the gentleman books was no good. What was an appropriate bland, quantitative question about your parents getting divorced? *What day was it official that your family was changed forever? How many times per week would your parents yell at each other?*

This is what came out: "How, um . . . ? How . . . ? You . . . Um?"

"It sucks, but it's . . . It had to happen."

"Yeah," I said, as if I knew her parents.

She shrugged and shook her head, like she was trying to clear the thoughts off an Etch A Sketch. "So, what do I need to know about your school? You haven't told me anything."

"Uh, not much has happened, really. I don't know. I try not to think about it during breaks."

"Yeah. I guess all schools are pretty much the same. Your school probably has the same crap mine has, just with a slightly different floor plan."

"Yeah, yeah, for sure." I nodded a little too vigorously. I'd had that exact same thought a few months before, which was further proof that we saw the world the same way.

"Have plans for New Year's?"

I told her about this party Luke and Will had just told me they were going to with the girls from homecoming. "I'm not gonna go, though," I said. I worried I sounded lame, though, so I tried to come up with some clever explanation — maybe something about how I'd rather stay at home reading Wikipedia pages about the 1999 Academy Awards nominees than have to watch those guys try to impress girls into giving them midnight kisses by wrestling each other or arguing about the best guitar solos or whatever other desperate masculine brutishness Sam and Patrick would start. But those images in my head never congealed into complete sentences that I could actually say.

Luckily she smiled and said she hated New Year's and all the pressure to have a good time that came with it. She wasn't doing anything, either.

I smiled and nodded, relieved. I didn't need to impress her with perfectly written excuses. She got me. A beat passed. Then another. Should I ask her more about her parents? Did she need to get that off her mind, or — No. She didn't want to talk about it. Shit, what was she talking about now? *Focus. Listen.*

She was telling me a story about a boring New Year's party she'd gone to last year. Wait, shit. Did I just miss my opportunity to ask her to hang out with me on New Year's? There'd be no party, just the two of us watching a movie together. Damn it. I'd missed the opening.

I listened to her as best I could over the noise in my head about blowing my chance, and before I had to say anything back, the nurse called for Alex and as she stood up, she said, "Weren't you gonna write a —?"

I whipped the packet of papers out of my hoodie pocket like I was unsheathing a sword. She smiled, took it, said, "Cool," and disappeared into the back of the office.

They called me back before Alex came out, and I figured I'd have to wait until January to hear what she thought of the story. But when I came back out to the waiting room, there she was, reading the last page. Smiling.

Like, while she read it, she was smiling. She even — Wait, could it be? Could this be real? She laughed. She laughed at something right there at the end.

Holy shit.

The words I'd made up in my grandma's house, then printed out in my room, then handed to Alex were now shooting into her brain and making her laugh. They were making her happy.

"This is funny," she said. "Did some of this actually happen?"

I told her that most of it really happened to me, except for all the interesting parts. I said I never really got to drive the driver's ed car.

"Want to drive mine?" she said.

"I mean, I only have my permit, so I can't, like . . . My mom or dad have to be in the car. . . ."

She shrugged. "I won't call the cops if you don't."

Right. Yes. What the hell was I doing enforcing the law that would keep me from alone time with Alex? *For god's sake, Kevin, get your head in the game.* "Um, yeah. Right. Yeah, let's do it."

I called Mom and told her a kid I knew from school was there and they'd drive me home. I kept the pronouns vague. Mom didn't need to know I was with a girl.

Alex and I snuck out a side exit to the parking garage and walked over to her car. She drove an old green Jeep. I'd never cared about cars before, but it was the coolest thing I'd ever seen. She opened the driver-side door for me and waved me inside.

I sat down, squeezed the steering wheel, and before she even got into the passenger seat my pits rained sweat. Pressure gripped me like vulture claws. The last thing I needed was to nervously spin out on a turn, flip the car, kill us both, and be the namesake of Kevin's Law, which forbids teenage guys from being in vehicles with the primary subjects of their compulsive daydreams.

She sat down, put her hand on my shoulder. "This is gonna be fun." Her touch melted the stress. I looked at her and we made eye contact. I wanted to live in that moment — buy a house, plant roots, open a small business, and have a family in it.

I backed out of the parking deck, merged onto the road. I didn't ask her any boring questions. We didn't need to talk.

We lowered the windows and felt the cold air rush into our hair, listening to the wind. The sun set. I drove a boring route around our strip-mall suburb I'd been on a million times, but it was different. Special. Magical. Signs on chain restaurants shone like stars. I'd look over at her when we stopped at red lights as much as I could without being a weird creep, trying to maintain the feeling that the whole world outside the car no longer existed. I wanted to keep going until we ran out of gas and had to spend the night in the back seat.

Eventually she said she had to get home and I drove to my house first.

I parked at the end of my street so my parents wouldn't see. "Good job," she said, nodding at the dashboard. "Seems like you learned something in that crazy driver's ed class."

I laughed. "Yeah, I guess."

"Keep writing stories. It made me happy."

Those four words made me feel so fucking good, I could have been flattened by an eighteen-wheeler and wouldn't have felt any pain.

She said, "Text me if you're bored."

"Yeah? Yeah. Defin — def — def — definitely. Wait. What's your —?"

"Oh, right. Here." She handed me her phone and I typed my number in. She texted me so I had hers: *Hey it's me.*

I got out of the car and smiled a real, unforced smile as she walked around and got into the driver's seat. She said through the open window, "I don't know why I didn't give you my number, like, a while ago. Sorry. See you soon, right?"

I nodded and she drove away.

Holy shit.

I sat in my room replaying every moment. My story made her smile. My ideas were worth something. She gave me the push I needed to stop outlining and stalling and overthinking. Just write. I was actually excited for next semester. Nothing at school would stress me out because I'd only care about writing the next chapter so I could give it to her and watch her smile when she read it. We'd make playlists together and press play at the exact same time every morning, connecting us across schools, keeping our heads in the same space until we could talk to each other next. School would become my B story, a subplot interrupting my real life with Alex, our intertwined existence in the waiting room, or talking on the phone, or being together on weekends. I'd write stories for her and Meyer would get them published. I'd be who I'm supposed to be.

We had each other's numbers. I wouldn't have to wait a month to talk to her.

She sent me a Facebook friend request that night and I accepted. It felt like an inside joke, like everyone at her school knew Alex June, and only I knew the real Alex Mae, since we didn't meet at school, we met in the real world. She hadn't posted anything in months, and she'd detagged herself from the homecoming pictures. My profile was almost entirely blank, too. No one from our schools would know what was going on between us. I liked that. It made what we had feel secret, undercover, pure.

On New Year's Eve I spent forty minutes drafting this text: *I hope you are having a nice night and that your blood is not diseased.*

Five minutes went by after I sent it while I analyzed every word, regretting each one individually, worrying that I'd accidentally said something offensive.

She responded: *watching TV with my dad. blood feels good. what are you up to?*

Me: *Hanging upside down in my gravity boots covered in leeches. Trying to freshen my blood for the new year.*

Excruciatingly long pause.

Me: *I was kidding.*

Her: *lol are you watching a movie or something?*

Me: *I'm downloading some old stuff I've been meaning to watch. Citizen Kane and Casablanca.*

Her: *of all the blood test places in all the towns in all the world, you walked into mine*

Me: *Stumbled in like a lost chimpanzee.*

Her: *that was a casablanca quote*

Me: *shit. right.*

Her: *lol I love that movie*

Me: *lol let me get back to you in two hours and I'll probably agree.*

Her: *don't make me wait that long I'll be so booooored*

I sat alone at my desk in my dark room, glowing blue-white in front of the computer monitor, having the best New Year's of my entire life.

22.

I cruised into school the first morning after Christmas break feeling like a new person. My face was a little clearer and less shiny since the cold January air dried the hell out of it. I looked like an old, dusty pencil eraser and I felt great. I was ready to ignore high school and think about writing stories for Alex all day.

Luke, Will, Sam, Patrick, and I stood in our usual spot before the bell rang and I was listening to them discuss what it would be like if our favorite children's cartoon characters had sex with each other when a hand tapped me on the shoulder.

I turned around and Alex was standing there.

Alex was standing there.

Alex.

Two separate universes colliding, the two spheres of my life T-boning into each other.

Alex was standing there. She had makeup on and was dressed differently, in a blue sweater and nicer jeans or something.

She waved at me. I nodded and my face felt hot. The guys would see us, ask who she was, ask how she knew me, ask why I'd never told them about her, ask what my —

"Hey?" she said.

I nodded at her again like she was as familiar to me as the guy who tears tickets at the movie theater. "Hey . . . Did, uh," I said, "you, uh . . . like, uh . . . you know?"

"Transfer here?" she said.

"Yeah. Uh," I said.

She nodded at me while squinting in a way that communicated I was insane. "I told you? Like, two appointments ago? When we were talking about homecoming?"

Shit. *Shit, shit, shit.* She must have brought it up when I was zoned out, tumbling through the storm of dark thoughts about her ex-boyfriend. Was *that* why she'd been asking me about my school at our last appointment? Goddamn. How had I survived as long as I had being so oblivious and stuck in my head all the time? I think I'm a good listener, but I'm really just good at staring at people while they talk.

"Right, no, yeah," I said, "I just . . . wasn't sure you were gonna go through with it. But . . . you did. Yeah, so . . . welcome, I guess?"

"Thanks," she said, still looking at me funny. But the bell

rang and spared me more follow-up questions. The guys all dispersed and she held her schedule out to me and asked if I knew where her first class was. I pointed down the hallway and told her to take a left and then she disappeared into the mass of idiots and morons I'd known since first grade. It was like watching a diamond ring fall into the toilet.

I zoned out through first period, wondering if Alex had been a mirage. Second period I sat through a world history lecture about the diseases Europeans brought to America, and I kept flicking my eyes over to the narrow window in the door, hoping she'd walk by. She wasn't in my lunch period and I didn't see her in fifth or sixth periods. In my last class I got a bathroom pass and wandered down every hallway, looking through classroom windows, trying to find her. I felt like either a cop who rescues kidnapped children or the guy who kidnaps the children. Ten, fifteen, or twenty minutes must have passed — enough time that my classmates were certainly debating in graphic, poetic detail the severity of my constipation and the ill-advised diet that caused it — when I found her.

She was sitting in a math class in the front row by herself. Everyone around her was talking in small groups — ignoring their assignments, catching up on what had happened over Christmas break. No one was talking to her. She was doing the worksheet, alone, leaning forward like she was trying to curl into a ball. She didn't care about socializing with the uninteresting characters around her. She wanted to get her work done. It was beautiful.

Eventually she looked up and saw me. I tried to act surprised, like I'd been passing by at just that moment and hadn't been deliberately ogling her for several minutes, slack-jawed like some barnyard animal. She stood up from her desk, got a bathroom pass, and walked toward the door.

"Hey—" she said.

"H-hey—" I stammered over her at the same time.

"Do you have a class now?"

"Yeah. I was just . . . going for a walk. Clear my head. Get out of the classroom."

"You do that a lot?"

"Sometimes," I lied. I had never done that. She nodded and then pointed to her bathroom pass and said, "Where's the, uh . . . ?"

"Like, to hang out for a while?"

"More like to . . . use the bathroom?"

"Oh. Right. It's this way."

I walked beside her to the bathroom like I was escorting her to a dance.

When she reemerged into the hallway, she looked surprised. "Oh. You waited for me."

Was I not supposed to wait? Was that weird and creepy? I changed the subject: "How's the, uh, the, uh, first day?"

"Kind of annoying. Something got screwed up on my transfer paperwork, so they're gonna have to change my schedule all around to put me in the right classes."

"You should transfer into all my classes."

"That would be nice."

Holy shit. Freeze those two sentences in amber and paralyze me inside them. *You should transfer into all my classes. That would be nice.* What a confident slam dunk of an all-star touchdown. She made me feel so confident that sports metaphors entered my vocabulary.

I walked her back to her class and watched her sit down all by herself, surrounded by kids who already had friends. She was starting new. She didn't have her posse of teen heartthrobs. She only had me.

The version of her I'd fallen for last August was becoming real right in front of me.

I went out to dinner with my family at a sports bar that night and zoned out in the corner of the booth, thinking about how it was like Alex and I were bound together in a storm, holding each other's hands to ride out the hurricane that is high school. But eventually Kate's rambling about seventh-grade birthday party drama got so loud, I couldn't ignore it.

She was going back and forth on her decision to get a horse-themed gift for her friend. Kate was straddling that line all girls face at her age, forced to choose between believing horses are majestic and glorious or accepting the objective truth that they're nasty and weird. I pictured this big field where thousands of twinkly-eyed twelve-year-old girls mingle with horses near the edge of some crazy cliff. And I'm standing at the bottom of this cliff, shouting and guiding the girls with a megaphone and orange flags to leap over the brink into the horse-free valley and never look back, because those filthy animals are strange and disgusting and a gateway to a smelly and off-putting subculture. That's all I'd do all day. I'd just be the guy in the vest encouraging girls to lose interest in horses and jump off a cliff and all.

I ate my grilled chicken wrap and watched Dad eat ribs with a napkin tucked into his shirt collar like he was a small boy. He smiled to himself and didn't say a word while he smacked his lips and licked the barbecue sauce off his face. A boy should never see his father quietly enjoying himself while eating ribs. It makes him appear too sympathetic and vulnerable, far more human than a father should ever appear.

I shook myself from that thought and went back to Alex. She'd get switched into my classes and she'd be my partner on every project. I wouldn't have to go up to teachers anymore and ask if Luke, Will, and I can be a group of three instead of two, and they say no, and then one of us has to partner with some kid who cusses way too much or won't stop summarizing TV episodes we've both already seen.

Alex and I would work together and the projects would give us things to talk about. We'd put jokes in the presentations that no one else would get and we'd wink at each other while standing up in front of the class and everyone else would be confused and not know what the hell we were talking about, but we'd get the joke and have our own secret language of references and we'd have to go over to each other's houses after school to work on projects and that would give us legitimate, not-weird reasons to be in each other's bedrooms, since that's where my computer is, and then we'd make out all afternoon under the cover of the greatest alibi of them all: *It's for school.*

The check came just as I was starting to get a boner, which is usually a good time to wrap up a family dinner.

23.

At school the next morning while I stood in the circle with the guys, I kept looking over my shoulder to check for Alex. Every passing minute made me more worried something had happened to her — car wreck? House burned down? She was so weirded out by me waiting for her at the bathroom yesterday that she transferred back to her old school?

The bell rang and my paranoia festered through every class until lunch. Since I brought food from home, I always sat down at our table first while the guys waited in line defending their crotches from Patrick's snapping fingers while he said, "Let me pinch that 'ner." I was at our table peeling my banana when Alex emerged through the swarm of generic kids crowding the cafeteria and walked toward me.

"I'm a bringer, too," she said when she sat down. "This looks exactly like my old school, but, like, completely different. I went up to the line and asked about you, and people told me this is where you sit. I just met Luke, Will, Patrick, and —"

Shit. They met her before I'd explained anything to them. I should have given them some reason why I knew her. They were probably making up stories right then that she'd helped me locate the extra-small condoms at CVS. I guess telling them the truth was an option: It wouldn't surprise anyone to find out I was on Accutane. But even if I was fine with people knowing I was on it, Alex probably wouldn't want that to be the first thing everyone knew about her.

"Cool, cool," I said. "Wait, so, what did you tell the guys about, like . . . how we know each other?"

"Oh, I didn't. I just asked if anyone knew you and they said they were your friends and pointed me this way."

I wasn't sure what to talk to her about when we were surrounded by random other kids who could hear everything we said. When I looked up, the guys were sitting down with their trays of chicken fingers, pizza, and fries.

"Sorry," Alex said to Sam, "but remind me what your name is?"

Patrick pointed to Sam and said, "Rickets. We call him rickets because he has rickets, like a guy from the Great Depression." Alex laughed.

Sam shook his head and pointed at himself and said, "Sam." I'd never heard that stupid nickname before. I think Patrick was just making up dumb bullshit in a desperate attempt to make the new girl laugh.

Luke said, "So you transferred into our ridiculous school?"

What was ridiculous about our completely average, normal school?

"Yeah, and they messed up my schedule and put me in the wrong classes yesterday, but they changed it this morning and now I'm in this lunch. Surprise!" She laughed nervously, looking at me.

"Cool . . ." I said again, and I realized this might be my only opportunity to find out why she transferred without having to explain to her I hadn't been listening when she told me at our appointments. "So, uh . . . why don't you, like, tell the guys why you go here now? Just to, like, catch them up and stuff?"

She squinted at me like she was confused or maybe even hurt. "Uh, all right," she said. "My parents just . . . they got divorced and my dad wanted a smaller place, so we moved. Now it's just me and him in an apartment."

She looked down and a silence fell over the table. Fuck. I was supposed to know that already, and now she must have thought I was a piece of shit for making her tell everyone.

Luke said, "Damn. Sorry."

She smiled at him and shook her head. "No worries. Anything I should know about this place? Kids to avoid? Teachers to be scared of?"

Luke's eyes lit up. "Our math teacher, Mr. Randolph, wears pants that are way too tight. Keep your eyes above his belt."

Alex laughed. Sweat drops fell out of my armpits, and my face got fifteen degrees hotter. I don't think what Luke said was true or even based on anything. All of them were like jackass chimpanzees trying to grunt the loudest for the new female.

"You're in their math class?" I said.

"I just got switched into it today," she said, and handed me her new schedule. The only period we had together was lunch. She was in the same math as Luke and Will and she had a couple classes each with Sam and Patrick.

"Since when does Mr. Randolph wear tight pants?" I asked Luke.

"Since, like, 1978, when he put them on. He probably hasn't been able to take them off since."

Alex laughed again. Even louder than before. It seemed like she was nervous and trying to make the guys like her.

I said, "I guess I just never noticed. He wore a suit to the last pep rally, so he must have changed out of them."

The guys glared at me, but I didn't care. Reality was wrapping its claws around me, perforating my daydreams from last night. I wanted Alex to be my secret girlfriend, but this wasn't the waiting room. I couldn't spill my emotional guts to her in front of an audience. The fantasies I'd had of us being in school together hadn't included Michaela Barton sitting four chairs down from Alex and staring at us, slack-jawed and unashamed, while picking god knows what out of her braces. They also didn't include Cody Dometti's blue-jean-shorted ass scraping the back of my head when he scooted by to get to his seat, or Tyler Liu screaming from the table behind us, "What if you could fart out of your dick?" There's a reason people in romantic movies don't go on dates in high-school cafeterias.

And forget about introspective Alex from the waiting room. Social Butterfly Alex — Alex June, from the pictures online — was there.

"Kevin told me about the movie you guys are making. About the singer, with the Russia stuff and the trains?"

Luke grinned. "Oh, you mean Kevin's film *Italian Hospital*, based on his intense knowledge of Italian hospitals?"

"What? No," I said. "We split up. We're not a group anymore." I really didn't want to get into an argument about our abandoned project in front of her. "Did any of you start the chemistry lab homewor —?"

"Wait, how do you two know each other?" Luke asked. "Kevin's never mentioned —"

"We, uh . . ." I muttered, but I still had no goddamned idea what to tell them. Alex looked at me. Neither of us knew what the other was comfortable admitting. So I blurted, "We're both taking this class in, uh . . . writing. This thing my mom signed me up for. It's nothing. Just . . . don't worry about it."

She looked at me for a second; then she shrugged, accepting the lie I'd roped her into. "Yeah . . . well, Kevin actually wrote this story I liked, this thing about the driver's ed class he was in and this teacher who . . . You should tell them," she said to me.

"It was nothing. Just this . . . thing. It was stupid. Seriously. Just forget it."

Alex's eyes widened. "Sorry . . . Jeez."

Patrick said, "Sounds cool," and I couldn't tell if he was being sarcastic or not. I stuffed my sandwich into my mouth. I'd written that story for Alex. I didn't want anyone else to see it or even know it existed.

I didn't say much after that. Alex filled everyone in on her old schools and the places she'd lived. She revealed more information in ten minutes than I'd been able to gather over the past six months. She mentioned a performing arts camp she'd gone to in sixth grade, and Will went to the same one. They didn't remember each other, but it still annoyed me. They had something in common that stretched back four years. It was like she'd technically known him longer than me.

The other guys told her ancient stories about kids from our school for the rest of lunch and I didn't really look at Alex the whole time.

In seventh period, I had to go to math by myself while Alex went to her class with Luke and Will. I couldn't pay attention. I could only worry about their conversation. What was she telling them about me? Or worse, what were they telling her about me? They knew every embarrassing and stupid thing I'd ever done. The time I woke Will up at a sleepover by squatting over him like a catcher and farting directly onto his face. The afternoon we spent at Best Buy drawing penises into Microsoft Paint on laptops. Things Alex didn't need to know.

Halfway through seventh period I couldn't take the worrying anymore, so I got a bathroom pass and wandered over to Alex, Luke, and Will's math class.

She'll be sitting apart from them. She'll be by herself. She'll be alone and quiet and mine again.

She wasn't sitting with Luke or Will, but she wasn't alone, either. She was at a desk in the front row, spun around to talk to the guy behind her — Jordan Breyer, a dumb-ass junior whose defining trait was a pair of orange sunglasses worn backward and upside down across the back of his greasy buzz cut. She was drawing on his worksheet. They were laughing together. Their faces were three inches apart.

It felt like one of her fingers slipped out of my grip in the hurricane.

She eventually noticed me and waved. Jordan Breyer looked up at me, too. I stood there with my mouth hanging open for a second, and then I walked back to my math class, thinking about how nothing was stopping me from walking out the doors, through the parking lot, onto the highway, and starting a new life for myself off Exit 11. I could become a silent man who works behind the scenes at Costco and has no interpersonal problems because he only interacts with cardboard cases of laundry detergent.

The worry that Alex wasn't *Alex* anymore wrapped around me. She was becoming the girl from the pictures online that everyone loved, and I was just one of a thousand idiots in khaki shorts at her school. We'd never be project partners, we'd never do homework together, she'd never have a reason to come up to my room.

I should have clarified our relationship the minute she showed up at school. I should have asked her to be my

211

girlfriend right there, instead of stuttering dumbfounded like I'd been fooled by a magic trick. It was messy now. She was at my school and she knew every person I knew.

The next morning I walked into the hallway where everyone loitered before first period and saw Alex standing with the God Squad. They laughed at everything Alex said. Their eyes were wide. They were just as enamored of her as I'd been. I didn't want to bother them, so I kept my head down and walked past.

I was a gawky disaster compared to everyone else she was meeting at school. I couldn't compete with them in the hallways; I couldn't prove I was worth her time with a mumbled self-deprecating joke that would be inaudible under athletes' confident laughter booming through their polo-shirt-filling chest muscles. There was no point in trying to make school feel like the waiting room. I had to focus on what I was good at and wait until I had the home field advantage again.

What she liked most about me was that story I'd written. I could do that again, no problem. I'd crush it. To stand out from the noise at school, I'd write her something new, something important, profound, blow her away with writing none of the morons in our grade could ever do and give it to her at our next appointment — in secret and away from everyone.

24.

Throughout January I worked at night and on the weekends on a story for Alex inspired by Meyer's assignments. I used interesting literary techniques and referenced books and poems I'd been reading.

At school I carried a small notebook everywhere and observed Luke, Will, Sam, Patrick, and every other kid, writing descriptions of how they thought and acted. I mined jewels out of nothing, putting a fresh perspective on the monotony surrounding us and turning it into something interesting, something profound.

My story was dark and kind of serious. It was the best, most interesting thing I'd ever written. It felt important, and I was proud. I revised it over and over, marking down the days until I'd get to show her at our appointment.

Sometimes she'd stand with us in the mornings before first period and eat lunch at our table, and I'd drop references the guys didn't get to *Rushmore* or Neutral Milk Hotel into conversations and she'd smile.

Gradually, though, she started spending more time with the God Squad. She handed out Veronica Wesson's unnecessarily aggressive "Don't Be an Idiot, You Moron. Just Recycle — It's Not Hard" flyers in the hallway and partnered with Haley Jackson on chemistry labs. I'd talk to her sometimes, but not for too long. I didn't want to say anything stupid and risk blowing whatever chance I still had with her before I could show her my writing.

The other guys were still dialing their jokes up to full blast when she was around, but I didn't make a big deal out of her. I put all my energy into writing at night, waiting for our next appointment, when we could be ourselves. I knew I could email her, but it wouldn't be the same. It had to be in our waiting room.

I found the good printer paper Dad used for work, printed my story onto it, hid it in a neat folder in my backpack all day, and brought it with me to our January blood test. When I stepped inside, Alex wasn't there. They called me to the back and I started breathing hard, worried I'd missed her.

But she was in the waiting room when I came back out.

"Hey, I was hoping I'd catch you," she said. "Want to head outside for a little while?"

I nodded stupidly and felt my heart hit my ribs like a mallet on a gong.

We sat across from each other. It was cold and gray outside and every bush was dead. I put my folder on the bench beside me and buried my hands in my black hoodie pocket. Her red sweater popped out of the dull background. Nerves rattled me from the inside. I blurted, "Finally we're away from all the riffraff."

"What do you mean?"

"Just . . . I like it here, when it's just us, you know?" My chest got itchy and my throat went dry; I was allergic to my own voice.

But she nodded. *She also likes it here when it's just us.*

She said, "Have you been writing more? Assignments for our . . . outside-of-school writing class? Our cover story? Isn't that where we are now?"

"Yeah, sorry if that was weird. I just . . . don't like the idea of the guys knowing I'm on Accutane."

"I get it. Your secret's safe."

"Oh, but yeah, I have been writing. A lot." I opened my folder and handed the pages to her. I savored the moment as her eyes took in my words.

She finished the first page of prose, and then quickly flipped past the page that only had three words on it, carefully designed for poetic impact. She barely glanced at the page covered in the phrase "it's all a performance" typed eighty times. She didn't laugh at anything in the conversation part that was supposed to be funny, and she didn't linger long enough on the two-page-long sentence comparing the social groups clustered in our school's hallways to the Dutch colonial empire to have actually understood it. I watched her blank face. When she got to page five, not even halfway through, she looked up. "It's interesting, yeah," she said. "I'm a little confused about what's going on or, like, where this is supposed to be. The characters all seem really mean to each other. Are they friends?"

"I mean, yeah, but I'm kind of playing with the perspectives, and —"

"It's just not clear, I guess. Maybe you could work on that. And the, like, sort-of poem stuff? I don't know. I mean, it's . . . interesting. But —I don't know, maybe this is just me, but it was kind of confusing. I mean, it's good. You should definitely keep —"

"Okay, sure. I'll fix it. I'll just rewrite it. Forget it." I took the pages out of her hands.

"You don't want me to finish?"

"Just forget it. It's fine."

The whole fucking world had crumbled under my feet. Everything seemed off. Wrong. I felt queasy and light-headed. The safe place where I was in control, where I was the best version of myself, was now just another location I'd ruined by embarrassing myself, stained my memories of it, turned them all warped and blood red.

I'd been such an idiot. I wasn't a natural at writing. That

first story I wrote was a fluke, a lucky shot. I was the one mon-key out of a million who'd accidentally written Shakespeare.

She looked into my eyes, disappointed. "You know this is my last appointment?"

"Wait, what? Like, *ever*?"

"Yeah . . . well, for now, anyway. I may go back on it at some point if my skin gets bad again, but this is the end of my treatment."

"Oh," I said. No more waiting-room conversations. No more picnic-table talks or aimless drives around town in her Jeep. I should've been devastated, but I felt . . . nothing. "All right." I told her I had to go and I'd see her at school tomorrow and walked back to the parking deck.

I asked Mom to drive and I sat there staring out the window listening to radio ads.

That night Alex texted: *you okay?*

I spent thirty minutes thinking about the right thing to say back, then decided it would be weird to respond after such a long delay, so I didn't.

I wasn't mad at her. Just annoyed at myself for denying reality for so long. She wasn't just out of my league. We were playing different sports. The disappointed look on her face as she read my writing made me feel like I was five and she was twenty-five. The gap between us widened and confirmed my crush on her was absurd and unattainable, a crush on a movie star or a babysitter, a childish dream of being an astronaut. She wasn't a speedboat pulling me forward in a tube behind her; I was an anchor holding her back from a life with better friends.

I was one of dozens of kids she talked to at school. I wasn't her boyfriend; I wasn't her crush; I wasn't her perfect match, her anything. I was just some kid at her school.

I sat at my computer but couldn't write anything. There was no point.

I had to force myself to even show up to school the next morning. I walked in on Alex and the God Squad laughing together in the hallway before first period, building a wall of inside jokes between them and the outside world. My locker was within eavesdropping distance, and I put my books away as slowly as possible and heard Alex say, "*A Walk to Remember* is, like, my favorite book. My friend at homecoming was weeping during the dance because she'd just finished it. It was hilarious."

Veronica Wesson laughed. I was confused. Last fall Alex had told me about her friend crying about a novel at homecoming. But it had been meaningful literature, not some mass-marketed garbage novel for twelve-year-olds. Hadn't it? How could that possibly be her favorite book? I'd seen her reading *Anna Karenina*, for god's sake. It didn't make sense. None of it added up and my mind raced, trying to put —

My chemistry textbook slipped through my fingers and slapped the tile floor. The hallway went silent while everyone stared at me. I swear to god I heard all my teeth grow an inch longer. I felt like I had a mouth full of crooked two-by-fours.

I picked up my book, which seemed to give everyone else permission to resume talking. I shuffled closer to Alex and mumbled, "Hey, but, uh, you're into, like, *Anna Karenina* and stuff, too, right?"

Alex shrugged. "I didn't really finish that.... It was assigned at my old school and I read half of it. Or, like, a quarter of it. I didn't hate it or anything. I just didn't have time."

Shit. Shit shit shit.

Jen Evans started singing a song I vaguely recognized from Kate's *A Walk to Remember* phase, and Alex laughed with her, then waved at me, turned around, and walked with them, singing with the other girls. I was confused for the rest of the day, wondering which version of Alex was real: the one I'd met in the waiting room or the one I'd seen pictures of online. I wanted her to be the shy, nerdy, premakeover Rachael Leigh Cook in *She's All That*, but at school she had the outgoing confidence of a postmakeover Cook. I wondered if I'd been wrong about her from the start. Had I ever been right about the movies and music I assumed mattered to her? I'd heard her listening to Elliott Smith at our first appointment. But what if that was an accident, a glitch in her playlist, and because of it I started listening to him and watching movies that used his music and reading forums where other lonely guys like me suggested more sad singers to listen to? I'd trapped myself inside this web of musicians she never cared about, listening to breakup songs that reminded me of a girl I'd never gone out with in the first place. I'd chased a mirage into the middle of the desert and now I was alone.

Maybe the reason I'd never let myself ask her for her contact info last fall was that some part of me, deep down, knew my dream version of her was too good to be true and the real version of her was always out of my reach.

That Friday afternoon I overheard Jen and Haley mention a sleepover at Emma's that weekend. From what I'd eavesdropped on, it wasn't clear if Alex was going or not, and I thought that what she'd decide to do that night would prove which version she was. There was a chance she'd lie to the other girls that she was busy and would stay in her room reading and listening to real music, a chance she was the Alex I knew, and that at school she was performing being outgoing to fit in, doing what I'd tried and failed to do at driver's ed.

Saturday night I texted Luke that I was busy and couldn't make it to his house, and once it was dark, I mumbled to Mom about meeting up with Luke, then took my bike from the garage and pedaled through the cold night toward Emma's house. I knew I could have just texted Alex to ask what she was up to, but I was paranoid she'd lie to me. I just wanted to see for myself.

Emma lived two neighborhoods down from me, and I cruised over in the darkness like a badass noir private eye. I'd do a quick drive-by to confirm Alex wasn't there, and that everything would be back to —

Motherfucker.

All of them. The whole God Squad plus Alex was in Emma's room with curtains open and lights on, music blasting, dancing in unison to "Bye Bye Bye." A synchronized expression of joyous pop music bullshit.

My front tire slammed into the curb, ripping a hole through the rubber and spilling me onto the asphalt. *Fuck!* My arms slammed into the ground and my forehead banged against my wrist. I was all scraped up and curled into a ball. I must have looked like a trash bag. Jesus Christ.

From the hard, cold ground, I stared up at the girls and watched them dance. They were carefree, floating above everything. They looked like angels. Weighed down by nothing. All light and freedom, swishing their baggy T-shirts like wings. A vision of heaven in a suburban bedroom, and my name wasn't on the list.

I lay there watching them and they never noticed me. I could have lain there forever and they wouldn't have looked. They were on another plane.

I limped out of Emma's neighborhood, hunched in the darkness, pushing my useless bike. I had to accept that Alex's hand had officially slipped out of mine; the hurricane of high school had pulled us apart. She'd been raptured, and I was stuck on the dirt. She didn't need me. I offered her nothing.

When I made it back to the garage, I leaned my busted bike against the wall, then shuffled through the kitchen and climbed upstairs into the bathroom — where Kate saw me, spat a mouthful of toothpaste onto the mirror, and shrieked at me like I had a forked tongue and cloven hooves. I looked past her at the mirror and I saw I did indeed look like the devil himself, with a face covered in dried, red-brown blood. A cluster of ripe zits had exploded when I went down, spewing blood all down my forehead, cheeks, and chin.

Mom sprinted upstairs and knocked on Kate's door asking if she was okay.

"We're fine!" I shouted to Mom, and told her I was just bleeding a little from a small accident I had on my bike.

Kate left the toothpaste foam all over the mirror, backed into her room like she thought I'd take a bite out of her neck, and shut the door. I turned the shower on and stood there, staring into the tiles, completely zoned out, until I couldn't feel the water anymore.

When I dried off and sat at my computer, I saw the time and realized I'd been in there for an hour.

25.

That Sunday I was locked in my room, seven hours into a movie marathon, when I heard Mom and Dad in the kitchen talking to some handyman who'd just cleaned out our gutters. "We have a son who's very creative," Mom said. "He's writing a book."

"Really?" the guy asked.

"He's writing all the time these days. Not just the book, but I think poems, too."

"Poems?" the guy said. "You know, I've always had this philosophy: Poetry is a lot like jazz. It's all garbage and no one actually enjoys it."

He erupted with laughter like a car engine exploding. My parents laughed, too, and I had no idea if they agreed with him or were just being polite by joining a stranger in making fun of their son.

Good. I was glad that guy hated poetry. It wasn't for morons like him. I bet his favorite literature was an ad for a dumb-ass pocketknife, full of tough-sounding fake words that made doughy guys with sunburns think they were in the military. He'd never understand the kind of stuff I liked reading and writing, which made me reconsider why Alex hadn't liked my last story. If she was into *A Walk to Remember* and NSYNC, it made sense she wouldn't have liked what I'd last written. Maybe my story didn't suck. I opened the Word doc and looked through it and didn't think it was bad. Maybe the issue wasn't my writing; maybe it was just that it didn't fit her taste. She was the wrong audience, and you can't please everyone. Terry Gilliam wouldn't give a shit about my dad's opinion of *Brazil*. If every artist quit after one bad reaction, no one would make anything.

So I put my earbuds in, cranked up ambient music to drown out the handyman's laughter, and wrote for the first time since Alex had read my story. The weirder and more obscure I could go, the better — abstract words and sounds splattered the page like blood. I wrote until the guy left, and I felt like I'd won an argument he didn't know he was a part of.

I fell back into writing over the next few weeks. More and more files built up — poems and scenes and conversations — and I decided my final project for Meyer would be a mixed-format book, all these elements woven together. Now that I was writing for myself instead of for Alex, the project kind of snowballed. I was looking forward to sharing it with Meyer. He'd love it. He'd send it to that literary magazine to be published. Then he'd introduce me to a world of art and inspire me to carpe diem and break rules. He'd be the first person to give me a beer. He knew how things worked, and he'd teach me to grow up — and the night we'd spend in prison together for trespassing into a symbolically significant graveyard would be worth it for the overly sentimental Academy Award–winning film our relationship would inspire. Meyer was the only interesting person I'd ever met in my entire life. He was the only person qualified to give me advice. He was who I should have been writing for the whole time. He was my path forward.

I worked on a piece about my blood tests, how I'd opened my veins and spilled blood for a girl and it got me nowhere. There was poetry and dialogue and descriptions that I thought were funny, and it ended with a scene of me at the blood-testing office, where I rip out the needle from my arm mid extraction, then go through a labyrinth in the back, following pipes until I find an Olympic-size swimming pool filled with teenage blood. I dive in and swim laps, staining my skin red, without realizing I'm still leaking from the little wound in my arm, until I pass out and die. It was a funny, weird ending, and I think it said a lot about the risks of opening up.

Meyer hadn't given us any creative writing projects, so I knew he'd be impressed when I attached it to the back of my essay about one of the George Saunders stories he'd assigned.

Two days later he handed us back our essays and I flipped to my story. He'd underlined a few sentences he must have liked. He didn't write any comments — no criticism, no suggestions for changes. There were only two words in red on the last page: *Let's talk.*

After the last bell rang, I packed my stuff up and went back to his classroom, ready to hear the next steps for submitting the story for awards. I stood in front of him at his desk, thumbs under my backpack straps, stretching my shoulders back. "Hey, so, uh, what's next for 'Out of Blood'?"

He nodded slowly. "Why don't you get the door?"

Weird. I walked over and shut his door, then walked back to his desk. There'd been hallway noise before, but now it was silent. He took a deep breath. "You did a nice job describing some strong visuals. Good word choice. And your cadence is playful."

"Oh, awesome, thanks."

He looked me in the eye. "There are a lot of references to suicide. Jokes about killing yourself."

"Oh? Um . . . not a ton. I guess a few? Just like . . . jokes."

"Are you doing okay? Is this school year going well for you?"

Jesus Christ. You hand a guy some words you made up looking for simple, vague praise that will motivate you to write more, but instead you get grilled about your psychological stability and have to lie to his face so he doesn't file an official report with the vice principal and force you to go to the counselor. How come the entire nation smiles into their eggnog every year when they watch Jimmy Stewart grip the railing of a bridge and come two seconds away from offing himself, but when a teenager writes some creative nonfiction, they get out their binoculars and observe you like you're a deer in their bushes who could charge straight through their sliding glass door at any moment?

"Yeah, everything's really good. I just, I don't know, I guess I have a dark sense of humor. I've been watching a lot of British comedy. The self-deprecating thing must have rubbed off."

"Have you shown your parents what you wrote?"

"Uh . . ." Why the hell would I show that story to my parents? "Yeah," I finally said, because I could tell it was the only answer he'd accept.

"Okay," he said, not believing me.

"Yep."

He folded his arms over his stomach. "I want you to express yourself, and if you have a dark sense of humor, then that's fine. You'd let me know if something was wrong?"

I told him that absolutely I'd tell him if I was having issues. Of course I would totally swing by his desk every day after school and describe every stalagmite of worry, fear, and doubt I'd accumulated in the previous eight hours. What a treat that would be for us both.

My story wasn't that dark, really. There were just a couple of jokes about yanking needles out of my wrists and spraying I REGRET EVERYTHING in blood on the doctor's office walls like Spider-Man's webs, and cannonballing onto hard asphalt from the roof of the mall, and putting a hose in my mom's car's exhaust pipe and sipping the fumes like it was a bendy straw in chocolate milk.

They were obviously jokes. I guess Meyer didn't know me that well. I hardly ever talked in his class. Maybe that stuff in my story would be kind of weird to someone who didn't know me. I never should have shown him.

"We cool?" he said

"Yeah, cool," I mumbled. I felt trapped. I would've cut my foot off to escape that classroom, but before I could search for a hacksaw, he leaned toward me.

"Look, I'll give you the best writing advice I know," he said. "Be yourself when you write. *Be. Yourself.* All right, dude?"

Dude? Jesus Christ. What an asshole.

"Okay," I said.

"Yeah?"

"Sure. Can I . . . can I go now?"

He nodded. I turned around and walked out of the room.

Everything I tried to communicate got misinterpreted. Maybe it was a relief Meyer had confirmed I sucked at writing, so I could stop wasting my time on more horribly embarrassing poetry about a fictional character who was obviously me, getting his heart broken by a girl he meets in a doctor's office, and turning that in as my final project. It was exactly what a weird perv would write and turn in at school, and word would get around about it, and the girl it was clearly inspired by would get a restraining order against him. Why had I come up with any of that shit in the first place? It seemed so horrible now. I didn't recognize the version of me who'd thought that any of it was a good idea.

I couldn't trust myself. My cells were dying and changing more rapidly than I could keep up with. Every few weeks it was like I was another creature on that evolution-of-man diagram, except I never become upright; I just devolved from one deformed, slimy fungus into another.

The next day at school Meyer wore a fedora and brought in his bass guitar and I knew it was over between us. "What's happening, cats?" he said with one foot propped up on his chair and his bass cradled on his nuts. "Poetry don't gotta be just on the page. In the sixties, the beatniks brought it to life. I used to make a little bread slaying this ol' ax back in the day."

He slapped out a few notes on his bass and I felt like I was in one of those nightmares where you're trying to scream but no noise will come out. Someone should have stopped him, but we were all too stunned to intervene.

Todd Lancaster finally stepped up to the plate. "You made bread with an ax?"

Meyer said, "Made some cheddar, baby. Cranked out some hot coin with the ol' four-string."

Christine Eller said, "I think he means he, like, made money playing his guitar."

"Bingo-bongo, sweet sister," Meyer said, and then he ripped into this awful bass line that made me sad. It sounded like the men's bathroom at an Olive Garden during an unlimited alfredo sauce promotion. Burbling, cream-fueled farts.

Whatever respect I'd had for the man crumbled. He decayed from a role model into a cautionary tale. I was finally seeing him as the weird guy my classmates had always known he was. Had he had that goatee all year? I swear it was the first time I'd allowed myself to notice it.

There was no longer any reason to try to impress him.

That night I looked up the Goose Creek Film Festival and the *Sopchoppy Review*. I'd never heard of a single movie that had won an award at the film festival and had never heard of anyone besides Meyer involved with that literary magazine. All I saw on their websites were dozens of pictures of desperate idiots who looked a lot like me, hoping to be discovered, hoping to be told they were filmmaking and literary prodigies, convincing themselves they'd accomplished something by winning meaningless awards no one had ever heard of. Great. Another goal of mine proven imaginary, another finish line turned to vapor.

What the hell was the point in doing anything?

Days smeared together in early February. I'd nod at Alex in the hallways, but she ate lunch with the God Squad, and we never really talked. Everything outside was cold and dead, and Georgia got no snow that year, so there was no physical evidence of time passing at all. Every day was the same shade of gray. My lips turned so dry, they looked white and dusty, so I rubbed Chap Stick on them constantly. My entire face was always in one of two states: powder-dry or dripping with moisturizing slime.

The thought of writing anything made me wince. I'd hear Meyer's misguided concern or see Alex's blank, confused face from that January appointment. Meyer and Alex had independently come to the same conclusion about my writing. I'd been peer-reviewed and the results were in: I sucked. I made a folder on my computer called "Bad Ideas" and moved all my writing files into it.

26.

The week before Valentine's Day, I got manhandled by a barber who grabbed my cheeks and chin and tossed my head around with his oily hands like it was a ball of bread dough. Each time he touched my lumpy jawline, I knew the grime and strangers' hairs on his fingertips were clogging every pore. But he wasn't getting any enjoyment out of this, either. I must have ruined the barber's day by bringing my pus-filled, chapped, bumpy face in there. I felt like my face had gotten worse over the past few weeks, but it was hard to know if that was real or just me feeling like shit. It looked redder than ever under the fluorescent lights, multiplied into infinity in the mirrors on every wall. I hated that he had to see my face, that I made him touch me. It was awful for everyone involved.

That night my chin was a mess — littered with bulbous, misshapen red bumps, all strung together like a giant bubble in a pizza crust. I knew I shouldn't, but I touched it. It felt plump and full. I rolled the fullest part around between my fingers. I wanted all that crap out of my face. It felt hard as a marble between my fingertips. I massaged it toward the surface, kneaded it into a cone, and then — *gush*. I swear I heard it break the surface of the skin. A ton of red-beige, pulpy goo shot onto the mirror. More leaked down my chin. My heart raced. Blood rushed out and coated my fingers. I dabbed the wound with toilet paper; the mound underneath was more swollen than before. It hurt, but it had felt so satisfying to get it all out of me. I'd felt clearheaded doing it; just for a second the pain had made all my other thoughts go away.

Luke asked me what happened to my chin. Will, Sam, and Patrick stared at me, concerned and grossed out by the giant scab. Alex pulled me aside and asked, "Is everything okay?" She sounded exactly like my mom. I told her what I'd told Mom: I was fine. My face still sucked. Whatever.

Emma was the only person who said my haircut was nice.

And even though I'd just learned a valuable lesson about not falling for girls who are out of my league — which pretty much rules out all of them — I found myself replaying that sentence in my head over and over again. I'd felt deflated for weeks, and that comment had been the only thing that lifted me up.

"Your hair looks nice, Kevin."

Now when I'd see Emma at school, I'd think about that night we spent in her hotel room watching that movie. Her legs beside mine on top of the covers. The way I'd impressed her by tricking Kyle into sprinting toward the promise of exposed breasts. It seemed unlikely that Emma would like me, but . . . she'd been so open and honest with me about breaking up with Kyle and being on birth control. Girls don't tell any random guy about their birth control weight gain.

Emma would make a great first girlfriend. Going out with her would be like training wheels. I could get my embarrassments out of the way with her, figure out how to eat pizza in front of a girl. Alex was a roller coaster, but Emma was consistent. Sure, she was into the same mainstream music and movies as all the other kids at school, but at least she'd never made me think otherwise. There was no drama with her. Alex was like *The Simpsons,* great at first and then disappointing, and you debate forever about her in your head, holding out hope that she will again be the version you fell for. Emma was *Scrubs* — never peaking as high as *The Simpsons,* but consistently pretty solid. And I'd come to realize the fantasy girl who'd seen every movie in the Criterion Collection didn't exist in my Georgia suburb, and probably didn't exist anywhere outside my imagination. Emma was there, we'd had our night together, and she was nice to me. *"Your hair looks nice, Kevin."*

The only hurdle was Luke. I should probably get his permission to ask out his ex-girlfriend. But after sitting through a forty-five-minute lunch period where he and Patrick did nothing but quote *Dumb and Dumber*, I decided I didn't care and would just go for it.

But I couldn't just ask Emma out with no warning. There were stories of kids who did that — crushed on girls for years, expecting that the girls had been taking equal note of them, and then they asked the girls out one afternoon by the lockers with no buildup or rapport established. The girls were mostly confused and always said no. You can't blame the girls — it's too startling, like if your dog suddenly asked you to drive him to the airport. You've got to ease into a switch like that.

I spent the week trying to strategize how I'd talk to Emma and plant the seed that would lead to us being a couple. I had absolutely no idea what to do. It must be great to be one of those guys who can casually talk to girls at school like it's not a big deal. Maybe it's because they have older sisters who give them advice. Kate had no advice, unless you want to know what to feed a horse.

Emma wasn't into a lot of the things I was, but maybe that was an opportunity. I thought about what else I knew about her and realized that her being religious was probably the main thing about her. I thought about how religion could be cool. The routine of it, having a place to go on Sundays, being able to analyze and interpret the Bible. I looked up a list of denominations online and scrolled through, thinking she'd be able to steer me in the right direction.

And I knew she liked that Blink-182 song in the movie we'd watched in her hotel room. I used to like Blink-182 when

I was a kid, but then again so does everyone. It can't be a defining aspect of a personality any more than enjoying pizza or *Jurassic Park*. But Emma and I could start there, and then I'd get her into Box Car Racer and Say Anything and American Football, guiding her through the bands I'd discovered, and then I'd introduce her to all the movies I loved while we lay side by side on top of the covers.

If I planted the seed visually, the pressure wouldn't be on me to conjure a conversation out of nothing, so I ordered a Blink-182 T-shirt online. I worried it'd be a step backward in my evolution to wear such a mainstream shirt to school, but the sacrifice would be worth it: a quick backtrack to put myself on the right path with the right girl.

The night the shirt showed up, I put on extra layers of nighttime moisturizer, and in the morning I did ten deodorant swipes before easing my arms through the shirt as delicately as possible to avoid streaks. I thought I actually looked pretty decent.

Mom stared at me while I ate cereal. "A smile," she said. "That's nice."

"What?"

"You've got a little smile on."

"No, I don't."

"Okay, okay, I won't ask."

Spanish finally came. Emma was sitting in her pod with her three friends when I walked in. I nodded at her. She didn't notice me. My desk was behind hers, and I watched her head all through class, feeling my pits moisten and praying to the deodorant gods to hold up their end of the bargain.

Señora Rosenthal stopped teaching and gave us our fifteen minutes of free time. This was my chance. I stood up and walked over to Emma. *"Hola."*

She didn't look up at me. Was I standing too far away? Had I mumbled? Probably both.

"Hola," I said. *"Emma, hola."*

Her friend tapped her on the shoulder and pointed to me. "Oh, hey," Emma said, and then she turned away from me.

"What, uh, what's up?" I said. Then I shook my head. "I mean, um, *qué pasa?*"

"Not . . . much?" she said, confused. "What's up with you?"

She wasn't noticing the shirt. She'd looked up at me twice and wasn't impressed by anything. Was this the price I had to pay for spending my entire life lying low and doing anything I could to avoid attracting attention? I want no one to ever notice me, except in specific situations when I want specific people to notice me, and in those cases I want them to really fawn and obsess over me.

Emma noticing the shirt was crucial, and it pained me to be so obvious, but I didn't have any other choice. "I just got this shirt, and, like, so what's your favorite Blink album, or song, or —?"

Before I could finish, the noise of a tool chest falling down a staircase rattled and boomed behind me. Everyone turned around. Todd Lancaster was lying on the floor on top of his collapsed desk, holding a screwdriver. A bunch of kids laughed, including Emma. Señora Rosenthal flipped out and dragged him into the hallway. Todd had unscrewed his desk just to see if he could do it. Fucking Todd Lancaster. I wished he would fall into a volcano and the whole thing would be videotaped and posted on the internet.

Emma and everyone rushed over to stare at the wrecked desk. I stood behind the rest of the class, frozen for I don't know how long, until the bell rang. Emma turned back around to pick up her stuff from her desk said, "Hey, that's, uh . . ." pointing at my shirt.

Oh, shit, here we go.

"My brother likes them."

Wait, what? "Don't you like them?"

"What do they sing?"

"Well, they do 'Dammit,' the song from the movie we watched in the hotel room."

"I like whoever sings the 'Time of Your Life' song. Is that them?"

She was talking about Green Day. She didn't know the difference. The music meant nothing to her. She only knew of the band because of her brother. So, technically, I had a crush on Emma's brother. Jesus Christ.

I shouldn't have assumed she was obsessed with a band she'd mentioned offhand one time. The same boneheaded blunder I'd made with Alex, assuming she'd memorized the *Royal Tenenbaums* script because she listened to one Elliott Smith song one time. Why had I let myself get my hopes up again? I shouldn't have tried. I wasn't ready even for a first-draft relationship.

I just wanted the school year to be over so I could lie to everyone that I was going to some summer camp and pass the time in my room alone.

That night I wadded up the Blink-182 T-shirt and stuffed it into the back corner of my closet on top of my old AC/DC shirt.

Valentine's Day happened and I acted like it didn't exist. A few girls got gigantic teddy bears they brought around to all their classes, which distracted everyone and negated the entire day's worth of education. The bears seemed incredibly inconvenient and must have been huge pains in the ass to get home. Like, the girls who got them must have had to call their dads, who had to call their brothers with the pickup trucks to get in the carpool line just to get the things home.

I was pretty sure no one got Emma or Alex anything. For a second, I wished I had — but then I reminded myself that neither of them actually liked me and I should save my energy for something I was qualified to do, like unloading the dishwasher.

On the day of my February blood test, Alex came to my locker while I was putting my books in my backpack.

She smiled and said, "How's it going?"

I shrugged. "Busy."

"Yeah?"

"Yeah." I didn't know why she came to my locker or what I was supposed to say to her, and the more I tried to figure it all out, the hotter and sweatier I got. Anything I might blurt out would probably sound stupid and wrong. Luckily I had a reason to leave. "I, uh, I gotta go to my blood test."

"Yeah, I know. Say hi to Kim and Jodie for me."

"Who?"

"The nurses?"

"Oh, okay." I shut my locker and turned away from her.

Say hi to the nurses? As I drove out of the school parking lot with Mom in the passenger seat, I tried to figure that out. Had Alex developed relationships with them? It was always the same women working there. I never knew it was an option to talk to them. I just closed my eyes, offered up my arm vein, and let them have at it.

I sat in the waiting room alone, happy to be away from everyone. There was no chance of me saying something stupid. No one knew me in there. I closed my eyes and appreciated the stillness.

The nurse called my name and I walked to the back, perfectly numb. Feeling nothing was preferable to hot, sweaty embarrassment.

The nurse put the needle in my arm and I stared at it without feeling queasy for the first time. It was like the blood wasn't even part of me.

I figured if I kept to myself for the rest of the year and didn't make any effort to impress girls or teachers or myself,

I wouldn't have to beat myself up all the time. I just needed to coast through the next few months and it would all be fine again in the summer when my face was clear and I was off Accutane.

27.

Weeks blended together. I'd smile and nod at Alex at school because I didn't want her to think I was mad at her or anything, but I limited myself to the kind of direct responses I gave my parents: "Yeah, everything's great!" "All good!" "Excellent, how about you?" If I let myself off my short leash, there was too big a chance I'd say something dumb and regret every word and hate myself for making the effort. It was better to stay safe and comfortable and out of everyone's way.

I wasn't bothered anymore that Sam and Patrick were in our group. I just didn't really care. The time it took for me to check out of conversations with the guys dwindled. It used to take ten minutes of uninteresting discussion of a football game I hadn't watched before I'd zone out and stop listening. Then it took five minutes, then three, then one. When I needed to, I could talk to the guys and make them laugh without thinking. Sam and Patrick cracked up at any dry, sarcastic reference to a teacher's testicles. That was all it took with them. It was like Mad Libs — [teacher's name] has [number that isn't two] testicles and an [adjective to describe burnt meat] penis.

I knew the routine, the dance moves and repetitive lyrics that made up the Kevin show: smile, nod, laugh when everyone else does. I could do it without thinking. It was easy.

My friends seemed to enjoy having me in their circle even though I didn't really care about their conversations. At home, my eyeballs bounced from my computer screen to my TV screen. I spent nights watching movies by myself in my room, working through a list I'd found online. But I wasn't taking any of them in. I'd put them on and stare at them until they ended. Sometimes I'd catch myself ten minutes into a Korean movie and realize I hadn't been reading any of the subtitles, but I wouldn't care enough to go back and start over.

Days fused into each other and I'd have no memory of them when I looked back in my agenda. My life became an endless white noise loop with nothing to mark one part from the next, this uninteresting run-on sentence, an awful, formless jazz performance every bit as bad as that handyman had said jazz always was.

Todd Lancaster, noted dumb-ass, swung by our lunch table one day and cryptically said, "Microcock." The guys laughed and told a story about some idiot getting his pants pulled down at Lauren Gordon's sweet sixteen party. Then they joked about how much vodka some older kid named Ivan would bring to Katie Lipton's sweet sixteen party. And apparently there had been a bonfire at Todd Lancaster's house. I had no idea what they were talking about. I hadn't heard about any of those parties. I certainly hadn't been invited to a bonfire at Todd Lancaster's house. I wished I could have gone. It sounded like it would have been an excellent opportunity to push Todd Lancaster into a bonfire.

Luke mentioned that the guys, Alex, and Emma had been talking about going to White Water, the water park, over spring break. It was the first I was hearing about that plan, too. Where were those conversations happening? Some online thread I wasn't looped in on? A meeting in some rich kid's massive tree house?

Events were happening without my knowledge. Things I'd never be able to be a part of. Those parties might as well have been the premiere of *Romeo and Juliet* or the day Weird Al's parents decided to have unprotected sex — monumental historical events that happened regardless of my being alive or dead. If I was there, nothing would change. If I wasn't, no one would miss me.

One Friday in March, Luke, Will, Sam, and Patrick decided to go to a movie. They said the girls would probably meet them there. They never explicitly invited me, but just in case they assumed I'd go, I texted Luke that I had some family stuff to do that night.

What stuff? You never do anything with your family, he responded.

Yeah, I know. That's why it's weird, I texted back.

There was just no way I could have gone with them. It would be too complicated. I had to take my pill at exactly ten every night. They were seeing a 7:45 movie, so if you factored in twenty minutes of trailers, ten would be during the climax of the movie. I'd have to walk out of the theater in the middle of the most important part, and on the ride home they wouldn't stop asking me why I'd left when I had. I'd have to lie about taking a dump, but the problem was we'd thoroughly discussed our defecating habits several times at our lunch table, and on more than one occasion I'd aggressively argued that the morning was the only logical time to shit, so my story wouldn't check out. I'd called Luke "one of the strangest people to ever live" because he pooped in the evening. If I *didn't* walk out of the theater, I'd have to dig through my pockets for my pill in my seat, pop it out of the plastic pack — since I couldn't put a loose pill in my pocket and risk losing it — then try to secretly swallow it. But I'd get caught. I'd push it out of the pack during the one second of absolute silence in the movie, and it'd snap as loud as a firecracker. They'd turn to stare at me, one head at a time, and demand to know what drug I was taking and what was wrong with me.

I had to stay home. It was calm in my room. There was no risk of embarrassing myself.

After I went through my face-washing routine and took my pill, I got in bed and wondered if the guys were having fun at the movie theater. I wondered what they were joking about. I wondered if they'd all be talking about the movie at school next week. On weeknights, I knew that at ten everyone else from school was just as bored and alone as I was, all of us stranded in our bedrooms. But when everyone except me was out on a Friday, I started to worry. I probably should have gone. I was stressed out lying there in my bed, kicking the sheets away and rolling from one side to the other.

But I knew that if I had gone, I'd be stressing out at the movies, too, wishing I was alone in my room.

No matter what path I chose, it always led to me being stressed out and anxious. I started to doubt that the solution to my problems was a clear face. I think what I really wanted was to be one of those guys who just doesn't care about anything. I fantasize about being a teenage guy from a Doritos commercial, the kind of dude who wakes up at two p.m. lying upside down with his head dangling off the foot of the bed. The kind of guy whose room is wrecked with guitar picks, video games, and dirty clothes all over the place — jeans draped across his drum set. He's got a big TV just sitting on the carpet and as soon as he wakes up, he pulls a Mountain Dew out of his band-sticker-covered minifridge, doesn't give any thought to its nutritional content, and chugs it while firing up his PlayStation. He finds a bag of Doritos under his skateboard and eats what's left of it just before his phone rings. It's his buddy Dirty Tom and he's on his way to the mall and he'll swing by the Doritos Dude's house. The Doritos Dude pauses his video game, leaves his TV on, pulls on one of his dozens of pairs of shoes, and leaps down the staircase. He hops into Dirty Tom's Jeep and they cruise down the highway in hot pursuit of more spontaneity.

At no point does the Doritos Dude wonder why he's going to the mall, if he really needs anything, or even what he'll do when they get there. At no point does he wash the Doritos dust off his hands, take a shower, brush his teeth, or wash his face. He doesn't think about wasting electricity by leaving his TV on. He doesn't consider what he's wearing or why. He doesn't rehearse conversations in his head with every person he might run into at the mall. And yet, despite all his insane inconsistency, he nails his guitar solo when his pop-punk band plays that night and he winds up talking to a midriff-revealing girl at a bonfire, casually making her laugh while taking a bite of the only constant in his life — a spicy, crunchy, cheesy Dorito.

I had to see my dermatologist for a checkup after my blood test at the end of March. She inspected my face like produce at the grocery store, turning it around to let the light shine on every side. The redness on my cheeks was fading to pink, but I still looked like I'd been stepped on by someone wearing lawn-aerating shoes.

She read through that same massive list of possible side effects she'd given me last summer and sat at her computer, clicking in my answers: Itching? *No.* Dry skin? *Nothing out of the ordinary.* Any rashes? *No.* Joint pain? *No.* Back pain? *No.* Dizziness? *No.* Dry eyes? *No.* Feeling depressed?

What? What a big question to throw at someone. *No.* Well.

I mean — god, no. What was I thinking? If I told Dr. Sharp I was depressed, she'd make me stop taking the pills and my face would get worse again. Not to mention, I wasn't depressed. Maybe I was bummed out sometimes, sure. But it wasn't a big deal. I was a kid from a crime-free suburb with no legitimate problems. I was on medicine that I knew might make me feel weird, so if anything was off, it was just temporary. Any sadness or whatever would get flushed out of my system along with the pus from my zits. I just had to ride it out until my face cleared up and it'd be fine.

"Nope."

She didn't even turn her head to look at me. She just clicked and kept going down the list.

Nosebleeds? *No.* Changes in your vision? *No.* Hair loss? *Nope.*

"Great," she said, turning to me. "So we're at the end of the standard course of treatment. I think there's been a gradual —"

"Wait, what?" I still had red lumps all over my face. I wasn't even close to the clear skin I'd been promised. "I mean . . . I don't think I should stop. Right?"

She tilted her head at me. "Well, you can't be on this forever. Normally I'd recommend taking a break for a few months before starting a second treatment."

And just like that, my dreams of having good skin by the end of tenth grade vaporized. I stared blankly at the floor and saw my bumpy reflection on the shiny tiles.

"But your blood work has always come back fine, so I'd be

open to extending you for a little while, at a lower dose. What do you think? Or do you want to go off it? Up to you."

Obviously I wanted to stay on it. I told her so and she wrote me a prescription for another three months. Even though technically I'd won, I left that appointment feeling even shittier about my face, which I hadn't thought possible.

28.

On the first morning of spring break, I made the unforgivable mistake of staring at the kitchen counter for thirty seconds after I finished my bowl of cereal.

Mom walked into the kitchen, stopped in her tracks like she'd caught me with a pistol in my mouth, and said, "How are you doing, bud?"

Bud? She hadn't called me that since fifth grade.

"Fine . . . ?" I knew I sounded defensive, but she was clearly convinced something was wrong even though I was just sitting there. God forbid I take half a minute to have a thought. Nothing freaks a parent out like a teen sitting quietly. Next Halloween I should sit on the couch for an hour, hands in my lap, smiling. My parents would shriek in terror and alert the media, and our home would earn a spot on a list of the country's ultimate haunted house experiences.

"You sure you feel okay? You look pale."

"Yeah," I said, choosing my words carefully, each one like pulling a wire out while dismantling a bomb. "I . . . feel . . . completely . . . fine."

She nodded at me, staring me down in a standoff. I nodded back, and while we held eye contact, my left hand slid toward an issue of *Entertainment Weekly* I'd been flipping through earlier. I pulled the magazine toward me and opened it to a page I'd already read. Mom smiled, then walked back into the laundry room, and I exhaled. I wondered if those girls who always carry around novels at school ever actually read them, or if they'd just discovered that pretending to be a voracious bookworm is the easiest way to get adults off your ass.

I got up to put my bowl in the dishwasher, and Luke texted me that he and the guys were on their way over to pick me up to go to White Water. Wait, what? When they'd talked about that plan in front of me at school, I assumed I wasn't invited, since they didn't directly ask me. I couldn't go. It was way too spontaneous. There wasn't enough time to run through every hypothetical scenario in my head and plan for all the —

Mom walked out of the laundry room and caught me staring into the sink. "Bud?"

Jesus Christ. I couldn't deal with that all day. *Okay sweet I'll be ready,* I texted Luke, then said to Mom, "Luke's coming to get me to go to White Water."

I rushed upstairs before she could comment or question, went into the bathroom, rinsed my cheeks and forehead with charcoal face wash, then patted dry and smeared on SPF-30 moisturizer with a cotton ball, rubbing it in until I stopped shining. I put on my bathing suit and took off my shirt and scanned my body in the mirror. Neck-down I was pale to the point of transparency. Neck-up I was red-pink. I couldn't help comparing myself to the guys from Alex's pictures online last fall, with their zit-free, nontranslucent skin. I looked like I belonged in a textbook about the circulatory system, not at a water park. Maybe this was a terrible idea. Maybe I was better off staying at home trying to dodge Mom's absurd concerns about me.

Ugh. No. I'd freak out and start hurling furniture through windows if I had to deal with her all day. I mean, really, how bad could it be? I pictured all of us at the water park. Luke, Will, Sam, and Patrick whipping towels at each other and acting like idiots. Alex and Emma walking around casually in their bathing suits. Alex and Emma lounging in the hot sun in their bathing suits. Alex and Emma adjusting their bikini bottoms when they got out of a pool . . .

I started to get a boner. Goddamn it. I looked like I was smuggling a strong-beaked bird in my swimsuit. I flipped it up into my waistband, but that time-tested solution to all school-yard boner crises was no good with my shirt off.

The clock ticked. Luke was speeding toward my house at a thousand miles an hour, blasting past stop signs and red lights, plowing over mailboxes. There was only one option: put my years of training to use by cranking one out in less than a minute. There'd be no enjoyment in it, no pleasure; a purely functional stroke, a task that had to be done not just for my own good but for the well-being of everyone around me.

I locked my room door and the door to the bathroom, got on my computer, slid into incognito mode, located pornography in a quarter of a second, and went through the motions automatically like I was a computer running my own virus scan.

Sixty seconds later it was like my boner had never existed.

As I walked to the toilet, I thought that I could have been a Revolutionary War minuteman. Only as I was walking out my front door toward Luke's mom's SUV did I start to feel like a repulsive pervert. The girls would see it in my eyes. One look at me and they'd know I was a no-good, dirty masturbator who'd just mainlined some objectively grotesque video content. But, hey, it had worked. I'd thrown myself on the grenade and saved us all from a horrific afternoon guest-starring my erection.

I took the seat behind Will in the middle row. Luke had the windows rolled down and awful pop-country music blaring, and I reminded myself that I was just here to get out of the house. I wasn't actually expecting to enjoy this day I'd be spending surrounded by hundreds of shirtless, jacked guys objectively better than me. *Just let the music play and the filthy water wash over me.*

Luke pulled into Sam's driveway, where Sam was laughing with Patrick, Alex, and Emma. The girls were wearing shorts and giant T-shirts and held big beach bags. I nodded at them while avoiding eye contact, certain they knew I'd just beaten off. Sam and Patrick rushed into the middle row next to me. Alex called Sam and Patrick assholes and laughed; then she and Emma crawled behind us into the way-back row.

I was crammed against the door, and Patrick's shoulder dug into my neck. He and Sam started punching the roof and grunting, "Water park! Water park!" Alex laughed, but I didn't hear Emma react. Maybe she found their desperate displays of masculinity as obnoxious as I did. I twisted my neck to the left as far as it could go, right up to the point where Patrick's shoulder completely blocked my air supply, and I could sort of see Emma behind me. "Hey, Kevin," she said, and I made eye contact with her while my nose bent ninety degrees against Patrick's neck. "I'm glad you came."

Wait, what? She was happy that I was there? She *wanted* me to be there? My brain slingshotted into an image of us discussing which bathroom tiles we'd want in our first home on *House Hunters* when she added, "What's your favorite ride?"

"Uh," I stalled, smashing back to the present. "The one with the least urine in it," I said without thinking, and she laughed. *Oh, shit.* She'd sought me out. She was glad I was there. She liked my piss joke. If I hadn't bombed trying to talk to her that day in Spanish class, I might take this as proof she liked me. When a girl talks to you and laughs at your jokes, how do you know if she's into you or just being nice?

I stared out the window, reviewing that awful day in Spanish. I'd always felt like it was my fault for blowing it, but thinking back, Todd Lancaster had been the one who ruined that moment by distracting everyone with his broken desk. Sure, Emma didn't recognize the band logo on my shirt, but if Todd hadn't thrown everything off, maybe I could have stayed in the zone and had that conversation with Emma, making her laugh with all sorts of references to urine.

I was trying to decipher the amount of romance that had been in Emma's laugh when Sam cut in: "Sucks Todd's not coming."

I was so surprised to hear Todd's name that it took me a second to respond. "Wait, Todd Lancaster was coming?"

"He was gonna, but he sprained his ankle bowling last night."

The words sprayed out of me, all carefree delight: "Hell, yeah."

Sam looked confused for a second, but then a new country song started playing and he and Patrick screamed the lyrics.

I saw Emma's reflection in the window beside me. She was looking out her window, ignoring the other guys, smiling. Maybe she was still thinking about my joke. I had a chance to talk to her again today. No Todd Lancaster, no school distractions. We'd step out of the group and forget about the world around us: me and a girl who was happy I was there.

Just be normal, keep cool, don't overreact.

We stood near the plastic lounge chairs while the girls put all their stuff in lockers. Without warning, Emma pulled her big T-shirt over her head.

Jesus Christ. She had on this pink-and-white-striped bikini

and, like, there were her boobs. She slipped off her shorts and there were her entire legs. And then she turned and her butt was right there, too. As she rubbed sunscreen on her legs like she was being directed through a radio earpiece by the members of Mötley Crüe, it took all my strength to keep my tongue from unrolling onto the ground in the shape of a staircase.

Shit. Be cool. I took a deep breath and tried not to think about getting to second base with her behind a maintenance shed.

I was staring into the concrete ground, reckoning with the fact that I was probably more of a stereotypically breast-obsessed teenage hound than I'd previously believed, when a tube of sunscreen smacked into my chest. "Moisturizer and sunscreen," Alex said. "It's rule one." She was in a black one-piece and I knew that if I looked directly at her, my nuts would pop like bottle rockets.

It'd been almost an hour since I applied sunscreen at home, so I figured I needed another coat. The sunscreen felt repulsive on my face. Some of it got into my hair and I knew I looked like a melting candle, all hot, dripping wax. There were no mirrors at White Water, but my fingertips rubbed across my face and confirmed how many lumpy zits were on it. It was braille for *slimy troll boy.*

When I opened my eyes again, the God Squad was there. No one had told me they were coming. Five more girls who fused into our group, laughing with Alex and Emma. They peeled their T-shirts and shorts off, morphing from random kids whose presentations I didn't listen to in health class into nearly nude babes. Caterpillars evolving into Kelly Kapowskis. They all seemed so confident, like they were ten years older than me. I couldn't help wanting them to like me, but they must have been confused to see me. *What's that kid from my math class doing here? I didn't ask to see his nipples. Why do I have to look at his nipples? I can just tell he masturbated an hour ago.*

A playlist on someone's iPod shuffled through Rhianna and Carrie Underwood and I sat there nodding, trying to look like someone who never masturbates. Blink-182's "Dammit" came on and my eyes shot over to Emma. She was talking to Jen Evans, telling some story with big hand gestures. I waited for her to react to the song. Was it dumb to get my hopes up? Their conversation stopped, and Emma turned toward me, and I saw it — just barely, but in perfect time, her lips mouthed the chorus.

Holy hell. She knew it. She remembered.

The signs were adding up. First she'd said she was happy I was coming today. Then she laughed at my joke. And then I found out Todd was supposed to come but couldn't because he'd injured himself in a wonderfully embarrassing way. And now the exact same song from our night at the hotel was playing? The bases were loaded and that was the pitch, slow and straight; all I had to do was swing.

I smiled, stood up, and took a step toward her. Her eyes met mine, like she'd been waiting for me. "Hey," I said. "This, uh, this song, right?"

"It's good," she said.

"I know."

"Yeah."

"Yeah . . ." I repeated. She wasn't lighting up at the memory. "You remember, right? It's, uh . . . Remember when we watched that movie? The one about high-schoolers on graduation night?"

"Oh, right. At Luke's house last year?"

"Er — no. When we were in the hotel? On the class trip?"

"Oh, yeah," she finally said. "Yeah, I don't remember what it was, either."

It was definitely *Can't Hardly Wait* with Jennifer Love Hewitt. I'd spent hours researching it online. "Right, uh . . ." I said. "I mean, this is, like, totally our song."

The words echoed back to me: *Our . . . song . . .*

Oh, no. Holy shit. *Shit. Shit. Sh—*

"What?" She looked confused. "Our song?"

My armpits liquefied. My face ignited. I wanted a lug nut to shoot off a slide like a sniper's bullet and take me out.

Our song.

Why the hell had I said that? We'd once watched the TV edit of a movie that had a popular song in it while lying like discarded mannequins on either side of a fully made bed. Why did my brain try to make a joke about that being the start of some romantic connection between us? She didn't even know I liked her, for god's sake.

"Huh?" I said. I considered sprinting into the woods, hoping I'd stumble onto an undetonated land mine. Instead I mumbled at my feet. "Don't worry about it. It was just a joke. Obviously it's not, like, *our —*"

258

Veronica Wesson shouting at some guys near a trash can cut me off. "Huh?" she yelled. "Don't you know how to read? Recycle, you ape! The bin is right there."

The guy and his friends hurried away, and Veronica spat on the ground behind them. The girls burst out laughing. Jen called over, "Hey, Emma, let's go."

"I guess I'll see you guys later," Emma said to all of us, then walked to the girls, who all disappeared down a hill toward the rides. I was left there at the lockers with Luke, Will, Sam, and Patrick.

Luke said, "You boys ready?" He nodded toward the most intense ride in the park — away from where the girls had gone.

"Wait, are we, like, not going with them?" I felt sick, wondering what Emma would tell the other girls about me when I wasn't there.

"They're doing the shitty rides first."

"But are we gonna . . . meet up with them, or . . . ?"

Luke shrugged. "I don't know. Come on."

Sam and Patrick started yelling and led the way. We sped from one ride to the next. Half were group rides, for two or four people to share tubes. Luke went with Will. Sam and Patrick called each other. I said I preferred stretching out on my own tube. On the four-person rides, the lifeguard would stick me with groups of three children from the line, who'd look at me like I lived in a swamp. But I didn't really care. All I could think about was how stupid I'd been with that *our song* comment. Was Emma telling everyone I'd said it? I was in shock and barely spoke the rest of the morning.

After a few hours, we met up with the girls for lunch. They wore sunglasses and hats and towels tied with these elaborate knots I'd never figure out, as put-together and grown-up as I wasn't. I braced myself for the onslaught, waited for them to shout "Our song!" at me in a snottily voiced chorus, then corner me in a shower stall and hurl tampons at my mouth, chanting, "Plug it up! Plug it up!"

But they didn't. They just laughed and joked with each other and the guys, and none of them even really looked at me. As everyone else finished eating lunch and I threw away the cardboard tray of fries I hadn't touched, Alex and Emma said they were going to ride back home with Jen in another hour or two. "Cool," Luke said. He turned to me, Sam, Patrick, and Will. "Now we can stay till the park closes and ride everything twice."

We walked back to Cliffhanger and while we stood in line on the ninety-foot-tall, wet, wooden staircase that seemed designed to collapse, it dawned on me that the girls didn't actually care that any of us guys were there. We weren't at the water park as a singular coed group of friends. The girls had probably planned the trip on their own, and then the guys decided to go, too, and just offered to give Alex and Emma a ride. These were two separate groups, and everyone was here for their own sincere, childlike enjoyment of the rides. I was clearly the only guy thinking about the girls, and I bet none of the girls were thinking about any of us — least of all me.

So maybe the girls weren't making fun of me behind my

back. I should've been relieved, but I was kind of disappointed. Even if it was negative, some part of me wanted to believe they were thinking about me at all.

I launched myself down the nearly vertical slide with a blank expression, feeling empty. I stepped out at the bottom and Patrick shouted "Woo!" into my face, and I limply high-fived him. The guys sprinted to the next ride and I lagged behind. The girls had all seemed so mature and carefree. And there I was, a wet, squinting twerp whose retinas were being destroyed because none of us guys had thought to bring hats or sunglasses.

I spent the rest of the day wishing a kid would take a dump on one of the slides and they'd have to send everyone home. Unfortunately the kids all held it in.

Despite convincing myself that afternoon that the girls didn't give a shit about me, as I was lying in bed that night, the conversation with Emma wouldn't stop replaying in my head. It was canonized in the constantly expanding blooper reel of stupid things I'd said and done. I was paralyzed by the certainty that not only had Emma told the others about the "our song" comment, but they were at that very moment laughing about me while they all sat around a crackling firepit.

I remembered her blank face when I reminded her we watched *Can't Hardly Wait* in the hotel room. She hadn't known what I was talking about. This life-defining event that I had thought about every single day since it happened had barely registered as a memory for Emma. Sometimes I feel like every single moment in my life is like that — so significant to me, but no one else cares at all.

Maybe the girls *weren't* actually talking about me, then. Maybe I hadn't earned a place in any of their memories of the day. They'd immediately forgotten everything I'd done, my face going blurry like in a photograph in *The Ring*. The good moments in my life, like the night in the hotel room with Emma, and the bad ones, like when Alex read my writing in January, were all equally meaningless to everyone but me.

If that was true, then maybe I should have tried harder with Emma and Alex both. Maybe I should have been more up front about my feelings. Sure, if I told them I liked them and struck out, the embarrassment at the time would have sucked, but if they were going to forget it had ever happened the second I walked away, then who cares? And maybe telling them how I felt would've worked.

Wait, no. Who was I kidding? The reason I wasn't going out with Alex or Emma wasn't because I hadn't been up front about my feelings; I'm sure girls are aware that the leering mouth-breathers loitering near their lockers are into them without hearing a speech. I wasn't going out with them because I was a hopeless daydreamer who misinterpreted every normal interaction, crossing his eyes to force a magic image to appear from nothing, misreading romance in meaningless head nods. No girl should have to deal with a guy like me, with wires so fucked-up that "Hey, Kevin" got translated into "I love you" between my ear and my brain.

I started to wonder if "girls" was a hobby I should give up on. I was desperately attracted to them, but I'd blown so many attempts I figured it was time to get out of the game. I felt like a little kid who loved basketball but never made a shot in his life slowly accepting the fact that his time was better spent sitting on the bench watching pornography.

What an insane process the whole thing was, of having crushes in high school. You're supposed to stew in your own midday pit sweat nurturing these absurd fantasies for years, getting your hopes up that someone may actually enjoy your existence, without knowing who may have a crush on you back, so everyone's randomly hurling darts in the dark, hoping to hit any target at all, never mind get a bull's-eye. There were about five hundred kids in my grade, and you figure each person had four or five people they could stomach the thought of sitting beside silently in a dark movie theater for two hours. So there must be at least a few perfect matches — storybook romances destined to last until the couple dies simultaneously holding hands watching a Hawaiian sunset — that never see the light of day because no one wanted to risk making an ass of themselves at this goddamned casino called high school where the only things on the line were your reputation and your happiness. Why couldn't we all just make a list of people we liked on the first day of ninth grade and then feed them into a computer program that would cross-reference all the lists and spit out a simple chart showing all the perfect couples in the grade? Problem solved! And if you weren't matched with anyone on the list, no worries! Enjoy four years of beating off all you like while not wasting your time daydreaming about girls who don't give a shit about you, and try again in college! You'll probably get into Harvard with all the extra time you'll have not imagining yourself making gingerbread houses with a girl who accidentally smiled at you one time.

No matter what I did, I always wound up in the same place: sweating in my bed at two thirty a.m., shackled with paranoia. Everyone else from White Water was sleeping soundly, bundled up in cozy memories of not being a world-class dumb-ass. Maybe it was time to admit I wasn't cut out for adolescence, weigh down my cargo shorts with old video game controllers, and walk into the ocean.

Was that a suicidal thought? Technically yes. But it made sense.

I stayed in my room for most of the rest of spring break.

29.

I couldn't bring myself to talk to Emma or Alex at school. I kept my head down when I walked past their lunch table on the way to mine, and hoped that since I couldn't see them, they couldn't see me. But Alex would always say hi to me, and Emma would sometimes wave. I tried to tell from the tones of their voices or the angle of their waves if they were actually mocking me, but I couldn't be sure.

I wondered who else knew about my "our song" comment at this point. The whole school? The entire internet? It some ways it didn't even matter. Even if no one else knew about that moment, I did and I'd never forget it.

I fell back into my routine and barely felt alive. In the mornings and at night I'd take my pills and wash my face and inspect every zit on my jawline. Were they getting smaller? Were there less of them? Had any of the scars healed? Most days it seemed like nothing at all had changed about me. It was impossible to tell when I'd check my face several times a day, this masochistic ritual of glancing in mirrors just long enough to remind myself I looked gross. I started to wonder if the pills had done anything at all but mess with my head.

It was warm and I couldn't wear my black hoodie to school every day anymore. I wanted to blend in and disappear, but most of my T-shirts had stupid graphics that drew attention and tried to claim an identity based on phrases I didn't come up with and had never said. So I'd rotate the two solid-color T-shirts I had, over and over. Blue and gray paired with khaki shorts. Generic guy camouflage.

I no longer brought anything to conversations with the guys. I'd stand there listening to Patrick making the guys and girls laugh at his bland story about how embarrassed he was when a waiter told him to enjoy his meal and he said, "You, too." Come on. A few months ago I probably would've pointed out that that was amateur stuff — the kind of conversational mishap that only mortified a fifth-grader. *You want to talk humiliating? Try telling a girl you like but who sometimes forgets you exist that a song everyone knows is "your song." That's how we do it in the big leagues.* But instead I just stayed quiet. Sometimes I'd see a video online I knew they'd think was funny or read something about a movie we'd all watched but I wouldn't bother telling them about it. What was the point? I knew how they'd respond. It felt like I'd already had all the conversations

I'd ever have with them. I didn't want to get stuck in an endless cycle of conversational reruns, so I'd limit myself to the predictable deadpan sarcastic comments they expected from me. They'd all laugh at my dark jokes and never think anything was different about me. I was a house being demolished on the inside, but the front yard looked the same.

I spent weekends in my room staring at my computer, compulsively refreshing movie forums for new posts and stalking kids from school online. By then, Alex's online persona had entirely fused with the God Squad. She switched to her real name online. Whatever separation had existed was gone; this was the one and only Alex. I'd flick through albums of them on road trips through south Georgia and at some country music concert in a field somewhere. She was wearing cowboy boots and a large hat. It felt like looking at Christmas cards from a distant relative I'd met once when I was five.

My April Accutane appointment happened. Mom drove me and I sat in the waiting room alone. There were five jaundiced people there, wasting their time waiting for the drug tests they were clearly about to fail. I sat with my eyes shut and felt relieved that I didn't have to pretend to care about Alex, whose interests were clearly polar opposites of my own, or worry that she was secretly thinking about the "our song" comment while we sat side by side in stony, judgmental silence.

Nights started getting warm in early May and I'd sit outside on the deck by myself after dinner. It was dark and mostly quiet out there. I'd play music, but sometimes I'd turn it off but keep my headphones on so my parents wouldn't bother me, and just listen to the crickets.

My parents and Kate would sit on the couch watching TV in the living room and I could see them through the blinds. We were all together, if you could ignore the brick wall between us.

One night I brought an old notebook out there with me, mostly as an excuse to give my parents if they asked why I was sitting outside doing nothing like a potted plant. I opened to a page that said MY LIFE SUCKS. I HATE MOM. Huh. There was a date on the page that placed it in seventh grade. I had no recollection of what had inspired it, but something must have really pissed me off. I tried to remember for a while but couldn't think of anything that had happened to me in seventh grade that was that bad.

I closed the notebook and considered trying to pursue some other kind of expression I hadn't failed at yet, like painting or forming a band. But what was the point?

It wasn't like I had anything to offer the world. I was just a collage of songs I'd heard and movie logos I'd drawn in my notebook, all other people's ideas. An 8-by-11 sheet of printer paper of a person whose main skill was wasting time trying to convince himself he was more interesting than everyone else, despite having done nothing but sit around inert, consuming media. I was pretty sure I didn't have a personality.

I took a sip of cold tea and was staring out into the trees, lost in my head, when Mom opened the deck door and scared the shit out of me. I made some guttural noise and leaped out of my chair an inch, spilling brown liquid on my T-shirt. Mom laughed.

"I'm sorry," she said. "I didn't mean to scare you. Just wanted to check if you needed anything."

I didn't turn around to look at her. "Nope."

She couldn't stop laughing. I imagine she wiped a tear from her eye. It might have been the funniest thing she'd seen in a decade. "I'm sorry, sweetie. It just reminded me of Dad. I swear, the same thing happened when we were first married. He was standing on a chair changing a light bulb and I opened the door and he screamed and fell flat on his back. Slammed on the ground. A picture fell off the wall. Once I realized he wasn't dead, we laughed for about an hour."

I laughed a little.

"You get your focus from your father. You both have that intensity. It's funny how much I see of him in you."

I nodded, not sure I agreed.

She closed the door behind me and I looked at the back of Dad's head through the blinds. He was watching baseball and had been for hours. I didn't get it. How could he devote so much of his time to a game that is basically the same thing every time?

I shrugged and felt my phone vibrate with a text. It was Luke. He and Will, Sam, and Patrick were on their way to pick me up to go sneak into our middle school. Goddamn it. They'd been talking about that incredibly dumb plan all week at school and I'd been ignoring them. I assumed I wasn't invited, just like

I hadn't been to most of the events they'd gone to on weekends the past few months. I wouldn't go with them. I'd made the mistake of spontaneously going with them to White Water and I wound up making an ass of myself. I wouldn't do that again.

Before I could text them a lie, Luke honked from my driveway. Shit. I sprinted through my house before my parents could get off the couch and told them it was just Luke picking something up.

"Dude, dude, dude, dude, dude!" Patrick shouted through the shotgun window as I walked across the driveway, slapping his hand on the side of the car. "Let's go, go, go, go, go!"

"Yeah, hey, I, uh . . . Nah. I'm just, uh . . . Nah."

"What are you talking about?" Luke said. "Come on. This is, like, the only interesting thing that's gonna happen all year."

"I'm just, I mean . . . we have finals coming up and . . ."

"There's, like, three weeks of school left," Luke said. "It's practically summer. Nothing matters. Come on."

Patrick said, "Dude, you're making this hard. It's very easy. The window around the back by the cafeteria doesn't lock. Everyone's been in there. It's a rite of passage. You can't move away from here to go to college without sneaking back into middle school."

"Seriously, dude," Sam said. "They won't let you graduate if you don't. If you haven't done it, when you try to get your diploma the principal chucks a baseball at your head and you have to start ninth grade again."

I took a deep breath. I thought about going. I really tried to picture myself slinking through that back window with the guys, tiptoeing across the tiles in the hallway where we used to play crab soccer in gym class. I got stressed out just thinking about it, picturing security cameras catching us, alarms blaring, me saying something stupid and embarrassing myself in front of everyone again.

I knew I should have been the Doritos Dude: *Get your flat ass off your beanbag chair and roll with the fun, you goddamned idiot.* But when I'd daydream about being a life-of-the-party guy who just doesn't care, no one in the daydream sees me that way; they know I'm only pretending to be laid-back. I shout, "Get in the pool!" and then I cannonball in and when I surface, I'm all alone in there and my bathing suit has come off and everyone looks down at my mediocre penis.

"Look, I just can't."

They all stared at me for a second. Patrick said to Luke, "I told you he wouldn't. There's no point in trying anymore." And then they drove away.

I walked back inside and my parents asked if the guys were there to surprise me the night before my birthday. The guys had no idea my birthday was tomorrow, and I didn't feel like telling them. I said no, they were going to a football team party. Most kids lie to their parents to sneak out at night; I lied to my parents to stay in my room.

Mom, Dad, and Kate decided to give me my birthday cards that night. They must have felt bad for me or something. My parents' gift was some cash inside a store-bought card because Mom said she really didn't know what to get me.

Mom asked me if I wanted to watch a movie or eat ice

cream or do anything special. I said thanks, but I was tired and just wanted a calm night at home before my driver's license test the next day.

I went up to my room, aimlessly browsed the internet for hours, then looked at porn, masturbated, said, out loud to myself, "Happy sweet sixteen, dude," and shut off the light.

30.

I got my driver's license on Saturday morning and I didn't look at the photo on it. I just took the license from the clerk and stuffed it into my wallet and tried to forget about it. I told my parents I had homework to do in my room, and I really did for a while. But as soon as I took my first break to browse the internet, I didn't get anything done for the rest of the day. I sat there for hours scrolling through pictures of everyone who'd snuck into the middle school the night before.

None of my friends were stupid enough to upload pictures of themselves breaking and entering on state property, but they were in the background of some of the shots uploaded by dumber members of our grade. Luke, Will, Sam, and Patrick were standing in the cafeteria, hanging around where Luke,

Will, and my old lunch table was. There must have been thirty kids there. Emma and Alex were there, standing with some juniors and seniors. They were laughing. Some of the older guys were holding cans that were probably beer.

Did the older guys get Alex and Emma drunk? I felt like a concerned mother. I don't know why I cared so much. I sat at my computer while the whole thing unfolded in my head: Luke, Will, Sam, and Patrick get there first and text everyone else that the coast is clear. Alex and Emma show up with the God Squad and other girls from our grade. Just before they pry open the window, a black pickup truck, overflowing with rowdy senior guys hanging off the sides like pirates clutching a sail, peels into the parking lot. They unload two beer kegs and an endless supply of twenty-four-packs that someone's desperate dad, in an attempt to seem cool, bought them with his Costco membership. More cars pull in, full of girls who look like they should be headed to Cancún for an MTV spring break party. Everyone flows through the open window like rainwater draining into a sewer. Luke, Will, Sam, Patrick, Emma, and Alex get swept up in the rapids. They're smiling, they're laughing, they're high-fiving people I've only seen in yearbooks. They march down the hallways pretending they're in a parade. Most of these kids didn't even go to our middle school. It means nothing to them. Luke and Will talk to some older girls in the cafeteria. They dance with them, sarcastically at first, and then it gets serious. They start making out. Some of the guys pick up Alex and Emma on their shoulders. They put the ends of those stupid beer-funnel things in their mouths and then they disappear around a corner. Alex and Emma are having fun and they're not thinking about me.

A senior named Carter Canton posted *socks* on Alex's wall and she commented *lol*. What the hell did that mean? Who were these people?

I kept clicking through pictures until I found the one I wish I'd never seen. In the background, behind a group of seniors I didn't know, Alex and Luke were leaning against a locker, their faces an inch apart. They might have been holding hands. What the fuck? How can a guy who had sex with a cinnamon raisin bagel be so irresistible to girls? Were they making out? Were they *going out*? Would they even tell me if they were? I'd known Alex from before she transferred; he should know I had dibs on her. But Luke clearly didn't care about crush-dib etiquette. Fuck.

Fuck!

Even though Alex and I didn't have anything in common, I wanted what Luke had in that picture so bad. If I'd gone, could it have been me? Was that my chance and I blew it? Was that the perfect situation, the night the universe had carved out for me and Alex to start a romantic relationship, and I'd screwed it all up again by being too scared and too shy and too nervous and too pathetic? Goddamn it. How is it possible to be mad at everyone, including yourself, equally?

I felt like I didn't even know Luke or Alex anymore — or maybe that I'd never known them. I thought I'd be the one to change that year, but it was those two and Will and

Emma — everyone but me — who morphed into people I didn't know, and didn't want to know. I'd lost them. There's no point in getting attached to anyone in high school. Everyone is the goo in a fucking lava lamp.

On Monday, everyone was talking about the middle school in hushed code words. The morons who'd uploaded pictures were all getting called into the principal's office, so everyone was paranoid about getting in trouble.

I watched Luke and Alex all morning. They didn't hold hands. It didn't seem like anything was going on between them. But they'd probably keep it a secret anyway. I didn't ask any questions when the guys whispered vaguely about the middle school at lunch. I didn't want to know. They kept saying that I should have been there and they'd never go back because they didn't want to ruin what was such a magical, once-in-a-lifetime experience they all shared. That made me feel great. They had a memory that would last forever, and meanwhile I couldn't even remember what I'd eaten for dinner that evening I spent alone masturbating.

I overheard two kids in the locker room talking about it. "Brett Wilson finger-banged Courtney Thorpe at the middle school, you know?" one of them said. Then the other said, "Logan Furman finger-banged Sarah Carter. Dude, everyone was finger-banging everyone. Luke Rossi finger-banged Veronica Wesson."

Wait, what?

The loud God Squadder who persuaded the school board

to put recycling bins in the cafeteria? Luke finger-banged her? Ugh, that word is gross. Luke "manually stimulated" the girl who convinced the school board to add all the recycling bins to the cafeteria? Actually that's worse. Whatever. There's no good term for that.

Had he made out with Alex *and* gotten with Veronica Wesson on the same night? How many girls in our grade wanted Luke? All of them? And this was Luke Rossi, the guy I knew for a fact had had sexual intercourse with a box of Honey Nut Cheerios?

What the hell had happened that night? Had everyone made serious sexual progress and I completely missed it? Did that ship sail, and now there was a clear dividing line between the sexual haves, who blossomed that night, and the have-nots, who would forever be treated as the eunuchs of the grade? Was that night my grade's Woodstock, and everyone would be wearing Middle School Night T-shirts for decades, and when I'm sixty I'll develop a false memory of it and lie to my grandkids that I was really there?

If Luke — and maybe the other guys, too — had done stuff with girls, and everyone knew about it, why hadn't they told me? How could they sprint to third base without even telling me the game had started? Did they think I wouldn't be able to handle it? By not going to this weird middle-school sex party, had I become some sort of little-brother figure in my group, only good for talking about cartoons and video games?

I started to wonder if Luke or Will had actually had full-on sex before. Or Alex or Emma? Emma'd made that God Squad abstinence pledge, but reading a sentence to some youth group leader with a chain wallet and frosted tips wasn't a legally binding contract. It was absolutely within the realm of possibilities that she'd had sex; it's not like she would tell me. She and Luke had dated for three months. I wondered how far they had gone. Will had never dated anyone, but he was always friendly with a bunch of girls, so for all I knew, he could have been hooking up with tons of them after school and on weekends. I had no idea what those guys were doing with their penises when they were out of my sight, and that upset me more than it should have.

All day I wondered about the sexual histories of everyone around me. I bet every other kid had at least already made out with someone. I started looking at all my teachers differently. Mr. Tilly, despite looking like he mutated in a riverbed, had a grown daughter, meaning that at some point his odd penis had been presented to a woman and for some reason she hadn't batted it away with a flyswatter. Mr. Meyer, as weird as he was, had probably wormed his dick past his bass guitar for a few minutes of intercourse with a woman. Or maybe several women — strange ones — all at the same time while wearing costumes at some unappealing poetry convention in a suburban hotel. I couldn't stop picturing his dong dangling through homemade steampunk cosplay.

It's difficult to focus on studying for finals when you've just realized that your school is teeming with sexual creatures who suppress the erotic sides of themselves for eight hours a day. It wasn't the building full of uptight prudes I'd thought of it as before; it was a den of porn stars.

Now that Alex and Emma were no longer options, there wasn't anyone in particular I wanted to have sex with, but with every hour that slipped by, I felt like I was losing ground in some race with Luke and Will. Like we started at the same time, but they were running at ten miles an hour and I was running at five miles an hour, so they kept getting further and further ahead of me, until they were at the finish-line orgy while I lagged behind, alone and preoccupied with the SAT math problem I'd written myself into.

31.

As soon as I got home that afternoon, I went to my room and closed the door. I lay down on the carpet and tried to think about nothing, but the images of Luke and Will getting hand jobs on top of the kidney-shaped table where we'd discussed *Tuck Everlasting* were hard to fend off.

Were they really comfortable whipping their dongs out in front of a girl who'd see them at school on Monday morning? Christ, can you imagine that confidence? If their shafts were bent even a single degree, if there was one blemish on the skin, the story would spread faster than any STD and their lives would be over. What was expected of their pubic hair? What styles were acceptable? Was there a popular cut I should have known about? Were they supposed to bring their own condoms? When were they supposed to buy them? Which stores had the best prices? Did Carter Canton's post on Alex's wall mean he'd used a sock as a condom with her?

If I'd gone and had the opportunity to finger-bang some unlucky girl from our grade, I wouldn't have had any idea what I was doing. Guys talked about sex all the time, but no one ever offered any legitimate advice. Porn was obviously a grotesque illusion with no application to the real world, and everything I was taught in teen movies growing up were just the sexual fantasies of male screenwriters with names like Adam Herz and David T. Wagner. How was I supposed to know what girls actually wanted? I'd only been trained to seduce Adam Herz and David T. Wagner.

I wasn't ready for sex. I wasn't ready for anything.

And apparently I was the only person in my entire grade that felt that way. Everyone else had moved on; they were zip-lining away from me butt-naked, popping wheelies on dirt bikes and furiously banging each other on a big grass field between a lake and a Red Hot Chili Peppers concert.

I had been left behind. Or had inadvertently chosen to stay behind.

Dad knocked on my door and asked if I had any donations for Goodwill and I told him no and to please go away because I had a ton of homework.

It was silent for a while, and my phone scared the shit out of me when it buzzed with a call from Alex. At any point before that week, it would have been the greatest moment of my life. But I let it ring four times. "Yeah?" I said.

"Hey, what's up?"

"Nothing."

"Cool."

"Yeah." A long pause. "Do you need something?"

"Oh, yeah. Can I ask you something?"

"Sure?"

"Is Luke, like, a good guy?"

I didn't know how to respond.

"Kevin? Are you there?"

". . .What?"

"He's really funny at school, but I was just wondering if he's, you know . . . nice? And sorry to sound like a middle-schooler, but does he, I don't know . . . *like* anyone?"

I knew it was coming, but it hurt worse than I expected. Whatever hope I'd maintained about her, that annoying nuisance of a crush buzzing around my head like a fly, had been shotgun-blasted to death.

"I don't know," I said.

"He's your best friend."

"I guess."

There was a long pause. "Well . . . okay. I don't know. Just . . . what's he like? Outside of school?"

"I don't know. He can be an asshole sometimes. I mean, everyone can. Haven't you hung out with him? Don't you already know what he's like?"

"Oh. Sorry. Maybe I shouldn't have —"

"Whatever. It's fine. Anything else I can help with?"

There was an awkward pause. I knew I was being a dick, but I couldn't bring myself to care.

She finally said there was nothing else, and we hung up.

I felt blank and numb, letting gravity shove me deeper into the floor, hearing my heart beat in the silence.

An hour went by while I lay flat on my back. Maybe more. How's it possible to feel frantic and dead at the same time?

At some point I got up to pee and blow my nose. When I flushed the tissue, the toilet clogged, but I didn't care enough to deal with it. As I washed my hands, I looked at my face in the mirror. Scars covered my chin and cheeks. Each one of them was a stupid mistake, a time when I should have held strong and been confident and not popped a zit. But instead I always caved and went for the stupid short-term solution that caused more problems in the long run.

Goddamn it. My skin was still so red, I looked as perpetually embarrassed as I felt, and it was flecked with a scab, bump, and scar for each bad choice I'd made in my life.

Kate was downstairs with some friend, and I stepped onto her side of the bathroom and looked through her makeup. I opened a case of the beige powder with the little pad you smear it on with, and I wiped it across my cheeks. Jesus, it was like a cheat code. I wiped more on my chin, my jawline, my forehead and nose. Everything was erased. For a minute it made me feel like the whole year had never happened. It helped me disappear. My heart sped up and I got scared I'd get caught.

I clicked the makeup closed and stepped back into my

room and locked the door. I felt like doing something, but there was nothing to actually do, and no reason to do anything. Even masturbating seemed like a waste. I already knew what it felt like. Why bother? I was sick of my computer. Nothing good ever came from sitting there. Video games and TV were a waste of time and I couldn't focus on a book.

The color was fading from the world around me. It had been for months. Was that what growing up felt like? Being disappointed over and over again, so often you get used to the numbness, and gauzy emotional scar tissue builds up between you and the world that washes out its color and smell and taste, a steady fade to black and white that starts in adolescence and ends when the last dots of light fizzle out and all that's left is darkness and silence and death?

Christ.

I was sick of my own thoughts. I needed a distraction, some way to get energy out of me without thinking. I dug that kid-size guitar I'd gotten for Christmas out of my closet. I'd barely thought about it, since it was made for a nine-year-old, but I sat on the edge of my bed and I banged out notes without knowing what I was doing, and it cleared my head for a second. A pure transmission of energy from my fingers into sounds that didn't require me to hear my own dumb thoughts. For a minute it felt good to be totally consumed, fully distracted.

I had no idea how to actually play it, but I landed on some notes that sort of sounded like Weezer's "Butterfly," and I started singing it, barely above a whisper. I'd heard the song about a thousand times and knew every word. The lyrics came out of my mouth like some head-clearing mantra, and for about thirty seconds I was completely lost, focused. The best kind of alone.

Then Kate and her friend screamed with laughter from the other side of my door.

My left hand choked the fret board and my teeth clenched, and I stood up and threw the guitar onto the carpet.

I pulled open the door. Kate and Courtney giggled more. Their laughter sounded like those kids in the football stadium bathroom last fall. They sounded like everyone at my school finally laughing at me, telling me what they really thought about me. Every individual giggle confirmed how pathetic I'd become.

"Shut the fuck up!" I slammed the door as hard as I could at them. My hands rolled into fists and I breathed hard.

They screamed and ran downstairs and I heard Kate crying to Mom.

Mom yelled upstairs, "Kevin. Kitchen. Now."

I stood there for a second, heart racing.

"Kevin!"

I shook my head and opened the door and stomped downstairs into the kitchen, where Kate and Courtney wiped fake tears from their eyes in front of Mom and Dad. Kate tilted her head at me and squinted. "Are you wearing makeup?"

I stared at the floor and walked past them, muttering, "This is bullshit." I opened the door to the garage and walked outside.

"That's my makeup, isn't it!" she yelled after me. Dad yelled something, too, but I kicked the door shut behind me and cut him off. I went through the garage, slipped on flip-flops, and stalked down the driveway and onto the dark street, lit up by just the streetlights.

My arms were tense and fists clenched and I breathed hard and could feel in my chest how frustrated and pissed off I was. I could have fought someone right then, if I knew how to do that.

I kept walking out of our cul-de-sac, down the first street in the neighborhood, through the side yard of the last house, into the woods, down the small path between the trees — feeling my way in the humid darkness — then huffed and stomped through the rough and finally made it onto the wide-open fairway of the golf course.

I could see stars in the sky. The anger vibrating through me settled as I walked, and my heartbeat calmed down. It was just me, alone on four hundred yards of moonlit grass, silent and away from everyone.

I tried to pinpoint what I was so mad about. Kate was the spark, but it wasn't just her. It was everything that had built up and compounded over the last year — the frustrations and annoyances and stress and anxieties and humiliations and people I hated and the hours I spent hating myself, doubting myself, wondering if Accutane was responsible for my thoughts. It was noise from every direction, inward and out. I wished I was pissed off at a *thing*. Then I could kick the thing and move on. It would have been so much simpler if Leatherface were chasing me with his revving chain saw. But my rage was obnoxiously unspecific. I was mad at every god-damned atom in existence, including my own.

Christ, what an original thought: *The universe sucks!* Everything I did was a cliché. Even my dream-girl version of Alex was the same generic romantic fantasy in a million other suburban losers' heads. Was I supposed to rebel against society somehow to differentiate myself? Become an anarchist punk? But there's a uniform for that, too; there might as well be a national convention of identical high-school punk kids to convene and realize they're all the same. But that observation was itself a cliché. Everyone knows punk is just as much of a pre-packaged group identity as playing lacrosse.

Goddamn it! My thoughts added nothing to the world.

Was there any legitimate reason for me to exist?

The terrible advice Mr. Meyer had left me with came to me: "Be yourself."

It's a cliché the floats around like the flu, a meaningless idea that infects adults who think they're being wise when they're just repeating shit from TV shows. They think it's a magic spell that'll get angry teens to embrace their inner freaks, start sporting blue Mohawks and baggy black pants covered in chains, and now they're smiling and alley-ooping basketballs with jocks, a whole school harmonizing into a utopia of self-actualized kids with no conflict or problems because everyone is *being themselves* so hard they forget to worry.

Being yourself isn't the hard part. Figuring out who the hell you are when you're morphing into a new brand of idiot every other week — that's the hard part.

Meyer's advice was just as annoying as Dad's advice last fall to "do whatever makes you happy." Sure thing, fellas! Comin' right up! And let me throw in a third for free: I'll live in the moment as well! Problem solved!

Why had I ever bought into Meyer's desperate-to-be-interesting bullshit? I hated that I'd thought his stupid poetry lecture was cool — the one where he'd spent five minutes repeating "crisp crunch" over and over as some example of the power of repeated sounds. What an idiot. How dare he trick me into admiring that. He convinced me to write awful poetry that made no sense. Fuck Meyer for making me believe there was some nobility in being obscure, some prize to win for confusing people with nonsense.

As I fumed, I walked to the end of the green and went down the cart path, through the tunnel under the street, and came out at the start of the next hole. I stomped down a big grassy hill and looked up at the stars, searching for something, anything, to let me know that things would be okay. That I was wrong about everything in the world being the dumbest bullshit.

But there was no constellation that looked like me in the future giving current me a thumbs-up. There was no Doritos Dude in the sky. There was no —

Plsshh!

My foot had caught on a root and I'd toppled face-first into a pond.

I thrashed and reached forward in the mouth-warm brown

water, touching the disgusting soft dirt at the bottom, knocking into debris and garbage all around me.

I crawled out, feeling like I'd escaped from a human stomach that stank exactly like the dump Luke's brother had taken in that pond three years ago.

I pulled myself onto my knees, felt something stuck to my lip, reached up to pull it off, determined it was a chunk of goose shit, and instantaneously vomited.

The makeup had undoubtedly washed off my face — and the illusion that the year hadn't happened had washed off with it. I lay back in the grass and looked up at the sky. I wished all the Accutane side effects would crawl out of the woodwork, all the different ones teaming up together to take me down. I wanted it all: Bring on the blurred vision and severe pain behind the eyes. Give me a hallucination and a seizure, too; the fast heart rate and spontaneous bruising; thick, bloody boogers; cracking and peeling skin — just let the whole epidermis fall off for good in one dry snakeskin piece. Give me some blisters and rashes, too; finger- and toenails turning to dust; bone fractures just for fun; and then bring on the good stuff, the stars of the show — I'm talking diarrhea; rectal bleeding; black, bloody, tarry stools — that's right, everybody in the arena, all together now: black! bloody! tarry! stools! And then let's put the cherry atop this pile of melted meat I've become with my favorite one of all, that classic from day one: dark urine, baby. Let it drip and drop and crawl out of my wilted dick like Dr Pepper syrup, black and sticky and thick.

I wanted to be pulled apart and melt and die out there, muscle and bones all turned to mush; to seep into the grass, spread out so thin the maintenance guys wouldn't even notice when they ground up my eyeballs and teeth in their riding lawn mowers first thing in the morning.

32.

I couldn't tell how long I was out there, but it was enough time to conclude that, unfortunately, my body was not going to turn itself into a pot roast.

I picked myself up and walked all the way back to my house and opened the door, hoping my family had written me off and had gone to sleep.

No one was in the kitchen, thank god, and I rushed upstairs, desperate for a shower. I opened my door —

Shit. Mom, Dad, Kate, her friend Courtney, and the jazz-hating handyman were all crowded in Kate's and my bathroom, watching a mechanical pump shaped like a trash can go to work on our toilet. It made a wretched squealing noise while it slurped up water, and a black plastic tube on the back end was aimed to shoot its catch into a large bucket.

I stood there, frozen. Kate sniffed the air and scrunched her nose. I couldn't tell if she thought the heinous shit smell was me or the toilet.

The handyman said, "Pump's still lookin' for the culprit."

Dad said to me, "It's *really* backed up."

I nodded, unsure if that was an insult or a compliment. I had no idea why everyone was gathered around the toilet like it was a giant radio broadcasting an FDR speech. What treasure did they expect the pump to find? Was Kate still eating coins?

I grabbed a change of clothes from my drawer and got in the shower in Dad's office bathroom. When I was clean and dry, I was still just as pissed off as I had been before; clearly whatever was actually wrong with me couldn't be rinsed off.

I stepped back in my room just in time to bear witness to the fruits of the pump's labors. It grunted and coughed and then vomited out a massive wad of white pulp into the bucket. It slapped the plastic with a wet thud, and all five faces peered at it. It was like a white jellyfish.

The pump choked again, and then spat another wad, and then a third.

"Anyone been flushing anything other than TP in here?" the handyman said. "Tissues?"

Oh, no.

Oh, no.

No, no, no, no. Please, no.

Everyone's heads turned to me in sync.

"I had a runny nose," I mumbled to the wall. It was not technically a lie. One percent of the tissues being sucked from my toilet were the product of a runny nose.

The pump squealed and hocked another wet wad into the bucket.

I was muttering something about hay fever when my eyes locked with Courtney's. Her foul little mouth twisted into a grin and she mimed jerking off. Kate saw it and screamed with laughter while my parents looked on, confused. The handyman winked at me, flashing a smile that was missing two teeth.

Fuck that. Fuck all that.

I needed to roll into an artillery cannon and blast my miserable body into any other situation; anything else would be preferable to the one I was in. "Mom, I need your car. Luke and the guys are doing a birthday thing for me tonight. They just texted me to come over. Okay?"

She sighed and told me I'd be grounded for the way I yelled at Kate, starting tomorrow, but I should go to the party. I stomped downstairs and took her car keys and got in the car with no clue where to actually go. It didn't matter. I pulled out of the driveway, sped out of the cul-de-sac, rolled through the bullshit stop sign, and then drove out of the neighborhood, watching the trees smear together in the black night around me while I wondered why I was such a goddamned idiot.

Why had I tried to sing my way out of my rut while strumming a child's guitar? No wonder Kate and Courtney had exploded in laughter. I must have sounded like a total fucking loser. And why was I putting myself through so much stress and pain for all these projects that didn't add up to anything? The movie, the book, the stories, the poems. They were all failed attempts to be interesting. No matter how hard I was on myself, I still maintained these dumb delusions of being something I wasn't. I was trying so hard to be unique, but I was just another spoiled kid from the suburbs with the misguided belief based on absolutely nothing that I was destined to be this great filmmaker, this writer, this storyteller. I couldn't stand to look at my own face, but I was obsessed with myself. A Narcissus who doesn't make eye contact is just a goddamned idiot staring at a lake accomplishing nothing.

The illuminated signs in the strip malls ahead of me smeared together, and I had a vision of big, shiny gold letters floating in front of my face: I'M AN AVERAGE, LAME FUCKING LOSER JUST LIKE EVERYONE ELSE. And underneath that, in rainbow bubble letters: STOP TRYING SO HARD, YOU JACKASS.

All the stress from all those projects last semester had probably shaved five years off my life. I'd gotten my hopes up and nothing had worked out. Why had I even liked Alex or Emma in the first place? I added up the total amount of time I'd actually spent interacting with each of them one-on-one. It was the most depressing math problem of all time. Each of my and Alex's blood test appointments were, like, ten minutes tops. And apart from the night in the hotel, I'd only talked to Emma alone in little thirty-second chunks during class changes at school. All added up, it was like seventy minutes I'd actually spent, combined, with the two girls in my imaginary love triangle. I'd spent more quality time with *Friday the 13th*

Part VIII: Jason Takes Manhattan. Was it possible I only liked them because they talked to me? The more I thought about it, the more it didn't just seem possible — it seemed obvious! If a woman kidnapped me, I guarantee I'd fall in love with her just because she'd shown me so much attention. I was no better than a trout lusting after a shiny piece of metal, desperate to sink my dumb lips into any rusty hook that acknowledged my existence. I was enchanted by girls who didn't care that I existed, no better than a fucking idiot in a bucket hat who's obsessed with toucans, devoting his life to creatures who see no difference between him and a goddamned scarecrow.

Last fall I'd had all sorts of metaphors about how I'd grow into a better version of myself because of Accutane and Alex, like I was a plant or something. But the time-lapse film of my year wasn't a flower blooming; it was roadkill decaying into bones.

I was pathetic and desperate and worthless, a plain guy who'd spent months trying to trick Alex into liking some made-up version of me. Thinking I was unique or interesting was a myth Alex unintentionally fueled when she'd accidentally let her eyeballs meet mine that first day back in the waiting room.

The car was almost out of gas and I didn't want to deal with it, so I turned around in a shopping center parking lot and drove back toward my neighborhood, running through mistakes from this awful year: *Forcing myself to watch pretentious French films. Pretending to read Russian novels. Trying to be outgoing at driver's ed. Taking Meyer's advice to quit the movie project. Writing the story about driver's ed. Writing poetry. Writing anything.*

So where did that leave me? I was a talentless, cliché-spouting, pretentious sixteen-year-old virgin loser with "severe recalcitrant nodular acne." If the strongest medicine known to man couldn't fix my face, what were the chances that there was anything in the world that could fix the rest of me?

I sped through the entrance to my neighborhood in a daze. Why was I even going back home? Did I really want to go to bed only to wake up and have to do this all over again, be *me* for another day, another week, another year? I wasn't sure I could do it. I wasn't sure I wanted to.

I kept driving toward home, passing that bullshit stop sign on my le —

Shit. *Shit!*

I wasn't moving. My ears rang — an endless, high-pitched dial tone. My window was shattered, the windshield cracked into a spiderweb. I coughed up dust rising off the deflated airbag. It smelled awful — sour, burnt rubber. Everything was blurry. All this white dust in the air stung my eyes. The airbag sagged in my lap. My car had been pushed to the side of the road, two wheels over the curb opposite the stop sign the other car drove through. That car was crumpled beside mine like an accordion, and mine was smashed in on the front left side, beside my door.

I turned the car off and stumbled out. I wasn't thinking about anything. My body was just moving. It was like watching a movie. My legs and arms felt jittery, like I'd been shot through with electricity. I stared at the other car. A guy was standing next to it under the streetlight. He said to me, "I didn't see the sign. Are you okay?"

I couldn't speak. I nodded.

"I'm okay over here," he said. "I called the cops. Are you sure you're okay? Should I call an ambulance?"

I stood there motionless. Staring at the smashed hoods of both our cars. All I heard was my own breathing. And then I stared into the ground and the police were there. I gave them my license. I told them I hadn't seen the other guy drive through the stop sign. It was hard to talk. My responses came out jumbled, sentences missing half their words. They asked if I was okay and I kept saying, "I'm fine. I'm okay. Really I'm fine."

Mom and Dad appeared. Dad talked to the police officers. Mom took the back seat of Dad's car and gave me the front. I told her I was really sorry about her car. She said she didn't care and kept asking if I needed to go to the hospital. Apart from the adrenaline coursing through me, I felt fine. My fingers tingled and my arms and legs bounced. My jaw quaked. I had to bite my lip to keep my teeth from clacking together. "Positive mental attitude," I said to Mom, all nervous energy through clattering teeth. She put her hand on my shoulder and squeezed it.

Kate was standing in the kitchen when I walked in. I couldn't stop smiling for some reason. I felt like I was on drugs. She stared at me like I was a ghost.

Mom led me to bed and told me that if there was anything at all I needed, I could just ask.

"Really, Mom, I'm fine."

I lay in bed in the dark for hours. Breathed slowly, stared forward into my bookshelf. Rubbed my hands over my comforter back and forth to the rhythm of my breaths. I was so happy to be there, to not have a mouth full of airbag. The memory of the crash tried to replay itself, but I forced it away. I didn't want to remember it. I didn't want it to be real. I was back in my room, where I'd been an hour ago. I was fine and the other guy was fine. You could chop the wreck out from the time line of my life and I'd still be there in bed that night. The wreck was irrelevant.

I focused on breathing. My wrists were red and chafed from the airbag. My ears were still ringing. I was alone, in my bed. It was calm. I wasn't dead. Everything was fine.

33.

Mom made me stay home from school on Tuesday. I told her the crash wasn't a big deal — some glass got smashed up. That was it. There was no tragedy — but she insisted, and I decided to stop arguing. Whatever. I was happy to take a day off from school.

All morning I lay in bed half-asleep, blissfully zoned out, watching movies. I got through three by lunchtime. It's crazy how productive you can be when you start watching movies at seven a.m.

I fell asleep in the afternoon, and when I woke up, the sun was shining through my windows and I had four texts. Will asked what happened. Luke asked when I was coming back to school. Emma and Alex both asked if I was okay. God. Mom must have told Luke's mom, and she'd probably exaggerated some absurd story about how I miraculously survived a forty-five-car pileup where everyone else died and all the other cars exploded into fireballs around me but her son was just so special he made it out. The texts annoyed me. This didn't have to be a big deal. I was gone from school for one day. I hadn't even broken a bone. There was no blood. I was unscathed and unchanged and there was nothing to talk about.

I didn't respond to the texts. I put in disc three of the *Clerks* DVD and watched all the special features, thinking I should wreck cars all the time so I could have more days off.

Mom drove me to school Wednesday morning, and I made the mistake of closing my eyes. She kept asking me if I was okay, which was annoying because I was honestly just tired, so I forced my eyes open so she'd stop questioning me.

Patrick hugged me in the hallway in front of the guys in the morning, and I stood there with my arms at my sides, waiting for him to start pretending to have sex with me. But when he didn't, I shrugged him off and told them all I was fine and there was no reason to even talk about it.

Alex and Emma sat with us at lunch. Alex asked if I was okay. Everyone turned to stare at me.

"What? Yeah, I'm fine — I'm totally fine. It's really not a big deal at all. It was like, really small."

Emma tilted her head. "My mom heard from Luke's mom that both cars got totaled. Like, completely destroyed."

I shrugged. "I don't know. I mean, moms exaggerate." I

stared into the table, waiting for them to start talking about anything else. I didn't want to think about it because there wasn't anything to think about.

The rest of the girls came by to see if I was okay. It was weird. I couldn't tell if they really cared about me or if I was just some freak show object for them to ogle at for the day. Someone told me Todd Lancaster was busy doing a project in the library but he'd said he was glad I was okay. Whatever.

"So, how did it, like, happen?" Sam said.

I shrugged. "I was driving through my neighborhood and the other guy went through a stop sign and hit me."

"Damn," Sam said. "It must have been terrifying. He drove straight at you?"

"Well, no. He, like, T-boned into me from the left. I didn't see him coming. My car was fine one second and then it was wrecked and then I went home and went to sleep. That's really all there is to it. Sorry this isn't interesting at all."

I kept telling them I was fine and after a while they finally started talking about other things.

By Thursday no one cared about the wreck anymore. Luckily some senior girl got arrested for shoplifting sports bras at the mall, so everyone was talking about that.

I knew I should have been studying for finals and figuring out something to turn in as my project for Meyer, but I wasn't in the mood to do work. When I got home, I watched movies in my room and stayed awake until I couldn't find any more websites to read.

Through my doorframe, I saw Kate creep out of her room at two fifteen a.m. My index finger automatically closed the browser window, even though the thread I'd been reading about symbolism in *A.I. Artificial Intelligence* was far from pornographic. "Why are you up?" I said.

"Hungry." She shrugged, heading downstairs.

She'd made me realize I was hungry, too, and I found her in the kitchen, standing in front of the open fridge, zoned out. The same way I'd stand there when there was something in my head I couldn't get out, and Mom would yell at me that I was wasting electricity. Seeing Kate do it, I saw what Mom was talking about. *Close that door before you ruin the milk, young lady.*

She sighed aggressively and slammed the door, almost like she'd been waiting for me to watch her do it.

She stomped over to the island and yanked the silverware drawer open loud enough to wake Mom and Dad.

"What's your problem?" I said.

"I'm hungry."

"You're obviously mad about something. Just tell me."

She sighed, closed her eyes, and spoke into the drawer. "Am I a bitch?"

Oh, no. "What?"

"Courtney's going to orchestra camp in two weeks and I'm not going because I'm not *in* orchestra."

"O-kay . . ."

"So Courtney found out Priya Leghari is going to the same camp, and we barely ever even talk to Priya Leghari, but all of a sudden they're best friends and they said they drank a beer at Priya's mom's house last weekend and they're making all these plans and talking about how it's gonna be the best summer ever and so I didn't give Courtney the birthday card I made for her and she found out and got mad and called me a bitch in front of everyone."

"Wait — you *made* her a card? For her birthday?"

She looked up at me. "Yeah . . ."

"Huh," I said, confused by such blatant displays of affection between friends.

"How come you and Luke and the other guy never fight?"

She had an interesting perspective on the perpetual pseudo-feud between me and my supposed best friends. "We do," I said. "It's just . . . different, I guess."

We stood facing each other for what felt like three hours. It was by far the longest amount of time I'd ever spent in a room with Kate by ourselves.

"So?" she said impatiently.

I jumped. "So what?"

She rolled her eyes. "So what should I do? About Courtney?"

"Oh. I guess . . . Why don't you, uh, just find some random other girl and start making plans with her, real loud, when Courtney walks by?"

Kate narrowed her eyes at me.

"Just say you're gonna, like, go on a life-changing cross-country road trip with this girl to meet whichever celebrity your grade thinks is cool. Then Courtney will be, like,

'Goddamn, I should've kept hanging out with Kate this summer. Priya Leghari's the worst.'"

Kate's face soured. "That's your advice?"

I shrugged. "Wait, do you still have the card?"

"Yeah. Why?" she asked suspiciously.

"You should just give it to her. You have the card made for her, so what else are you gonna do with it? It's pretty much just trash to anyone except her if her name's on it."

"My card's not *trash*."

"No, no, no, no, no," I said, holding my hands out to tame her like she was a lion. "I just mean you can't do anything else with it, right? So just give it to her and you'll be the better person. Take your emotions out of it and take the high road."

She balled her hands into fists, grunted, "Ugh!" and stomped past me upstairs.

Jesus. Sorry for trying to help. I took a Pop-Tart from the pantry back to my room. I scrolled through more forum posts, but after a while I was only thinking about Kate

What had I told her? *"Take your emotions out of it and take the high road"*? I'd said it without even thinking, factory-produced nonsense that had infected my mind from movies or books or made-for-TV movies based on books. A pre-programmed script like "What's up? Not much. You?" that our brains use to coast through life. Realizing the advice had spilled out of me the same way it would from an unprepared substitute teacher freaked me out. How much longer until I loaded up more of these manufactured slogan bullets and suddenly I'm an adult sleepwalking through workweeks while my esophagus burst-fires, *How are you? I hate Mondays. It's hump day. I'm working for the weekend. Thank god it's Friday.*

What the hell was I doing giving advice, anyway? The highlight of my week was receiving an email from Amazon about other DVDs I might enjoy.

I licked the last Pop-Tart crumbs off my fingers and vowed to stay out of Kate's middle-school business.

34.

On Friday, Will offered to drive us all to a movie after school. But the idea of packing into Will's car and letting him drive in after-school rush-hour traffic freaked me out. Every way I imagined it, we'd be smashed up and sprawled out in bloody heaps on the side of the road. The more I thought about it, the concept of driving seemed insane. We let any jackass who stayed awake long enough to get a driver's education certificate blast around in two-ton chunks of gasoline-filled metal, ten inches apart, on narrow, unlit two-lane roads? Honestly, why aren't lanes forty feet wide? There should be wrecks all the time. It's a miracle anyone ever makes it to the grocery store alive.

At lunch I just told the guys I had a family thing and couldn't go. They walked past me in the carpool line that afternoon. Mom would drive me home, nice and slow.

By six forty-five that night I was in my uniform, pajamas and earbuds, stationed at my post in my room behind the keyboard, cruising through the internet. Kate had been in her room with the door shut all afternoon. When she hadn't come down earlier to get the pizza Mom ordered, I started wondering about her. She shared a lot of my DNA, so there was a good chance she was lying on her floor, listening to music, and soaking in her own misery. But she was younger, and a girl. Maybe it wasn't the same. I'd spent every night of my life sleeping twenty feet away from her, but I felt like I barely knew her and didn't understand her. I'd never really taken her seriously. I still felt bad about giving her terrible advice the other night. If someone had said that to me, it would have annoyed the shit out of me. And she was probably still torn up about her friend drama, but she'd never open up to me again. If she was like me, she was probably stuck in a storm of self-hatred, and I felt sick about that.

I walked over to her closed door and hesitated. I wanted to knock on it and reach out to connect with her, but I had no idea what I was doing. Beside her door was a trash bag filled with junk for Dad to take to Goodwill. Maybe there was something in there that'd connect us. I dragged it back into my room, eased the door closed, and rooted through.

There was a bunch of horse-related garbage. Thank god,

that phase was ending. There was a sweatshirt from some acting camp I had no recollection of her attending. The *Sisterhood of the Traveling Pants* movie soundtrack. A bunch of plastic rings. Did those mean something to her? Had she loved everything in this bag at some point, or was it just trash?

At the bottom of the bag were a bunch of books — all by Judy Blume. Kate had been obsessed with these books when she was in third or fourth grade, and all the girls in my elementary school had read them, too. Maybe if I consumed the media she did at a formative age, I could start to understand her. It was worth a shot — and it's not like I had anything else to do. I sat against the wall on my bed and started reading.

Huh.

I got sucked in.

Hours passed. Every few chapters I'd look up to confirm I was alone, nestle deeper into the covers, and fall back inside the minds of young girls.

I rushed from one book to the next as soon as I finished. I read *Deenie* and *Blubber* and *Are You There God? It's Me, Margaret.*

Man. The girls in those books go through some serious stuff. Margaret worries about stuffing her bra and thinks she's weird for not getting her period when her friend does, and she has the balls to question her parents' religion. In *Blubber*, Jill realizes she's a bully, then gets bullied back and has the sack to stand up for herself. Deenie has scoliosis and defies her mom, who wants her to become a model. Plus, not that it's the point of the book or anything, but Deenie strokes off like she's captain of the varsity masturbating squad, which is the kind of detail anyone can enjoy.

Girls have it so much worse than guys in middle school. Their puberty is on full display. Everyone at school can see how big their boobs are and compare them to the other girls' instantly. What a goddamned nightmare that must be. If it was normal for guys to wear spandex bicycle shorts all the time and everyone could see how tiny our dicks are in sixth grade, every boy would be openly weeping in the hallways, begging for mercy, going to the bathroom in groups to console each other, telling the other guys their shirts are cute because we're desperate to have someone say something nice back to us. Girls can't just exist; they're also on display. They have to be beautiful and smart and caring and sexual enough to not be labeled strange but not so sexual they violate the dress code. If I had to face the added pressure girls do, my body would have compressed itself into a walnut years ago. Every girl should be given a medal on the last day of each grade from sixth through twelfth for the accomplishment of not leaping to her death from a cliff.

I tore through pages of those books faster than I ever did when I read what Meyer had given me — the short stories that were poetic allegories and metaphors mixed with opaque social commentary and had won awards no one had ever heard of. Ugh. Why couldn't those writers just get to it like Judy Blume does? It wasn't just that those books were a window into all the secret things girls have to deal with, though. It was the clarity those narrators had about their own feelings that floored me. They could grasp what was like vapor to me.

I thought about myself when I was Kate's age and how emotionally stunted I'd been. Seventh-grade me was a blob that rolled around from my house to the bus to the classroom, searching for snacks and the sounds of other guys making jokes about penises. I didn't know anything about what went on inside my friends' heads the way Kate knows and constantly rambles about every emotion Courtney's ever felt. Middle-school me was a human corn dog incapable of making decisions, whose strongest memories are the times kids accidentally farted in class.

In seventh grade, Luke, Will, and I made Rebecca Kleene cry. We were just bored in class one day, and she sat next to us, and we saw her write her name on a worksheet. Luke said, "Kleenex." Will and I started saying it, too. "What's up, Kleenex?" She turned red and walked out of the room, sniffling back tears. I had no idea what had happened. I just thought we were being dumb and saying something stupid for no reason. After it happened, we never talked about making her cry. We didn't feel like we'd done anything wrong.

But Rebecca Kleene had feelings. It didn't matter that we were just messing around about her name and not actually making fun of anything specific about her. We'd made her feel like shit. If she hadn't moved to Montana three years ago, I would have tried to apologize.

Goddamn it. What else had I done that I should feel terrible about? I felt like up until then the only feelings I understood in myself were anger, self-loathing, and frustration. I had the emotional breadth of a Limp Bizkit album. I'd gone sixteen years without truly addressing my emotions like a developed human being. In the book, Margaret develops boobs over her year. I was starting to develop basic emotional intelligence. I needed to stop being such a coward and stare down my feelings like Margaret did.

I pulled up the texts Luke, Will, Alex, and Emma had sent me on Tuesday, asking me where I was and how I was doing. I'd been mad that they cared about me? I was annoyed they acknowledged the most notable thing that had happened in my entire life, and were confirming I wasn't dead?

How much of my shitty year was my fault? I pictured everything I'd done all year from Luke's and Will's and Sam's and Patrick's and Emma's and Alex's perspectives. Alex and Emma waved and smiled and talked to me all spring, and I barely reacted. I was paranoid they were secretly making fun of me or that they pitied me or something. I didn't let myself believe they might actually just be being nice.

How many times had Luke and Will tried to invite me to things and I'd turned them down? How many times had they made an effort to include me, and I'd blown them off? And what had staying home alone gotten me? I'd only made myself sadder.

Objectively I had a good life, and I was wasting it wallowing in self-pity. Sure, I had bad acne. But who gives a shit? Plenty of kids around the world have bad acne *and* are fleeing from war. I had high-speed internet in my room. And it's not like acne was the only reason I didn't have a girlfriend. I didn't know anything about girls, or how to be a decent human being around them. I remembered the time a few weeks before when I'd sat at my desk looking up religions and fantasizing about having Emma "help me choose one." I was such a clueless dumb-ass. I thought I could try on faith like it was a baseball cap. And what the hell was I doing putting on a Blink-182 T-shirt to attract Emma, like a peacock showing off his colorful butthole to a potential suitor? My grand plan after she fawned over my T-shirt was to teach her about more obscure bands? What kind of pretentious dick would I have been, lecturing this uninterested girl about Sunny Day Real Estate? And why couldn't I just admit I genuinely loved Blink-182? Why couldn't I bear the idea of admitting I liked a band everyone else liked? How'd I benefit from denying myself all the things I had in common with other people?

And what was wrong with me that I thought Luke couldn't go out with Alex because of some nonexistent rule about having dibs on her? Alex was never mine and she wasn't Luke's, either. This wasn't the 1700s — girls didn't *belong* to anyone. I bet Luke didn't think Emma was off-limits to me just because they'd dated last year for three months, and I bet it never crossed his mind that someone would think he had dibs on a girl just because he'd supposedly met her at a writing class before anyone else met her. No wonder Alex preferred Luke over me! He treated girls like human beings, not like trophies in some unspoken contest with his friends. Plus, he didn't vibrate with stress like a fucking tuning fork 24/7 — and he didn't spend hours sitting around trying to come up with the perfect TV shows to compare real people to in these metaphors no one should ever know about. Had I really compared Alex to *The Simpsons* and Emma to *Scrubs*? Jesus Christ, those were the thoughts of a dangerous, deranged virgin.

I'd assumed I was better than other guys my age because I wasn't obsessed with porn-star-looking babes, but how was fetishizing Alex's taste in music and movies last fall any different from ogling some supermodel's massive rack? My eyeballs blasted out of my skull at Alex's imagined reading habits the same way Luke's did at his mom's Victoria's Secret catalogs.

How well did I even know Alex, anyway? She'd had more of an influence on my life than anyone, but how much did I actually know about her? I knew who her friends were and some movies and music she liked. I knew that she had bad skin and she'd transferred schools. The more I thought about each fact I knew, the more hollow it all felt — an unfinished connect-the-dots outline of her. I'd been too stuck in my head at all of our appointments trying to think of ways to impress her to actually get to know her.

For months I'd been scrutinizing my face to see if the Accutane was having an effect, but what if the thing it had been changing was my mind? What if the reason I couldn't get out of my head and engage with her was the medicine?

The list of potential side effects was so long and so broad, anyone could see themselves in it. It was like a horoscope. Were my mood swings, anxiety, and dark thoughts because of the pills, or were they all just side effects of being sixteen?

Had I been sad before the pills? I'd written those words in my notebook in seventh grade about my life sucking and hating Mom, but I didn't describe any specifics or bother to address those feelings beyond writing my own dumb clickbait headlines that linked to nothing. I didn't have the courage to think my anger through. I used to stay home from school with fake stomachaches, telling myself I just felt like lying in bed all day because it was fun. But it was never fun; I was just trading stress for loneliness. How many times had I convinced myself I wanted to be invisible, and then felt disappointed when no one looked at me? Was something off about me, years before I ever had acne? How many feelings had I been in denial about, from when I was a kid up through the car wreck?

As soon as those words crossed my mind, I pushed the thoughts of the car wreck out of my head again.

No. Stop being a coward. Think about it. Let the memory back in. Hold on to it.

I closed my eyes and took a deep breath and put myself back in the car the night of the wreck. All week I'd convinced myself the car wreck wasn't a big deal. But both cars were destroyed beyond repair. How bad had it actually been? And why was I afraid to confront it?

I breathed harder. I felt the airbag punch my face, scrape my arms. My hands quaked. The airbag dust stank like eggs and felt like sand on my lips.

I rewound the memory, trying to focus on the moments just before the crash. The other driver had gone through the stop sign. He'd made the mistake. Legally it was his fault. But why didn't I see him and stop? I knew people ran through that stop sign all the time. I'd done it. If I hadn't been so stuck in my head, obsessed with my own thoughts . . . if I'd taken driver's ed seriously and remembered to not drive when angry and distracted . . . I knew everything I needed to know to avoid that wreck, but I hadn't used it. Why?

Was that the question I was scared of? What I hadn't wanted to acknowledge all week? Had some part of my brain taken over my body, distracting me with awful thoughts about myself, hoping I'd get in a wreck that looked like an accident?

If that other driver hadn't hit me, would I have kept driving until someone else did? Would I have taken my hands off the wheel and let the car drift off the road and into a tree?

I choked up and squeezed my eyelids shut. Those were more than suicidal thoughts; they were subconscious suicidal plans.

Something was off about me. Maybe the pills made it worse. How could I know? I had already been planning on starting a second round of treatment at the regular dosage as soon as Dr. Sharp would sign off on it, but would it be worth it if the side effects got worse and the grand prize at the end of all this was having a clear face at my open-casket funeral?

Or maybe the pills were just an easy excuse to not deal with my shit.

I opened my eyes and made a vow to myself: I would do my best to take control of my life and crawl out of the hole I'd buried myself in. But if I made the effort and still felt stuck in this invisible trap all the time, I'd stop taking the pills for good. If that meant sacrificing my skin to save the rest of me, then so be it.

35.

I knocked on the locked door from our bathroom into Kate's
room.

"What?" she said from behind it.

"It's me," I said.

"Why?"

"Do you want to talk?"

"About what?"

"Can you just open the door? This is weird."

She opened it and stared at me.

"I'm sorry," I said.

"For what?"

"Well, I guess, first for, like, my terrible advice about the birthday card thing. But, also, when I flipped out and yelled at you and Courtney the other day."

Her face didn't move. "Oh. Yeah."

"That was mean. Sorry."

"Uh . . . okay."

She was unimpressed. She looked at me like I had the plague, and I cracked up.

"What?" she said.

"It's just funny. You find me disgusting."

"Correct."

I laughed again.

"What are you laughing at?"

"You and me are pretty similar."

"No."

"We'll probably be friends one day."

"Okay . . . ?"

"Oh, I pulled your Judy Blume books out of your Goodwill bag. You should keep them."

"Who gave you permission to touch my stuff?"

"It was in the Goodwill bag. It wasn't yours anymore."

"It wasn't *at* Goodwill yet."

Normally I would've spun around and abandoned her after a comment like that. Instead I said, "Can I sit down?"

She shrugged and I sat on her bed. She stood in front of me with her arms crossed.

"Tell me again what's going on with you and Courtney and that other girl."

"Priya?"

"Yeah, sure."

She frowned. "They're the worst. Like, since when do they drink beer? I don't get it. Do I have to drink, too? Is that just what we do now?"

"Yeah, that sounds frustrating," I said.

"Yeah," she said, sitting down beside me. "I mean, do they even want to? Or do they just, like, think they're supposed to?"

"That's a good question, yeah," I said.

"*I* don't want to drink. I don't care about beer! Why would I care? But now it's like I'm some loser if I don't. What if they go away to camp and drink and, like, do drugs in the woods and stuff while I'm stuck at home?"

"Do you want to do drugs in the woods?"

"No! I don't think they want to, either. It's not even peer pressure, since no one is telling them to do it. It's just, like, *pressure* pressure. Like some voice whispering to everyone. It's annoying. I *don't* want to do that stuff, but I feel left out when they do it. It doesn't even matter what it is. If they, like, started playing the saxophone and I didn't, it'd be the same thing."

"That'd be very cool if instead of drugs, everyone at your school was pressured into taking up the saxophone."

"I just feel left out, but I know it's stupid, since they're only at camp for two weeks. So I should just find other stuff to do while they're gone and I'll be okay, right? Like, they'll come back and if they're really my friends we'll keep being friends and if they're not, then I don't want to be their friend anymore."

I nodded. "Yeah. I think that's right." Is that the secret to advice? Just listen to someone until they figure it out themselves? Do we all have the answers lodged inside us like deep-rooted blackheads we have to squeeze out ourselves? "You know, me and Luke and Will had kind of a similar thing this year."

"No, you didn't. You guys never have drama."

"Eh . . . our drama might not be as, uh, *obvious,* I guess, as the stuff with you and your friends, but just because you don't see it doesn't mean it's not there. They joined the football team and I got lonely and sad. I felt left out. But it was all me. They never stopped trying to include me and be my friend, but I kind of made it hard for them."

It all sounded so simple and dumb when I said it out loud. She looked up and smiled at me, like she respected me for the first time in her entire life. "So it's okay now?"

"Uh, not yet. I still need to, like, talk to them. But it'll be good. I'll come clean and be honest and we'll all feel better."

She nodded and I stood up and wondered for a second if we should hug or something, but decided that would be too weird. I went back to my room and lay in bed thinking about how I'd always dreamed of having some fantasy older sister who told me how to interact with girls, who gave me all the secrets. But maybe that sister didn't have to be older. Maybe Kate could be the kind of sister I'd always wanted, if I gave her the chance. And I could be the emotionally available older brother who'd tell her how to talk to boys and get through bad times. She'd get acne and I'd pass on my wisdom about face washes. And she'd remind me to confront my sadness and anger head-on.

The advice I'd been looking for all year had been on Kate's bookshelf — and in Kate's head — the whole time.

I picked up the trash bag Dad had left in my room and dumped the Gentleman books into it.

They hadn't helped me; they'd just added more noise in my head. There weren't rules and instructions to follow for having conversations and connecting with other people. Why are guys bound to keep repeating this dumb quest to codify everything into lists and brackets and instructions? If I believed in those rules for being a guy and kept ignoring my feelings, suddenly I'd be fifty years old and thinking I'd accomplished something by watching a movie about cancer and not crying.

Saturday morning, Mom walked downstairs while I was eating cereal in front of the family room TV.

"Hey, Mom?"

"Yeah?"

"When I was in middle school, did I, like, yell at you? In seventh grade specifically, was there some time I was really mad?"

She raised her eyebrows. "You'd yell sometimes, but it's fine. We knew it was hormones."

"Huh. I'm . . . I'm really sorry."

She laughed. "It's fine."

"No, seriously. I'm so sorry."

"It's okay, bud. It's normal."

I laughed a little. She said, "Want to see a movie? Your pick. Anything you want. My treat."

That was usually my cue to mumble that I was busy and then slump in front of the computer to read online movie trivia with headphones on for six hours. But I said, "Sure, let's do it."

She opened the newspaper to the movie listings and I looked through them with her and said, "I'll see whatever you want. Promise. I'll honestly be happy with anything."

"Really?" she said, curling her mouth into a devilish smile.

I smiled back — a living, breathing positive mental attitude.

The movie was bad. On the way out, I told her I had a good time and I was happy we saw it together. I wasn't lying.

That night Kate had Courtney over and Mom read a romance novel on the couch while Dad watched baseball with his Braves hat on.

"Hey, Dad?" I said after psyching myself up for twenty minutes.

"Yeah?" he said, looking at the TV.

"Why are you, uh, a Braves fan?"

"I've lived in Atlanta my whole life. Hometown team."

"Yeah, I know, but, like, don't the players change every few years? So isn't it kind of weird that people are just fans of, like, a team name and logo?"

"It's the spirit of the team," he mumbled at the screen. "The hope of being great stays consistent, passes through every new player. The team evolves gradually, always looking for the perfect combination of players."

Huh. From what I understood, baseball's primary purpose was to provide metaphors for everything in life. I considered opening up to him, explaining how just like the Atlanta Braves I'd also maintained some hope of becoming better all year while the cells in my body gradually changed. But it wasn't the right time. Maybe someday I'd explain all that. Instead I said, "How long is a, uh, typical baseball game?"

"Around three hours."

"Cool."

I turned to go to the basement, but I stopped and asked Dad if he wanted to play golf next weekend. We hadn't done that since I was in sixth or seventh grade. That got him to look up from the TV. "Really?" he said. "I'd love that. I didn't think you wanted to play anymore."

"It'll be fun. Good to get outside."

"Absolutely. Next Saturday at ten?"

There wouldn't be much conversation between us, but there's depth when Dad talks logistics. He's all subtext, a puzzle for me to decipher. To hear him analyze the layout of a parking lot is like watching a French new wave film. I told him ten was perfect.

Late that night, I heard Mom, Dad, and Kate laughing at the TV downstairs. I shut down my computer and sat on the couch beside Kate to watch an unbelievably unfunny sitcom with them. It felt like we were a family again, for the first time in a while.

Sunday night I tried to figure out exactly what to say to everyone at school. I thought about calling Alex and telling her I was sorry I'd been acting so weird and I'd let my emotions and screwed-up hormones get the better of me, and I was going to try to be normal from now on. Then I'd call up Luke and Will and tell them the same thing, and we'd start talking about some hilarious memories from the greatest hits of our friendship and then we'd roll into some new ideas for things to do, and then we'd close with some words of mutual respect for one another. I'd skateboard into school with my hands out for high fives, cruising toward anxiety-free friendship, and we'd wrap up the school year having squirt-gun fights and making sincerely silly faces at the lunch table for the yearbook photographers.

Eh.

Call everyone and tell them I'd try to be normal from now on. That sounded like the kind of thing a psychopath says. Besides, I can't call my friends just to chat. That's bizarre. Only our moms do that to talk about us. Luke and Will would have found it weird and creepy and word would spread that I was calling people in the middle of the night and must be standing on the roof of my house about to throw myself to my death. I didn't need to make any big announcements. I would just go to school tomorrow and stop being an asshole.

I turned on my TV and the idea of calling everyone for heart-to-heart conversations was gradually replaced by footage of a driveway getting pressure-washed on a home renovation show.

36.

I'd told myself everything would be different on Monday since I'd snapped myself out of my rut and had a fresh, clear outlook on life. But even though I'd been able to start acting normal around my family, it was impossible not to fall back into my routine at school. In that setting I was locked in the habits I'd honed over a decade, a supporting character trapped in the nine hundredth episode of a sitcom. I nodded at Luke and Will, hoping that subtle motion conveyed that I'd made a big personal step forward over the weekend, and that they'd all understand and forgive me, and we could move on without having to say anything. They nodded back, but I didn't get the sense they fully understood my emotional arc.

* * *

On the way to lunch, I found an opportunity to try again. Emma stood with Jen Evans at a table selling doughnuts to raise money for the club of Christian athletes to go on some mission trip to build a school in Costa Rica over the summer. Did it sound like a bullshit charity to pay for wealthy kids' vacations? Of course. But I had two dollars and instead of ignoring them and rushing to my table, I bought a doughnut. I smiled at them and Emma smiled back and said thanks. The girls didn't look at me like my "our song" comment had been the subject of the God Squad's favorite inside joke for the past month. The interaction felt normal. It seemed like a step forward.

When I turned away from them, I realized I didn't want to eat the doughnut, so I walked to Todd Lancaster's table and said, "Do you want a doughnut?"

"Yeah."

He stuffed the entire thing in his mouth and I wondered if I was about to witness someone asphyxiate right before my very eyes. Was this a cry for help? A desperate —? Nope. He swallowed it all; reared back to burp, didn't; leaned over to fart, couldn't; gasped, opened his eyes wide, and sprinted toward the bathroom.

That was two out-of-character steps forward: buying the doughnut from Emma and Jen and giving it to Todd. It wasn't much, but it felt like progress.

From my table, I smiled at Alex. She smiled back. I forced myself not to overthink it. She was happy to see me and I was happy to see her. It felt like things were back to normal between us, but I knew I still needed to explain how sorry I was for acting weird toward her over the past few months. And then I needed to shut up and actually *listen*. Not zone out and wait for a gap to make a sarcastic comment. Stop trying to impress her. Stop trying to win her over, stop thinking of conversations as competitions. Ask her how she was feeling and listen.

I had to find the right moment to prove I was finally ready to be her friend.

Tuesday was my last Accutane blood test appointment. It felt monumental, like the end of an era. I decided to try to apologize to Alex that day at school. No matter what, I knew I'd be thinking about her when I sat in that waiting room alone. I didn't want to have to sit there regretting how I'd treated her for the past six months; I wanted to be able to think about how we'd reset and were okay.

All day I plotted where and how I'd find a quiet moment to talk to her. But she was always with other people. I thought about tapping her shoulder and asking if we could talk privately, but I worried everyone would think I was trying to kidnap her if I led her underneath the staircase by the gym. My only shot would be right when school ended, as the God Squad dispersed like a gas leak throughout the building toward their extracurricular activities.

After the last bell rang, I went straight to her locker, but she was already gone.

I thought about rescheduling my appointment. It didn't *have* to be on a Tuesday, now that I wasn't trying to align with Alex. But what if I couldn't talk to her tomorrow, either, or the next day? I bit my lip and told myself not to spiral into a hundred similes about how doomed our friendship was and how pathetic and hopeless I was. We'd missed each other by a minute. It meant nothing. I'd suck it up and call her that night. It would be awkward at first, but then it'd be fine.

Mom drove me to the blood-testing place and I told her she could come inside with me. I felt bad that I'd made her wait in the car at every appointment all year. Why had that never bothered me before? What a weird thing to do.

She did sudoku in the waiting room while I signed in at the desk. A nurse took me back and I squeezed my eyes shut, but after she pulled the needle out, I looked at the two vials of blood. It was just as disgusting as I remembered from the first time, but I guess it was a relief that it was the last time I'd have to do that.

"Thanks," I said to the nurse. She looked confused. I'd never spoken to her before. "You've always done a great job taking my blood."

"You've always been good," she said. "Or, wait, no. Aren't you the one who puked in the sink?"

"I did, yeah. Sorry about that."

She shook her head, deeply disappointed. I shrugged and walked back into the waiting room —

Where I found Alex sitting three chairs down from Mom.

Mom looked at me and closed her sudoku book, but I flashed her a "Just a sec" sign and walked past her to Alex.

"Hey," I said quietly. She smiled at me and stood up. I could feel Mom watching us. "What are you —? Are you back on . . . ? You don't look —" I took a deep breath. "Hi. What are you doing here?"

"I knew today was your last day. Felt like I should be here."

Mom walked over to us, her face glowing with joy at the sight of me interacting with a girl, and I only hesitated a second before saying, "Mom, this is Alex. She's a friend — from school. And . . . outside of school. From here, actually. Just, like —"

"It's nice to meet you, Alex."

Alex smiled back. "You, too."

"Do you need a ride home or anything?"

"Well, if it's all right with you, I was hoping Kevin and I could hang out for a little while. I can drive us back home."

"Sure, sweetie. You two have fun." She winked at me in this disturbing way that almost seemed like she was hoping I'd have sex with Alex, and then she left.

37.

I followed Alex to that picnic bench around the back of the office. It was painfully bright and so hot that I started sweating instantly, but I didn't mind.

"How was the last one?" she said. "Feel good to be done?"

"I guess. I mean, it doesn't feel like that much changed on my face, but I don't know. It was so gradual that maybe it did."

"Your skin looks better. I can confirm."

I smiled, then took in a deep breath and told myself to nut up and channel the emotional bravery of a twelve-year-old girl.

"I, uh, I . . . Look, I'm really sorry. I've been a weird jerk these past few months. I didn't . . . I wasn't actually listening when you first told me you were transferring to my school, so when I saw you that day, in the hallway, I kind of freaked out. I was embarrassed for my friends to find out I was on Accutane and I—" I winced, but plowed ahead: "I kind of didn't want to share you with anyone. You were like this secret I had, and this place"—I gestured vaguely to the park and the doctors' offices and parking deck behind it—"seemed kind of, I don't know . . . special. I didn't want to lose that."

She didn't say anything for so long that I started to wonder if I had only imagined spewing all of that at her. Was the heat melting my brain? Or maybe it was the Accutane. Was I having hallucinations? It wasn't too late to tell Dr. Sharp to cancel my last month's prescription.

But then Alex tilted her head. "Why didn't you just tell the guys you were on Accutane? I don't think any of them would actually care, do you?"

I shrugged. "Probably not. But, like—I know this is gonna sound stupid, but we never really talk about my acne. And if I told them I was on Accutane, well, suddenly it's this thing that's out in the open. I mean, my face is already visible to everyone, but just . . ." I smiled weakly. "Like I said, this is all stupid."

"No, I get it," she said, looking thoughtful. "I just wish you could've told me all this earlier. I wanted to hang out with you when I switched schools, but instead it always felt kind of . . . weird. Like you resented me for being there or something."

"I guess I did," I admitted, hating myself for it. "But not because you were, like, meeting my friends or whatever. I guess I figured you'd stop wanting to be friends with me once you had better options. I mean, you fell in with the God Squad almost instantly. . . ."

"What's the God Squad?"

"Jen and Haley and Veronica and Emma and all them?"

She laughed. "Why do you call them the God Squad?"

I shrugged. "Just because they make this big point of being Christians and whatever. Like with all their fake charities and church camp T-shirts and stuff."

She stopped laughing. "You know they all volunteer at the hospital every Saturday, right? And they really do raise a lot of money for homeless people and stuff."

"Huh. For real?"

She nodded. "They raised enough money for Mark's surgery."

"Who?"

"Emma's brother? He had a brain tumor?"

"What?"

"You didn't know?"

"How was I supposed to? No one tells me anything."

"Did you ask? Or did you just assume that their fundraising was, like, part of some elaborate scam . . . ?"

"Yes . . . ?"

"For their final project for Meyer's class, they're making this video about some of the people they helped with all the different fund-raisers they did this year. They did coat drives and programs to get people to recycle or donate books or money to help build schools around the world."

"Jesus Christ. Shit. Welp." I could no longer consider myself superior to the God Squad because I'd seen *Being John Malkovich* and they hadn't. "Hang on, though. Like, is it true that Haley's dad was an extra in the rave scene of *The Matrix Reloaded*?"

"What?"

"The Zion rave. With Morpheus."

"What?"

"I've spent a ton of time on IMDB and, like, I don't think extras get credited, so there's no way for me to know for sure."

"I have no idea what you're talking about."

"It's the only thing anyone knows about Haley."

She narrowed her eyes. "It sounds like it's the only thing you've chosen to know about Haley."

I nodded. "Yeah. Fair point." I squinted against the sun. "Hey, can I ask you something else?"

She shrugged. "Sure."

"Well, what about their music? Like, the pop-country stuff? And, like, NSYNC or whatever. Are you into that or are you into, like, Elliott Smith?"

She looked confused, and for a moment I thought she had somehow figured out that I'd creeped on her and the other girls dancing along to "Bye Bye Bye" from the darkened street below Emma's window. But what she said was "Uh, all of the above? What, am I not allowed to like different types of music?"

"Huh." I had to stop asking her questions because the answer to all of them was that I was a dumb-ass. There were never two versions of Alex. She was just herself. And anyway, it's not like taste in media has anything to do with being a good person. If there is a heaven, it will one day be full of people who saw *The Fast and the Furious: Tokyo Drift* opening weekend.

"One last question . . ." I said, taking a deep breath. She nodded gamely. "Are you and Luke . . . ? I mean . . . Like, what's going on between you two?"

She rolled her eyes. "Oh, that. No. I was interested for, like, a few days, but then I came to my senses. I mean, I know he's your friend and all — and he's not a bad guy or anything — but sometimes you talk to somebody and just realize it doesn't click, you know?" She bit her lip. "Sorry if that put you in a weird position or something. I probably shouldn't have called you like that."

"No, I get it. It's okay." I nodded and turned away to hide my smile. I knew it was dumb to continue this made-up competition with Luke, but goddamn did it feel good to see him strike out. "Oh, wait, so what does 'socks' mean?"

"Is that, like, a riddle or something? And what's with all the questions? You realize that there wouldn't be all this mystery if you'd just talked to me these past few months."

"I know. I'm an idiot. But I'm working on that."

"So, what about socks?"

"On Facebook, Carter Canton posted 'socks' on your wall after the middle-school thing and it's been kind of bugging me trying to figure out what that meant."

"Oh, that. At the middle school we saw a pair of socks on the floor by the lockers and he laughed at it."

"That was it?"

"Yeah."

"Was it funny?"

"No."

"Why'd you respond 'lol'?"

"Did I?" She shrugged. "Probably because I didn't know what to say, but I felt like I had to respond."

"Wow. All right. Well. Good to know."

"Yep. Sorry it wasn't interesting."

"No, this is good." I laughed a little and said, "I feel left out of that whole night or something, but it was my fault. I could have gone. Just . . . the last few months, I thought I was better off being by myself, watching movies alone on weekends. I thought there was something noble about ignoring high school."

"Yeah," she said. "It's probably not healthy in the long run to romanticize loneliness."

"Uh-huh."

She bit her fingernails and we both sat there for a few seconds. I felt cleansed somehow, unburdened of months of doubt and resentment and anger and baggage. I felt, finally, like a new version of myself — a better version.

"Do you, uh . . ." I squinted. "Do you want to talk about your parents?"

In the background of some of our waiting room talks had been this plotline about her parents' divorce, but I'd been too focused on myself and on trying to win Alex over to actually listen to her.

"Oh, uh . . ." She sounded surprised, and I worried that I'd weirded her out. But then she shrugged. "Sure, I guess. It might be nice to talk to someone about that stuff. If you really don't mind listening?"

I shook my head.

And so she told me about how hard it had been, watching her parents' relationship crumble. At first they fought all the time, but toward the end they barely talked to each other, and that was worse. She told me how she'd had to choose who she wanted to live with, and what an impossible position that put her in, and how she worried that her mom would never forgive her for choosing her dad. "I'd rather live with her, actually. But my dad's struggling with some stuff and I didn't feel right leaving him alone."

"Wow. That sounds super shitty. I'm really sorry. I didn't know you were dealing with . . . whatever, too. I just thought . . . I mean, you always seem, like, good."

"It's probably best to never assume anything is easy for anyone."

"Yeah."

She shrugged. "I mean, some days my life feels super shitty; other days it's fine. At least my parents aren't alternately screaming at each other and ignoring each other anymore."

I nodded, thinking about how lucky I was to have two parents who seemed to genuinely love each other, even if Dad did pare Mom's stories down to size, and even if Mom made fun of Dad for being so impatient.

I looked at Alex, and she was looking at me, too. Our eyes met and held, and we both smiled. How long had it been since we'd actually looked each other in the eyes? For a moment, a flicker of hope burned in my chest. Maybe now that she was seeing the new me, she'd realize that—

"You know, you kind of remind me of my dad," she said.

"Huh?"

She laughed. "Don't look like that. My dad's a great guy."

I was starting to float on those words, imagining her dad was a wildly successful and attractive man, when she followed them up with "But some of the things you've said to me in the past about all your anxieties and stuff . . . well, it made me think of my dad. And I . . . I worry about you sometimes. When I saw you at our first appointment . . . I thought you might be, like, legitimately depressed."

"Wait, what?" My brain was frantically replaying our first appointment. "Is that . . . why you talked to me? Because you were *worried* about me?"

She looked worried now. "I'm sorry! I don't mean to freak you out. I'm not a therapist or anything, obviously. So I could be totally wrong. I just recognized some similar behavior and stuff from things my dad has said and done, and . . . please don't be mad. It's nothing to be ashamed of — assuming I'm even right. Which I might not be."

I was still evaluating my memories of our early meetings, reframing those interactions as interventions rather than proof of her budding love for me.

I blinked and tried to clear my head of the old noise. *Be honest,* I reminded myself. *Don't shy away from your emotions.* I met Alex's eyes again. "Maybe you were right to worry. I think I *was* depressed. I thought maybe it was the Accutane, but I wasn't even on it when I first met you, so if you were noticing the signs then . . ." I shrugged. "Anyway, it doesn't really matter anymore. My car wreck kind of snapped me out of it. Well, that and Judy Blume. I've been figuring out my feelings more. I think in some way the crash, like, cured me."

"Cured you?"

"Yeah."

"Of what?"

"Like . . . I don't know. Sadness or . . . depression, like you said. I confronted it, and things are different now. Better."

She looked at me steadily. "That sounds good, but a car crash isn't really a cure. Even if you feel better now, those other feelings might come back. Depression isn't a thing you can just fix, but you can learn how to handle it." She cringed. "Sorry, I sound like an ad for an antidepressant."

I nodded. "Right. Yeah. Well, I guess I just mean that I figured it out. I figured out what was wrong with me. It wasn't really *depression* or anything as dramatic as that. I just need to stop being an asshole."

She stared into my eyes. I looked back at hers. She didn't look away, and neither did I. Locked in a game of chicken.

Was I being honest with her? With myself? Finally I caved. "I mean, I might have been depressed or whatever." She kept looking into my eyes. I cleared my throat. "Like, even before this year. For a while. And I guess there's a chance I might still be depressed," I acknowledged. "Maybe not as bad as your dad or whatever," I added quickly. "But, yeah, I was having really bad thoughts about myself the night of my car wreck, and . . .

337

I mean, I feel good right now, but . . . I guess that if that urge was real and it just sprung itself on me, that maybe it could happen again."

She nodded supportively. She'd pulled it out of me, but I didn't feel embarrassed or ashamed. I felt relieved.

"You don't have to compare yourself to anyone," she said. "It's not a competition. However bad you feel is how bad it is. And you can't blame everything on yourself. It might be more complicated than that. There's chemical and genetic stuff that's part of it."

I knew she was right. It was easier to take the concern when it came from her. Advice always sounds like bullshit when it's the wrong person or the wrong time, but it's magic when it's the right person at the right time, and you're open and vulnerable and ready to accept it.

"If you want, I can text my dad and get his therapist's number?"

"Oh, uh . . ." It was one thing to talk about my hypothetical depression. I wasn't sure how I felt about taking concrete steps toward addressing it, though.

"Look," she said, "if you want pizza, you call the pizza place. If you're feeling really down, you call this guy and get an appointment. It's as simple as that."

"Yeah. Okay. I guess I probably can't just fix myself. Thanks." It felt monumental and casual at the same time, the way she always made me feel.

"And if you start seeing the therapist and feel weird about

it and want to keep it a secret, I'll tell everyone that you're taking another writing class."

I smiled.

"Wait," I said, sounding more serious than I was. "You said depression can be genetic?"

"Yeah."

"That's interesting because now that you mention it, I'm remembering my dad sawed his head off in front of me on Christmas morning, my mom drowned herself, my grandfather flew a helicopter into a mountain, and then my three other grandparents made a pact and stood in a triangle and all shot each other at the same time. Does this put me at risk?" She looked scared for half a second and I laughed. "If this is a real thing I have to deal with, I hope I'm at least allowed to make fun of it."

She smiled a little and shook her head at me. I realized the reason I'd liked her was never because she wore a perfectly fitted T-shirt or understood my movie references. I liked her because she was nice to me and she cared about other people.

She said, "So, what else is going on with you recently? You haven't told me, like, anything about your life in months."

"Oh, yeah, um . . . I guess . . ." I didn't know where to start. "Not much. I mostly just sit around in different chairs."

"Come on. *Something* must have happened."

"Not really," I said instinctively. And then I remembered that wasn't true at all. "Wait, no. Something did happen to me recently."

"Oh, yeah?"

"I was stomping around the golf course all pissed off and alone one night, and I tripped and fell into a pond full of goose shit."

She laughed. "Are you serious?"

"Yeah. And then, I swear to god, I went home and my entire family plus my sister's friend and a plumber were in my room unclogging a year's worth of tissues from, uh . . . you know—from my toilet." *Oh, no.* A second too late, I realized that was a way more embarrassing story than I'd realized when I'd started telling it.

"Wow."

"Yeah."

"Wait. You flushed tissues?"

"Yeah."

"You're not supposed to flush anything but toilet paper."

"How does everyone know this but me?"

"They drill it into girls' heads about tampons."

"Unbelievable. Girls are always five steps ahead."

She laughed. Talking to her, *really* talking to her, felt great—natural and easy and fun. "I'm sorry, again, that I screwed everything up. We had these appointments together where we had each other and could ignore everything else, and I screwed it all up the last few times. I shouldn't have ruined this. I guess we can hope we'll both get some blood disease and wind up back here together."

"There's nothing magic about that waiting room," she said.

"It was special because we were honest with each other. It can be like that out in the real world, too."

I looked at the ground, biting my lip and smiling.

"You wanna get something to eat?" she said.

"Yeah, let's do it."

She pulled my hand open and slapped her car keys into it. "You're driving."

I held them out to her. "I, uh . . . I still feel weird about . . ."

"I know. That's why you have to drive. We won't play music. You can go ten under the speed limit. I'll be there to help."

Her face was bright and open, in a way that reminded me of the first time I saw her. I couldn't help smiling. "All right."

We walked into the parking deck to Alex's Jeep. I put the keys in the ignition, took a deep breath, squeezed the steering wheel, and eased out of the parking space as slowly as possible.

Alex applauded.

At the intersection to turn onto the road, I waited until I got a green left arrow, made sure no one was coming from either side, then crept out and made the turn. I breathed steadily and felt calm. I was by far the slowest person on the road. Everyone else could go around me and have fun slamming into each other. I was perfectly fine back where I was, driving twenty miles an hour.

I must have looked like an idiot with my goofy grin, but I didn't really care. I wasn't obsessing over what I assumed Alex thought of me. I wasn't scripting my next line. I wasn't scared to drive. I was present.

It felt how I always wanted it to feel with her. It felt right.

I'd call Alex's dad's therapist. There was a chance he'd tell me I was just your typical stressed-out sixteen-year-old kid with acne and normal problems everyone experiences and it was fine for me to go back on Accutane. Or maybe he'd tell me there was more to it than that; something serious was off about me. Maybe he'd say the pills messed with my head and I shouldn't go back on them. I could deal with that. I'd easily choose being able to laugh again with my friends through my bleeding, zit-ridden face over sitting in my silent room with perfect skin, alone and feeling nothing.

Or maybe the therapist would tell me to stop searching for some simple explanation for how I felt. If I was depressed, I probably had been for a long time, and it was more complicated than a pill. What's the point of obsessively searching for some clear-cut excuse when there was no way to know for sure? Whatever caused it, I knew I had a problem and should work to get help and move forward instead of stalling, stuck in my head searching for a scapegoat in all these vaporous feelings.

Whatever happened, I'd deal with it head-on. And I knew Alex would be around if I needed her, just like I'd be around if she needed me. We were two people who seemed to get each other — maybe better than anyone else could.

38.

The second-to-last week of school, Meyer handed out a worksheet to everyone with just one sentence at the top: "If you could rename the school's football team, what would it be?" Luke and Will turned their desks toward each other and I stared at the paper by myself for a few minutes, trying to figure out what deep, hidden meaning Meyer thought this meaningless busywork assignment had. Was this a reference to some book no one had heard of? I wondered about what kind of intellectual nonsense he'd want us to write, but nothing came to me.

I got up and dragged my desk over to Luke and Will, and when I sat down, I saw a detailed, grotesque drawing of a man teabagging a cast-iron grill Will had drawn on the paper under the heading "The Sizzling Scrotums." It was the sort of image that makes you wonder what other people think of your group of friends. How did he draw it so quickly? Was that image stored in his muscle memory? Was that what Will did all day at school?

I laughed at it.

"You're into this name?" Luke said.

"Definitely," I said. "I mean, if there's one unquestionable, slam-dunk name that would unite the student body and get approved by the school board without making anyone uncomfortable, it's the Sizzling Scrotums."

The paper asked for an explanation of the suggestion. "Oh, and here, for the explanation part, say . . ." And I took Will's pen and wrote without thinking, just making dumb stuff up to entertain myself like I had done back when I first started writing: "At the stroke of midnight, an army of students surrounds the football field under spotlights and punishing rain, clutching George Foremans at their crotches. Orange extension cords run up the stadium steps like jungle vines and the grills hiss, a chorus of a million snakes. Angry and determined, we chant: We are no longer bristling, dwindling, middling, sickening. We are thickening, stiffening, and it's greatness you are witnessing, for our scrotums now and forever shall be sizzling."

It felt like doing a prank call with them like we used to. It was the only time I'd enjoyed writing in months. I was sure Meyer would immediately send us to the principal's office. Whatever. It was fun.

"Did you learn that stuff in that writing class thing you took with Alex?" Luke said.

Oh, shit. "No, uh . . . not exactly." I needed to explain that that whole thing had been a lie. But there never seemed like a good opportunity at school. "I was just kind of making fun of the weird poetry crap Meyer likes."

Luke laughed. "Oh, yeah. It's like rap, but worse in every way."

Will took the paper up to turn in and I cringed, turning my head away from Meyer but glancing out of the corner of my eye to watch him read it. He leaned back. He laughed a few times. Huh.

He came over to our group and said, "Assonance. Words that resemble each other because of their vowel sounds. You wrote this, Kevin?"

I tilted my head up at him. "I, uh, well, I mean it was, like, a group —"

"It's disgusting," he said. "But it's good to see you're finding practical ways to apply my lessons."

"Oh. Uh, thanks."

Huh. He wasn't as clueless as I'd thought. He had some level of self-awareness about his own weirdness. Why had I let myself get so annoyed with him? Why had I judged him for volunteering at film festivals and literary magazines? He went out of his way to help people be creative. So what if he worshipped artistic eras he'd never actually known? I spent most of the year fantasizing about girls I barely knew. So what if he loved jazz and nonsense poetry? I loved slasher movies and prank calls about searing my penis on a grill. Everyone's interests are equally ridiculous, just like he'd told us at the beginning of the year with that pie chart.

Right then I knew what I wanted to do for Meyer's final project. Plus, it would be the right time to come clean to the guys and apologize for being an asshole all year.

"Hey, you guys wanna come over Saturday night?" I asked as we stood up at the end of class.

They looked surprised, but neither hesitated. Luke said, "All right."

Will said, "Yeah."

"Cool," I said.

"Cool," Luke said.

"Cool," Will said.

It felt good to be back.

At the end of the day, we got our yearbooks and I saw the picture of myself with the digitally altered skin Mom paid for. They'd sanded the bumps off my forehead, erased blackheads from my nose, and blended my skin from its red-purple shiny swirl into flat beige. This hollow, lifeless-looking guy who never existed and never would, a shared hallucination between me, Mom, whoever at the picture place retouched it, and everyone else who ever thought it was a good idea for high-schoolers to have professionally Photoshopped yearbook pictures. A collective fantasy of the ideal teenager based on daydreams and movies, not reality: It was like looking at the Doritos Dude.

39.

After Dad and I went to the driving range, I spent Saturday afternoon setting everything up in the basement for the guys to come over. I put on the Blink-182 T-shirt because I realized it was sweet and I'd actually wanted it all along. With the money Mom and Dad gave me for my birthday, I got pizza and soda and cookies and all the other garbage we ate at sleepovers, but I wanted it to seem more important or special, so I put a tablecloth over the pool table and set up three place settings for me, Luke, and Will. But something felt off. I dragged two more chairs over for Sam and Patrick, and I texted them to come over. Then I turned off the overhead lights and put on some lamps, so the lighting was soft and nice. It felt good. Mature and grown-up. Everything was in its place.

The guys barreled through the side door into the basement and stopped in their tracks, staring at the table. "What the hell?" Luke said. "Is this, like, a dinner party? This is unbelievably weird."

"It's just us hanging out," I said, trying to sound casual. "I just wanted to eat at the table instead of the couches."

"This tablecloth is creeping me the fuck out," Luke said. "This honestly feels like a trap and you're gonna murder us."

Will took a slice of pizza and sat down, and the rest of them apprehensively followed. I sat at the head of the table and badly tried to act casual while sitting just far enough away from everyone to feel extremely uncomfortable. "Have a slice. We're just hanging out."

Only Will ate. Luke, Sam, and Patrick stared at me.

"Dude," Patrick said. "Please tell us what's going on. You said you had something to tell us?"

"This is so goddamned disturbing," Luke said.

"Yeah, all right, fine. Fine. Sure. Just, uh . . . Look. I'm sorry I acted like a weird asshole all year." I looked at Luke and Will. "I guess I got annoyed that you both started playing football and that you were suddenly best friends with these guys." I nodded at Sam and Patrick. "I felt like a fifth wheel, even though you always tried to include me. But I also felt weird because I had this . . . secret all year." They all stared at me, waiting for the reveal. "I, uh, I've been taking Accutane."

They all blinked.

"Okay," Luke said. "And you, like, got cancer from it?"

"No, I just took Accutane."

"So what's the secret?" Patrick said.

"What do you mean?"

Luke said, "My brother's been on it, like, three times. And Alex was on it, right? Why is this a big deal?"

Alex had told him? She wasn't embarrassed to admit it? Was I the only one turning this into a big deal? Christ. I was pulling a Mom. "I, uh, I just . . . I was, like, embarrassed because . . ."

Sam said, "Will saw your mom drive you to that doctor's office after school one day, so we figured you had some serious problem and didn't want to talk about it, so we didn't ask."

Patrick said, "Yeah, we just figured you had, like, Lyme disease or something."

"No . . . it's just the, uh, acne medicine."

Total, unimpressed silence.

Luke said, "This is the worst secret I've ever heard."

I started laughing. They didn't give a shit and it felt great. "Good. All right, well. Anyway, that's how I met Alex last year. There was no writing class. She was on Accutane, too, and we met at the place where you get your blood tested."

"All right," said Patrick. "Is there any other uninteresting secret you'd like to reveal to us?"

"Yeah," Luke said. "Want to confess that you ate cereal this morning?"

"You know, what? Sure. Here's some honesty I should get out in the open: I've never done anything with a girl. Never even kissed one."

"Right," said Luke. "And you're not really gonna get any

closer to it by hosting formal pizza parties for four dudes."

"Should we invite girls over tonight?" The idea of hanging out in one group with the guys and girls didn't terrify me anymore.

Luke thought for a second. "No. This bizarre thing you set up is at least entertaining."

I had to ask. "Did you guys, when you snuck into the middle school, like, do stuff with girls?"

Will said, "We wrote our names on the wall. I think some girls saw us do it. That's not that scandalous, though."

"No, but did you, like, finger-bang anyone?"

"What the hell?" said Luke. "At the middle school? We'd get arrested."

"Some kid at school said that everyone was finger-banging everyone that night."

"Nobody finger-banged me," said Will. "Should I feel left out?"

I laughed. "I heard it was basically an orgy in there, where the entire grade had some sexual awakening and I missed it."

"No . . ." said Luke. "The only mischievous thing I did in there was fart in Mrs. Garrett's chair, and that's not really something that turns girls on."

Patrick said, "You seriously feel like you missed out on something that night?"

"Yeah."

"It was honestly, like, one of the lamest things I've ever done. We stood around a middle school in the dark. You made a good call ignoring the dumb-ass peer pressure to go."

"Huh," I said. "Well, have you guys ever . . . ?"

"Had sex?" said Luke. "No."

"Only with a sock," said Will, licking pizza grease off his thumb. "Oh, wait. There was also a Ziploc bag."

"What about with Emma?" I said to Luke. "I always thought that when you were going out you guys, like . . ."

"We made out a lot. And once I felt one of her boobs through her shirt. But we broke up before I got to the other one. I'm, like, caught in a pickle between first and second base."

"The five of us masturbate way too much to have anything left over for actual girls," said Will. "Oh, or guys. Sorry, Sam."

Sam shrugged, reaching for a slice of pizza. "It's cool."

"Wait," I said, putting my hands on the table. "Wait. What?"

"Wait, were you not there the night I told everyone I'm gay?" he said through a mouthful of cheese.

"*What?*" I screamed.

"Kevin?" Mom yelled from upstairs. "Everything okay?"

"Yeah!" I shouted, and then, softer, "You've all known this? For how long?"

They all shrugged. Luke said, "Yeah, he told us, like, a few months ago. Some night you weren't there. It was a big deal for, like, a day, but no one gives a shit anymore."

"Wow," I gasped. "Wow. Holy smokes."

Sam said, "I'll be honest with you, since we're friends, dude: You're acting like a huge idiot right now. I'm glad you're not being a dick, but you're really sounding like a dumb-ass."

"Right, yeah. Sorry. I just, uh . . . this is a surprise and it's cool we can be honest with each other. But yeah, I guess you liking dudes doesn't actually change anything between us."

"Nope," Sam said, stuffing the rest of the crust in his mouth. He turned to Will. "Wait, what about you and Lauren Gordon? Did you do anything after homecoming?"

Will burped. "She invited me to her house once, but when I got there her dad was all sweaty and pissed off at the top of a ladder and he yelled at me to help him clean out their gutters, so I did that for, like, three hours." He shrugged. "What base is that?"

There was a pause until Patrick said, "I honestly feel like I'm at a six-year-old's birthday party right now. So before you fucking idiots bring out the musical chairs, I'd like to announce that I got a hand job last spring break."

"Holy shit," I said.

"What was it like?" Luke asked.

Patrick said, "It's pretty much like jerking off, but the hand isn't yours and it has no idea what it's doing, so it takes forty-five minutes. And I'd never thought about my dick being sweaty before, but that was mostly what I thought about the whole time."

I cracked up, feeling this sense of relief. They hadn't all been drafted into the big leagues of teen sexual encounters yet. Luke had made out with a girl and felt one breast, but that wasn't nearly as far ahead of me as I thought he'd gotten. Will had only had sex with a sock and a sandwich bag. Was I jealous of Patrick's hand job? Absolutely. But my moment in the spotlight would come; one day I'd be the chosen one worrying about my sweating penis. I tried to hold back my smile.

We all ate pizza while Patrick detailed the physical ecstasy he'd experienced under a towel between a sand dune and a dumpster at the Myrtle Beach Embassy Suites. It was like hearing a firsthand account of the moon landing.

After the pizza was finished, I cleared my throat and stood up. "Oh, so I didn't just invite you guys over to tell you about Accutane and apologize for being a jackass."

"I knew it," said Luke. "You're gonna cut our heads off with an ax."

I smiled. "Maybe. I was thinking . . . do you guys want to, uh, make our movie? For Meyer's project?"

"You mean that black-and-white French film from the sixties you've been writing? *Italian Hospital? Antonio Gets His Colon Cleansed?* How are we gonna make that in a week?"

"No, let's make a horror movie," I said. "I've got the title: *The Goose-Shit Killer.*"

"Does he kill goose shits? Or is he made of goose shit?"

"It's a guy who falls in a pond on a golf course and when he comes out, he's, like, half goose shit, and he starts going back in time to kill past versions of himself when he was an idiot."

"Yeah, all right, sure," Luke said. "And I'll be the first guy he kills. I need a weapon. The, uh, Pool Cue Man. That's our first victim. Let's go. Let's start."

Patrick said, "Sweet, and I'll be the, uh . . . the . . . the Bread Stick Boy." He swung two pizza crusts through the air. It looked really dumb. For one, crusts aren't bread sticks. And they were so small, you'd barely even see them on camera. The Pool Cue Man was already not exactly a groundbreaking idea, and—

Stop.

Who cares? Don't take it so seriously. Have fun.

"Yeah. Bread Stick Boy. He's in there. Let's do it."

"Why Bread Stick Boy?" Will asked. "Why not a guy named Dick Sweat?"

Patrick shook his head but laughed. Luke sprang off his chair and paced, spewing ideas. "Okay, okay, okay, so we gotta start with the goose guy's origin. We gotta go out there and Will's gonna fall into the shit pond."

Will shrugged and said, "Yeah, all right."

I took the video camera out of the cabinet. I had no goals or expectations or plans. I would just make the movie. Get lost in it. So what if it fell apart halfway through, or if we lost interest? That was okay as long as we were laughing while we were doing it. The experience mattered more than the product. Most horror films made by sixteen-year-olds suck and most memories with your friends don't.

Whatever we made, we'd turn it in to Meyer. If it was unwatchable, then our story would be about how it fell apart. Anything could be a story — that was Meyer's whole point with this vague assignment.

I set up the camera while Luke and Patrick talked through ways the first scene would work. Patrick went to the bathroom and walked back saying, "That bed in your guest room has the same sheets Sam pissed in."

"Sweet," Sam said.

"You pissed in your sheets?" I asked.

The other guys all laughed. "Couple weeks ago," Sam said.

"Had this dream I was standing at a urinal and then I woke up and realized I was mistaken." He shrugged. "Felt great. You guys are wasting a lot of time walking from your beds to the toilet. I might have to relive the magic with the setup you've got in there."

"We should make him sleep in a bathtub tonight," Will said. "He's like a wild animal."

"Put him outside by the garbage cans," said Luke. "Let the raccoons piss all over him."

I asked Sam, "Why do you tell the guys about this stuff when you know they'll give you shit?"

Sam shrugged. "If I don't own up to this stuff, you assholes would find out somehow and give me shit anyway. It feels better to take charge of it instead of being crippled with shame and fear like you pussies."

He made a good point.

"I gotta pee," I said. "The camera's ready. Figure out what you'll say and we'll go out to the golf course and just start filming."

I stepped into the bathroom and closed the door behind me. I heard them coming up with lines for Dick Sweat and I smiled.

That Doritos Dude I fantasized about being — the smooth slacker who wakes up at two p.m. on his beanbag chair and is only concerned about scoring some nachos — doesn't exist. Everyone's worried. Everyone's paranoid. Sam acts so confident about his embarrassing moments because he worries we'll make fun of him if he doesn't own them first. Patrick wishes he could stand up to peer pressure and he's nervous about his penis sweat. Luke and Will worry they'll never do anything with girls, too. If the Doritos Dude did exist, he'd be stressed out about the way his cargo shorts fit or about the other dudes at the skate shop thinking his deck sucks or about the orange dust on his fingertips leaving handprints that ruin his girl-friend's tank top when they make out.

We see the pieces of other people's lives they choose to share. The calm, composed parts where things are going well. But everyone is stressed out. Everyone worries. Probably half my grade regularly considers tying cinder blocks to their feet and pencil-diving into a lake. But if we could just open our eyes down there at the green-brown bottom, we'd see that we're not alone. We could reach out to each other and swim to the surface together. Just another classic teen mass suicide turned lake party.

The girls who'd come to White Water had seemed so care-free and mature in their bathing suits, but they must have been just as nervous and paranoid as I was — maybe more. I mean, their whole bodies were basically on display in their swimsuits. At least guys get to maintain some mystery about the mess between our belly buttons and our knees.

And really, who was I to ever judge the God Squad and their abstinence pledges? They were weird virgins, just like me. Meyer's pie chart wasn't right about everything. Sure, everyone likes different books and bands, but when it comes to real life, we all have a lot more in common than not. A few weeks ago I would've thought that meant we're all bland and uninteresting, but I was coming to realize it meant we could all understand each other's problems if we just took our goddamned headphones off for a minute. Being interesting is a stupid goal. Being a fully formed, engaged person isn't.

Going forward, I'd try to remember that no one is just one thing—an obnoxious new friend or a weird teacher or a girl who's too cool for me. I'd take the time to hear someone's whole story. To acknowledge they exist and they matter. Listen. Do what Alex did for me.

She made me feel seen when I didn't even know I needed it. Maybe connecting with other people isn't about having the same taste in movies or saying the perfect joke as much as the feeling you can give someone by showing them that you care. The one thing that helped me the most all year was Alex looking me in the eye.

I know I'm terrible at that. I'm the guy who stares at his shoes because he's shy and nervous to show his face, and then probably comes off like an asshole who doesn't care about other people.

I looked up at myself in the mirror. The lighting was bad—awful fluorescent overheads brighter than they needed to be. The kind of light I used to instinctively shut my eyes at. But I kept them open. I stared at myself in the mirror, looking over my face. My cheeks were smooth, but dry and scratched with pink and purple scars. My nose had some blackheads, and my jawline was streaked with red track marks from where I'd been squeezing. A bulging whitehead sprouted from my temple.

I could hear the guys laughing outside.

My face looked nothing like the Photoshopped fantasy. But unlike in that picture, I was smiling. My reflection here wasn't the whole story any more than my reflection in a room with soft, forgiving lighting would be. The truth about myself and how I felt, or how any of us feel, is more complicated than one image, one angle, one moment of eye contact can show. Those things are a start, but real feelings take effort to understand and express. I need to pay attention, to not get distracted. To keep my eyes open and see myself from all angles, under the best and the worst lights, and have the courage to ask for help when I need it.

Right then, under those terrible fluorescents, I was able to look straight back at my face.

I'll probably be okay.